Dog Will Have His Day

Dog Will Have His Day

Translated from the French by Siân Reynolds

Fred Vargas

W F HOWES LTD

This large print edition published in 2014 by
W F Howes Ltd
Unit 4, Rearsby Business Park, Gaddesby Lane,
Rearsby, Leicester LE7 4YH

1 3 5 7 9 10 8 6 4 2

First published in the United Kingdom in 2014
by Harvill Secker

First published with the title *Un peu plus loin sur la droite* in 1996
by Éditions Viviane Hamy, Paris

A CIP catalogue record for this book is available
from the British Library

ISBN 978 1 47127 157 1

Typeset by Palimpsest Book Production Limited,

Pr~inted and bound in Great B~ritain
by TJ I~n~ternational, Lt~d P~adstow, ~Cornwall

CHAPTER 1

Paris, November 1995

'And what the hell are *you* doing in this neck of the woods?'

Marthe liked picking quarrels in her old age. That evening, she hadn't found anyone to argue with, so she'd devoted herself to a crossword, standing up at the counter with the barman. He was a nice enough guy, but exasperating when it came to crosswords. He missed the point, didn't follow the rules, couldn't adapt to the number of letters. And yet he ought to have been helpful; he was good at geography, which was odd since he had never left Paris, any more than Marthe had. When the clue was 'River in Russia, two letters', he had suggested 'Yenissei'.

Well, it was better than having no one at all to talk to.

Louis Kehlweiler had come into the cafe at about eleven o'clock. Marthe hadn't seen him for two months, and she'd actually missed him. Kehlweiler had now put coins into the pinball machine and Marthe was watching the ball bounce

1

around. This crazy game – with its special oubliette for the ball to get lost in, and the uphill slope it took huge efforts to climb, and as soon as you got there the ball tumbled down into the oubliette – had always irritated her. It seemed to her that the machine was designed purely to give people perpetual lessons in morality – and an unfair, austere and depressing morality at that. If you quite understandably gave it a bang with your fist, it went *Tilt!* and shut down the game. And on top of that, you had to pay! People had tried to explain to her that it was meant to be fun, but she wasn't buying that, it reminded her of catechism classes.

'Well? What the hell are you doing here?'

'I just came to take a look,' Louis replied. 'Vincent has noticed something.'

'Something worth your coming over for?'

Louis broke off the conversation, it was an emergency: the pinball was heading straight for the pit. He caught it and flipped it rattling back up, rather incompetently.

'Pathetic,' Marthe said.

'I know, but you keep talking.'

'Have to, don't I? When you're at catechism class, you don't hear what people are saying. You didn't answer. So. Worth your while?'

'Could be. Have to see.'

'What is it? Politics? Gangland? Bit of both?'

'Don't shout so loud, Marthe. It'll get you into trouble one day. Let's just say it's this far-right politician, who's somewhere we weren't expecting him to be. And that intrigues me.'

'Serious?'

'Yep, Marthe. Authentic, certified, chateau-bottled. But we have to check it out, of course.'

'And where's this? Which bench?'

'Bench 102.'

Louis smiled and flipped another pinball. Marthe stopped to think. She was getting confused these days, having the odd senior moment. She was mixing up bench 102 with benches 107 and 98. Louis had decided the simplest policy was to number the public benches in Paris, which he used as observation posts. Only the interesting ones, of course. It's true that it was more convenient than giving details of their exact location, especially since that's sometimes hard to get quite accurate. But in twenty years there had been changes, some benches had been retired, new ones had come into play. They'd had to number the trees too, when there weren't any benches at key points in the city. Add in some temporarily used benches for minor cases. The numbers had reached 137, because they never reused an old number, and all this got muddled in her head. But Louis had made it a rule not to have anything written down.

'Is 102 the one by the florist's?' asked Marthe with a frown.

'No, that's 107.'

'Oh shit,' said Marthe. 'At least buy me a drink.'

'Get what you want at the bar. I've got three more goes here.'

At seventy, Marthe could no longer roam around the city, between two clients. And she mixed up the benches too. But, well, she was Marthe. She might not bring in much information any more, but she had some excellent hunches. Though her last important lead went back a good ten years. Still, that one had really made the shit hit the fan, which was both salutary and the whole point of the exercise.

'You're drinking too much, old lady,' said Louis, working the flipper.

'Keep your eye on the ball, Ludwig.'

Marthe called him Ludwig, other people called him Louis. It was up to them, he was used to it. For fifty years, people had been dithering about which name to use. Some even called him Louis-Ludwig. He thought that stupid, nobody's called Louis-Louis.

'Did you bring Bufo?' Marthe asked, as she came back holding a glass.

'You know he gets panicky in cafes.'

'Is he all right? Are you still friends?'

'Love of my life, Marthe.'

There was a silence.

'We don't see your girlfriend around these days,' Marthe began again, leaning her elbows on the pinball machine.

'She walked out. Move your arm, I can't see what I'm doing.'

'When?'

'Just move it, for heaven's sake! This afternoon. She packed her bags while I was out, and she left a note on the bed. Now look, you've made me lose the ball.'

'It was you that was clumsy. Did you have some lunch at least? What kind of note?'

'Pathetic. Yes, I had some lunch.'

'Not easy to write a fancy note when you're walking out on someone.'

'Why not? And she could have said something, instead of writing.'

Louis smiled at Marthe and hit the side of the machine with the flat of his hand. Yeah, it really had been a pathetic note. OK, Sonia had walked out, she had a perfect right to, no point going over it again, ad infinitum. She'd left, he was sad, end of story. The world was full of horrors and bloodshed, you couldn't blow your top just because a woman had walked out on you. Although, yes, of course, it was sad.

'Don't break your heart over it,' said Marthe.

'I have some regrets. And there was that experiment, remember? It failed.'

'What did you expect? That she'd stick around for your film-star looks? I didn't say you were ugly, don't make me say anything I haven't, mind.'

'I'm not making you do anything.'

'But look, Louis, it's not enough, the flashing green eyes and all that. I used to have them too. And your gammy knee, frankly, that doesn't help.

Some girls don't like a man who limps. It annoys them, can't you get that into your head?'

'Yeah, job done.'

'Don't break your heart.'

Louis smiled and patted Marthe's wrinkled hand.

'I'm not breaking my heart.'

'If you say so. Do you want me to go to bench 102?'

'You do whatever you want, Marthe. I don't own all the benches in Paris.'

'Can't you give some orders, from time to time?'

'No.'

'Well, you're doing yourself no good. Giving orders, that settles a man down. But there it is, you've no idea how to obey anyone else, so I don't see how you can order other people about.'

'Stands to reason.'

'Haven't I told you that plenty of times? In so many words? And it's good advice, isn't it?'

'A hundred times, Marthe.'

'A good piece of advice never wears out.'

He could have avoided having Sonia walk out on him, of course he could. But he had wanted to try the ridiculous experiment of hoping she'd take him as she found him. As a result, she'd left him after five months. OK, that would do now, he'd been thinking about it quite long enough, he was sufficiently sad, the world was full of horrors and bloodshed, there was work to be done, in small matters of the world as well as big ones, he wasn't going to go on thinking about Sonia and her pathetic little note for hours and hours, he had better things to do. But the trouble was that up there in the damned Ministry, where he had once spent so long as a free electron – needed, hated, indispensable, and highly paid – they now wanted him out. New faces, new expressions on old idiots (not all of them were idiots actually, that was the trouble), and they no longer wanted the help of a guy who was a little too clued up about everything. They were getting rid of him, they distrusted him: with reason. But their reaction was absurd. Take a fly for instance.

'Take a fly for instance,' Louis said.

Louis had finished his game, only a moderate score, these new flippers were really annoying, you had to watch the screen and the ball all at once. But sometimes the balls popped out three or four at a time and it was interesting, never mind what Marthe said. He leaned on the counter while Marthe siphoned up her beer.

When Sonia had shown the first signs that she might leave him, he'd been tempted to tell her: to let her know all his achievements, in several ministries, on the street, in the law courts, in cafes, the countryside and police stations. Twenty-five years of bomb disposal he called it, tracking down men of iron with toxic ideas. Twenty-five years of vigilance, and he'd met too many men with calcified brains, working alone, or in groups, or screaming in hordes, the same rocks inside their heads, and

7

the same murders on their hands. Hell's bells, Sonia would really have loved him, if she'd known he was into bomb disposal. She might have stayed, even if he did have a knee that was shot to pieces: he'd got that in Antibes, during a showdown in a blazing hotel owned by the mob. That tells you something about a man, doesn't it? But no, he had held out, he hadn't told her anything at all. He had hoped the only attraction was his physique and his conversation, just to see. As far as the knee was concerned, Sonia thought he'd fallen down the steps in the metro. That doesn't tell you anything about a man. Marthe had warned him he'd be disappointed, women were no better than anyone else, you couldn't expect miracles. Possibly Bufo hadn't actually helped.

'Shall we have another, Ludwig?'

'You've had enough to drink. I'll walk you home.'

Not that Marthe was running much of a risk, since she carried no money, and she'd seen it all, done it all, but when she'd had a drop too many, and it was a rainy night, she had a tendency to fall over.

'What's that about a fly?' Marthe asked as she left the bar, holding a plastic bag over her head. 'You said something about a fly?'

'You've got a thing about rain now?'

'It's my hair dye. If it runs, what'll I look like?'

'An old hooker.'

'Which I am.'

'Which you are.'

Marthe laughed. Her laugh had been well known

in this *quartier* for half a century. A man turned round and gave her a little wave.

'See that guy?' Marthe said. 'Should have seen him thirty years ago. I won't tell you his name, I don't do that.'

'I know who he is,' Louis said, with a smile.

'Hey, Ludwig, I hope you haven't been poking your nose into my address book. You know I respect professional secrecy.'

'And I hope you're just *saying* that, but you don't mean it.'

'No, I don't mean it.'

'All the same, Marthe, your address book could be very interesting for someone less scrupulous than me. You ought to destroy it, I've told you that a hundred times.'

'Too many memories. All the high and mighty who used to come knocking at my door. Just think—'

'Destroy it, I'm telling you. It's dangerous.'

'Get along with you! All those famous names, they're old now. Who'd be interested in a lot of has-beens?'

'Plenty of people. And it isn't just a list of names, is it, Marthe, you have your little comments, don't you?'

'And you don't have some little comments written down somewhere yourself, Ludwig?'

'Marthe, keep your voice down, we're not out in the country.' Marthe had always spoken too loudly.

'Eh? Little notebooks? Reports? Souvenirs of cases? You've thrown them out, have you, since you got the sack? You *did* get the sack, didn't you, is that official?'

'Apparently. But I've kept a few contacts. They'll have a job to get me out entirely. See, take a fly for instance.'

'If you like, but look, I'm dead beat. Can you just tell me, what's that damn river in Russia, keeps coming up in crosswords, two letters, know what that is?'

'The Ob, Marthe, I've told you that a hundred times too.'

Kehlweiler dropped Marthe off at her place, listened as she climbed the stairs, and then went into a cafe on the avenue. It was almost one in the morning, and there weren't many customers. A few nighthawks like himself. He knew them all. He had a thirsty memory for names and faces, perpetually unsatisfied and eager for more. Which had been a cause of some anxiety in the Ministry.

Just a beer, and then he wouldn't worry his head any more about Sonia. He could have told her about his grand army too, about the hundred or so men and women on whom he could count, a representative in every *département* of France and a score in Paris, you can't do everything yourself in the bomb disposal business. Sonia might have stayed then, perhaps. Oh, let it go.

Anyway, back to the fly. This fly comes into the house and it's irritating everyone. Beating its wings, hundreds of times per second. A persistent little creature, a fly, but really annoying. It buzzes everywhere, walks on the ceiling, no special equipment needed, goes places it shouldn't, and in particular it zooms in on every single spot of honey lying around. Public enemy number one. Exactly like him. He used to find honey in places people thought they'd cleaned up so well no trace would remain. Honey – or shit, of course, because to a fly it's all the same. And what's the dumb reaction? Shoo the fly outside. Big mistake. Because what'll the fly do, once it's outside?

Louis Kehlweiler paid for his beer, said goodnight to everyone and left the bar. He didn't want to go home. He'd go and sit on bench 102. When he'd started this, he'd had four benches, and now there were 137, plus sixty-four trees. What with the benches and the chestnut trees, he'd picked up masses of stuff. He could have told her about that too; he'd resisted. And now it was pouring with rain.

So, what'll the fly do, once it's outside? It bombs around for a few minutes, naturally, then it copulates. Then it lays eggs. Now there are thousands of little flies growing up, bombing about and copulating in turn. So there's nothing more illogical than getting rid of a fly by shooing it out of doors. It just multiplies the fly, to the power of x. You should let it stay inside, doing its fly-type things, and have patience, until age catches up with it and it gets tired. Whereas a fly outside is dangerous, a

11

real menace. And those cretins had shooed him outdoors. As if, once he was there, he'd give up. But no. It would be worse. And obviously they couldn't swat him with a tea cloth like you can a fly.

The rain was torrential as Kehlweiler came within sight of bench 102. It was a good lookout post, opposite the home of the nephew of a notably discreet politician. Kehlweiler knew how to look like a tramp, it came naturally to him, and people weren't suspicious of a large man, if he was lolling on a bench. Not even when the large man slowly started to shadow someone.

He stopped and pulled a face. A dog had made a mess on his territory. Right there, on the metal grid round the base of a plane tree, alongside the bench. Louis Kehlweiler didn't like his lookout posts to be fouled up. He almost turned on his heel. But the world was full of horrors and blood-shed, he wasn't going to give up just because some passing dog had dumped its wretched excrement there.

At midday, everything had been OK, he had eaten his lunch sitting on this selfsame bench: the surroundings were perfectly clean. And tonight, a woman had walked out on him, a pathetic note had been left on the bed, he'd only managed a moderate score on the pinball machine, and his territory had been crapped on, a vague despair was setting in.

Too much beer this evening, perhaps that was

true, he wasn't going to claim the contrary. And there was nobody on the streets, with this drenching rain coming down, which would at least wash the pavements, the metal grid and lookout post 102. It might wash his troubles out of his head as well. If Vincent had been correct, the politician's nephew had been receiving at his house an obscure person who interested Louis. He wanted to take a look. But this evening, there was no light in the windows, no sign of life.

He sheltered himself with his jacket, and wrote a few lines in his notebook. Marthe really ought to get rid of *her* book. It would be doing her a favour to take it away from her by force. Marthe, although you wouldn't think it now, had once been the most beautiful taxi girl on the Left Bank, according to what he'd been told. Kehlweiler glanced at the grid again. He wanted to go home. Not that he was giving up, but this was enough for tonight. He was sleepy. Of course, he *could* say he'd be there tomorrow morning at dawn. People were always telling him how beautiful the dawn was, but Kehlweiler liked his sleep. And when he was sleepy, there were very few pressures that could prevail against it. Sometimes, even if the world was full of horrors and bloodshed, he was still sleepy. That was how it was, he was neither proud nor ashamed of it, although, well, that wasn't quite true, he couldn't help it, indeed it had got him into quite a lot of trouble, and even some massive failures. He had paid a price for his beauty sleep. The future belongs to those who get up early, he'd been told. Stupid, because the future is also watched over by those who get up late. He could be back here by eleven in the morning.

CHAPTER 2

Killing like that, not many people could have done it. Watch out, though. Now's the time when it's important to be clever, precise, excellent indeed, for the next stage of the operation. The secret is to be discreet while being excellent. You wouldn't believe how pathetic people can be. Georges is a good example, well, I say Georges, there are others. Still, what a waste of space!

But as I say, just an example.

Careful, don't smile more than usual, practise, pay attention to detail. The method worked fine before, all you have to do is apply it strictly. Relax the jaw, let your cheeks go slack, eyes blank. Perfect detachment from ordinary life, under cover of being normal but a bit tired. Not so easy when you're feeling pleased with yourself. And last night, it was more than feeling pleased, it was close to ecstasy – and quite right too. Pity not to be able to enjoy it, don't get that many chances. But no, absolutely not, not that stupid. When some halfwit's in love, you can tell at once, and when a murderer is satisfied, you can see it from their body language. Next day the police notice, and it's all over. To kill, you've got to

15

be the opposite of a halfwit, that's the secret. Training, attention to detail, discipline, and people won't notice a thing. You'll get the right to celebrate, take advantage of it later, but a year from now, and discreetly.

You've just got to cultivate detachment, hide the pleasure. Killing someone like that, on the rocks, quick as a flash, no witnesses, how many people could have done that? The old woman never knew what hit her. Excellent in its simplicity. People will tell you murderers want everyone to know that it's them. 'They can't help making themselves known, that's how they get their kicks.' And it's supposed to make them feel worse, if someone else gets arrested instead of them, an old trick to tempt them out of their hole. 'They can't bear anyone else to steal the credit for their murder.' That's what people say! Bollocks! Maybe there are some pathetic losers like that. But not this one, oh no, not that stupid. You could arrest twenty other people, and it wouldn't make this one lift an eyebrow. That's the secret. But they won't arrest anybody, they won't even think it was a murder!

Feel the need to smile, enjoy the benefit? Yes, quite legitimate. But no, stop, absolutely not! Be clever. Relax the jaw, look calm. That's the long and short of it. Think about the sea, for instance. One wave, another wave, tide comes in, goes out, and so on. Very soothing the sea, very regular. Much better than counting sheep to relax, that's just for morons without a thought in their heads. Sheep number one, OK, jumps the gate and goes off to the left of your head.

And where does the stupid creature go? Just hides in the left of your head, above your ear. And by the time the second sheep comes along, the game's spoilt because there's less room for it. You soon get the sheep piling up on the left of the gate, the later ones can't jump it at all and the whole herd crashes, bleating away, might as well slaughter the lot to start with. The sea's much better. In and out, never stops and all for nothing. Bloody stupid, the sea, actually. In the end, the sea's irritating too, because it's huge but useless. Pulled in and out by the moon, can't even make its own mind up. Best of all would be to think about the murder. Just going back over it again in your head makes you laugh, and laughing's good for everything. But no, not so stupid, big effort to forget, don't think about the murder.

Work it out. They'll start looking for the old woman tomorrow. By the time they find her body on the rocks, where nobody goes in November, that will probably give another day, perhaps two. By then they won't be able to fix the time of death with any certainty. What with the wind, the rain, the tide coming in, not to mention the seagulls: perfect. Still smiling? Just don't! And stop your hands clenching and unclenching, always that way after a murder. Murder's got to come out through the fingers for, oh, about five or six weeks. So relax the hands too, as well as the jaw, no detail uncontrolled, discipline in all things. All those pathetic half-witted killers who give themselves away by nerves, tics, looking too pleased with themselves, being exhibitionist or too nonchalant, just weaklings, not even capable of self-control. Not so stupid. When they tell you about it, seem interested, even concerned. Let your arms swing naturally when you walk, act calmly. Let's work it out. The gendarmes will start looking tomorrow, and volunteers will help them. Join the volunteers. No, not so stupid. Murderers join the volunteers all too often! Everyone knows that, even the most bone-headed gendarme knows that, they make lists of the volunteers.

Work hard at being excellent. Work as normal, smile as normal, keep your hands relaxed and ask what's the news, that's all. Correct that clenching of the fingers, it's no time to get uncontrolled spasms, no, no, no, and anyway not your style, certainly not. Keep a watch on lips and hands, that's the secret. Hands in pockets, or fold your arms, loosely. But not more than normal.

Watch what's going on, watch other people, but look normal, not like those murderers who imagine every little thing is about them. But pay attention to little things all the same. Every precaution was taken, but there are always nosy parkers to reckon with. Always. Be aware that some damn nosy parker might have noticed something. Be prepared, that's the secret. If someone takes it into their head to poke their nose into this business, they've had it. The fewer pathetic losers there are on this earth, the better it would be. Finito. Like the others. Think about that now.

CHAPTER 3

Louis Kehlweiler sat down on bench 102 at eleven in the morning.

Vincent was already there, leafing through a newspaper.

'Nothing better to do today?' Louis asked him.

'Couple of articles on the way. If anything happens in *there*,' Vincent said, without looking up at the building opposite, 'can you let me report on it?'

'Of course. But keep me posted.'

'Of course.'

Kehlweiler took a book and some paper from a plastic carrier bag. The weather hadn't been warm this autumn, and it was hard to find a comfortable position to work on the bench, still damp from the overnight rain.

'What are you translating?' Vincent asked.

'Book on the Third Reich.'

'Which way?'

'German to French.'

'That pay well?'

'Not too bad. Will it bother you if I put Bufo on the bench?'

'No, go ahead,' said Vincent.

'But don't disturb him, he's asleep.'

'I'm not daft enough to start a conversation with a toad.'

'People say that and then they do.'

'You talk to him much yourself?'

'All the time. Bufo knows everything, he's a safe-deposit box, a living scandal. Tell me, have you seen anyone come to this bench this morning?'

'Are you talking to me or your toad?'

'My toad wasn't here before me. So I'm talking to you.'

'Right. No, haven't seen anyone round here at all. Well, not since seven thirty. Except old Marthe, we exchanged a word or two, and she went off again.'

Vincent had taken out a small pair of scissors and was cutting articles out of his pile of newspapers.

'You doing like I do now? Collecting press cuttings?'

'The pupil has to copy the master till the master gets fed up and boots him out, and that's the sign that the pupil's ready to become a master in turn, yeah? Am I bothering you?'

'Not at all. But you're not paying enough attention to the provinces,' said Kehlweiler, shuffling through the pile of newspapers Vincent had collected. 'This stuff's too Parisian.'

'Haven't got time. I'm not like you, I don't have people sending me their discoveries from all over

20

France, I'm not a veteran chief. One day, I'll have my own secret squad. So who are the people in your grand army?'

'Guys like you, or women like you, journalists, activists, the unemployed, troublemakers, whistleblowers, judges, cafe owners, philosophers, cops, newspaper vendors, chestnut sellers, er . . .'

'OK, I get the picture,' said Vincent.

Kehlweiler looked quickly at the iron grid round the foot of the tree, then at Vincent, then around them.

'Have you lost something?' Vincent asked.

'In a way. And what I've lost on the one hand I get the feeling I've found on the other. You're sure nobody else has been sitting here this morning? You haven't nodded off to sleep over the stuff you're reading?'

'After seven in the morning, I never go back to sleep.'

'Good for you.'

'The provincial press,' Vincent went on obstinately, 'is full of common or garden crime, going nowhere, just small-town incidents, time after time, and it doesn't interest me.'

'And you're wrong. A premeditated crime, a private slander, an arbitrary denunciation, they all go somewhere, to a big dunghill where bigger things are fermenting, large-scale crime, collective operations. Better look at it all, without weeding it. I'm a generalist.'

Vincent muttered something, while Kehlweiler

got up to go and stare at the flat metal grid round the base of the tree. Vincent knew Kehlweiler's theories by heart, including the story of the left hand and the right hand. The left hand, Louis would announce, lifting his arms and spreading his fingers, is imperfect, clumsy and hesitant, and therefore a salutary source of muddle and doubt. The right hand, firm, assured, competent, is the driver of human genius. Mastery, method and logic all proceed from it. But look out now, Vincent, this is where you have to follow me carefully: lean just a little too far to the right, a couple of steps further, and you see discipline and certainty looming up, yes? Go further still, three steps, say, and it's the tragic plunge into perfectionism, the impeccable, then the infallible and the pitiless. Then you're only half a man walking, leaning over to your extreme right, unheeding the great value of muddle, a cruel imbecile closed to the virtues of doubt: it can creep up on you more sneakily than you imagine, you think you're safe, but you have to watch it, you have two hands, we're not like dogs. Vincent smiled and flexed his hands. He had learned to watch out for men who walked leaning one way, but he wanted to concern himself entirely with politics, whereas Louis always wanted to have a finger in every pie. But now, Louis was still standing with his back against the tree, looking down at the grid.

'What the heck are you doing?' asked Vincent.

'That little white thing on the grid round the tree – see it?'

'Sort of.'

'I'd like it if you could pick it up for me. With my knee, I can't crouch down.'

Vincent got up with a sigh. He had never challenged any suggestion by Kehlweiler, the high priest of muddle, and he wasn't about to start now.

'Use a handkerchief, I think it'll be smelly.'

Vincent shook his head, and handed Kehlweiler the small object in a piece of newspaper because he didn't have a handkerchief. He sat back down on the bench, picked up his scissors and seemingly paid no further attention to Kehlweiler: there are limits to one's tolerance. But out of the corner of his eye, he observed him looking at the little object from every angle, in the piece of newspaper.

'Vincent?'

'Yes.'

'It didn't rain early this morning?'

'No, not since two in the morning.'

Vincent had started doing the weather report for a local paper and he kept an eye on it every day. He knew a lot about the reasons why water sometimes falls from the sky and sometimes stays up there.

'And this morning, nobody's been here? You're sure? Not even someone walking their dog and letting it piss against the tree?'

'You keep making me say the same thing ten times over. The only human being who came near was Marthe. Did you notice anything about

23

Marthe, by the way?' Vincent added, bending over the paper, and cleaning his nails with the tip of the scissors. 'Seems you saw her yesterday.'

'Yes, I went to catechism class in the cafe.'

'And you saw her home?'

'Yes,' said Kehlweiler, sitting down again and still contemplating the small object wrapped in newspaper.

'And you didn't notice anything?' asked Vincent with an edge of aggression.

'Well. Let's say she wasn't on top form.'

'And that's all?'

'Yes.'

'That's all!' cried Vincent brusquely. 'You spout lectures about the planetary importance of small-town murders, you look after your toad, you spend a quarter of an hour fiddling with some bit of rubbish from under the tree, but about Marthe, whom you've known for twenty years, you didn't notice anything. Bravo, Louis, bravo, well done!'

Kehlweiler looked at him sharply. Too late, said Vincent to himself, and anyway, what the hell. Kehlweiler's eyes, green with long dark lashes that looked as if he was wearing too much mascara, could move from dreamy vagueness to painfully incisive intensity. His lips became a straight line, all his habitual mildness disappeared like a flock of sparrows. Kehlweiler's face looked then like those majestic profiles carved on to cold medals, no fun at all. Vincent shook his head as if chasing away a wasp.

'Tell,' said Kehlweiler simply.

'Well, Marthe has been on the streets for a week now. They took over all those attics to make them into fancy apartments. The new landlord has chucked everyone out.'

'Why didn't she tell me? They must have been given notice ahead of time. Stop that, you'll hurt yourself with those scissors.'

'The tenants campaigned to keep their lodgings, and they were all chucked out.'

'But why didn't she tell me?' repeated Louis, louder.

'Because she's proud, because she's ashamed, because she's frightened of you.'

'The bloody idiot! And what about you? Couldn't you have told me? For God's sake, stop it with the scissors, your nails are quite clean enough, aren't they?!'

'I only found out the day before yesterday. And no one knew where you were.'

Kehlweiler stared again at the object wrapped in newspaper. Vincent gave him a sidelong glance. Louis was good-looking, except when he was irritated like this, with his hawklike nose and jutting chin. Irritation didn't improve anyone's looks, but with Louis it was worse: his three-day stubble and his staring eyes with their heavy lashes could be scary. Vincent waited.

'Know what this is?' Kehlweiler asked finally, passing him the bit of newspaper.

Louis's face was getting back to normal, emotion

25

was returning under his brows and life to his lips. Vincent examined the object. He couldn't concentrate. He had just shouted at Louis and that didn't often happen.

'I've no idea what this piece of shit is,' he said.

'Getting warm. Carry on.'

'It's unrecognisable, funny shape . . . oh hell, Louis, I couldn't give a toss what it is . . .'

'Go on, try harder.'

'If I make a big effort, it might remind me of what was left on my plate after my gran cooked pigs' trotters for me. I hated them, she thought it was my favourite food. Grans are funny sometimes.'

'Wouldn't know,' commented Kehlweiler, 'never knew my grandmother.'

He bundled his book and papers back into the plastic bag, pocketed the object still wrapped in newspaper, and slid the toad into the opposite pocket.

'You're keeping the pig's trotter?' asked Vincent.

'Why not? Now, where can I find Marthe?'

'The last few days she's been sheltering under the awning by tree 16,' Vincent muttered.

'I'm off. Try to get a shot of our target.'

Vincent nodded and watched Kehlweiler disappear with his slow steady steps, leaning a little to one side because of the knee that had been demolished in a fire. He took a sheet of paper and wrote: 'Didn't know his grandmother. Check if same for grandfather.' He made notes of everything. He had

26

picked up from Kehlweiler his mania for wanting to record everything except domestic crime. It was difficult to find out anything about the man though. He didn't give much away. You might know he came from central France, but that didn't get you very far.

Vincent didn't even hear old Marthe, as she dropped down on to the bench.

'Any luck?' she said.

'Christ Almighty, Marthe, you frightened me. Don't talk so loud.'

'So, any luck? The fascist?'

'No, not yet. I'm patient. I'm almost certain I recognised him, but people's faces get older.'

'You ought to take notes, my boy, plenty of notes.'

'I realise that. Know something? Louis never knew his grandmother?'

Marthe shrugged her ignorance.

'So what?' she muttered. 'Louis can buy himself as many ancestors as he wants, so . . . If you listen to him, he's got millions of them. Sometimes it's this fellow Talleyrand, he talks a lot about him, or that other one, what's-his-name . . . well, millions anyway. Even the Rhine, he says that's his ancestor. He's got to be kidding.'

Vincent smiled.

'But his real ancestors,' he insisted, 'not a whisper, we don't know anything.'

'Well, don't mention it, you shouldn't embarrass people. You're just a shit-stirrer, aren't you, my little lad?'

'I think you know a lot of things.'

'Just shut up,' said Marthe sharply. 'This Talleyrand's his grandad, OK? Got that? Satisfied?'

'Marthe, don't tell me you believe that. You don't even know who Talleyrand is. He's been dead 150 years.'

'Well, I don't give a toss who he is, or who he was, OK? If this Talleyrand slept with the Rhine and they came up with Ludwig, then they had good reasons for it, and that's their own business. Couldn't care less about anything else. I'm feeling pretty fed up today, so tell me what it is you're watching for.'

'Oh my God, Marthe, here he comes,' whispered Vincent suddenly, clutching her arm. 'The one I'm after. The sleazy fascist. Just look like an old hooker and I'll be a drunk, we'll get him.'

'Don't worry, I know your methods.'

Vincent slumped drunkenly on to Marthe's shoulder and pulled a corner of her scarf over him. The man was coming out of the building opposite, they had to be quick. Under cover of the scarf, Vincent focused his camera and took several pictures through the gaps in the damp knitted fabric. Then the man vanished from sight.

'Got him, have you?' asked Marthe. 'He's in the can, is he?'

'I think so. See you, Marthe. I'm going after him.'

Vincent went off, still looking wild-eyed. Marthe smiled. He was good at acting like a drunk. At twenty, when Ludwig had picked him up in a bar and rescued him, he was in a bad way, a long story behind him. Nice guy, Vincent, and good at crosswords too. But it would be just as well if he stopped trying to nose about into Ludwig's life. Affection can become a bit intrusive sometimes. Marthe shivered. She was cold. She didn't want to admit it, but she was really cold. The shopkeepers had expelled her from under the awning that morning. Where on earth was she going to go? Come on, old girl, get up, start walking, don't freeze your backside off on 102, get walking. Marthe was talking to herself, which was not unusual.

CHAPTER 4

Louis Kehlweiler walked into the main police station of the 5th arrondissement, ready and prepared. Worth a try. He glanced at his reflection in the glass door. His thick dark hair, a bit too long at the back, his three-day stubble, plastic bag and jacket creased from sitting on the bench would all work against him, and that was exactly what he wanted. He had waited till he got inside before starting to eat his sandwich. Since his friend Commissaire Adamsberg had left this station, taking with him his deputy Danglard, there was no shortage of imbeciles in there, and others who just put up with them. He had a bone to pick with the new commissaire, and he might have found a way of doing it. It wouldn't hurt to try. This was Commissaire Paquelin, Adamsberg's replacement. Louis would willingly have decommissioned him, or at least sent him far away, in any case somewhere different from Adamsberg's old office, where he had in the old days passed some good moments, some peaceful ones and some intelligent ones.

Actually Paquelin was far from being an imbecile,

that was often the problem. God, as Marthe would say, had distributed a good dose of intelligence to the mean bastards of this world, so you had to wonder about God.

For two years now, Louis had had Commissaire Paquelin in his sights. Paquelin, a petty sadist, didn't like the Justice Ministry to meddle in his affairs, and he let that be known. He considered that the police could do without investigating magistrates, and Louis considered that the police should urgently consider doing without Paquelin. But now that he was out of the Ministry, the fight was rather more complicated.

Kehlweiler planted himself, arms crossed and sandwich in pocket, in front of the first policeman he found sitting at a computer.

The officer looked up, made a quick estimate of the man in front of him, and reached an anxious and unfavourable judgement.

'What do you want?'

'I wish to see Commissaire Paquelin.'

'What about?'

'A little thing that might interest him.'

'What kind of little thing?'

'It wouldn't mean anything to you. It's too complicated.'

Kehlweiler didn't have anything against this particular cop. But he wanted to see the commissaire unannounced, in order to start the duel in a manner of his own choosing. And to do that, he needed to be sent from lowly constable to sergeant to inspector, until, by forcible means, he would land up face to face with the commissaire.

Kehlweiler took out his sandwich and started to munch it, still standing up. He let crumbs fall everywhere. The policeman got cross, not unnaturally.

'So what's this little thing, what's it all about?'

'Cooked pigs' trotters. Look, it won't interest you, it's too complicated to explain.'

'Surname, first name?'

'Granville, Louis Granville.'

'Your papers?'

'Haven't got them on me. I didn't come for that, I came in to cooperate with the police of my country.'

'Get lost. We can do without your cooperation.'

An inspector approached and took Louis by the shoulder. Louis turned round slowly. It was working.

'Is it you causing this trouble?'

'Not at all. I want to make a statement to Paquelin.'

'Commissaire Paquelin?'

'The very same.'

The inspector made a sign to the first cop and pulled Louis towards a glass-fronted office door.

'The commissaire can't be disturbed. You can tell me about whatever piddling nonsense is on your mind.'

'It's not piddling nonsense, it's pigs' trotters.'

'Surname, first name?'

'Gravilliers, Louis.'

'Just now you said Granville.'

'Don't let's quibble over it, inspector, I haven't much time, I'm in a hurry.'

'Oh really, is that a fact?'

'You've heard of Blériot, the guy who got it into his head to fly the Channel, so as to get there quicker? Well, he's my ancestor.'

The inspector put his hands to his cheeks. He was getting pretty cross.

'So,' Louis went on, 'you can imagine the problem. It's in my blood. Has to come out, as Paquelin says.'

'You know the commissaire?'

'Yes, well. Very well in fact. But he doesn't know me. He can't remember faces, which is a drawback in your job. Tell me, were you here when there was that regrettable incident in the cells over there?'

The inspector passed his hand across his eyes. This one didn't look as if he had had much sleep, and Kehlweiler understood that kind of suffering better than anyone. While waiting for the inspector to decide to push him higher up the hierarchy, Louis took Bufo out, and held him in his left hand. He couldn't allow Bufo to suffocate in his pocket, police station or no police station. Amphibians have their needs.

'What the hell is that?' asked the inspector, recoiling.

'Nothing,' replied Louis, a little snappily. 'Just my toad. He's not bothering anyone, as far as I can see.'

It's true that people are very disappointing in their attitude to toads, they make a huge fuss about them. And yet they're a hundred times less of a nuisance than a dog. The inspector passed his hand over his eyes again.

'Right, off you go, out of here,' he said.

'Impossible. I wouldn't have come in if I'd wanted to go out again. I'm a persistent guy. You know the story of the man who wouldn't leave even when threatened with bayonets? Well, never mind him. All you need to know is, he was my ancestor. I don't say it's an advantage but that's just how it is. You'll have a job to get rid of me.'

'I don't give a damn about your ancestors!' shouted the inspector.

'Please yourself,' said Kehlweiler.

He sat down and munched the sandwich slowly. It had to last. It wasn't very praiseworthy to be harassing a cop who was short of sleep, but he was enjoying himself all the same. Pity the cop didn't want to enjoy himself too. Anyone can play the ancestor game, it's not forbidden. And as far as ancestors were concerned, Louis was prepared to lend out as many as you like.

Silence fell in the office. The inspector dialled a number. His superior officer no doubt. He was saying 'captain'.

'There's a guy here, won't go away . . . Yes, perhaps . . . You can come and take him and cook him in a pie if you want, you'll be doing me a favour . . . I don't know . . . Yes.'

'Thank you,' said Kehlweiler, 'but it's Paquelin I wanted to see.'

'What nationality are you?'

'I beg your pardon?'

'Bloody hell, are you French?'

Kehlweiler spread his arms evasively.

'Could be, Lieutenant Ferrière, it's quite possible.'

Now was the moment to bring out 'lieutenant'.

The inspector leaned forward.

'You know my name?'

The chief inspector opened the door quietly, with aggressive calm. He was a small man and Kehlweiler took immediate advantage of that to stand up. Louis was about one metre ninety, and it often helped.

'Please get rid of him, sir,' said Ferrière, 'but you may need to check him out first. This guy knows my name, he's playing games.'

'What did you come in here for? Lunch?'

There was something about the chief inspector's eyes that seemed to hint that he might not greatly appreciate the doings of his boss. Kehlweiler decided it was worth taking the chance.

'No, I've got something for Paquelin, to do with pigs' trotters. Do you get on with Paquelin? I find him a bit severe, a bit prejudiced.'

The other man hesitated briefly.

'Follow me,' he said.

'Not so fast,' said Kelhweiler, 'I have this damaged knee.'

Louis picked up his bag, and they went to the first floor; the chief inspector closed the door.

'Did you know Adamsberg?' Louis asked, putting Bufo on a chair. 'Jean-Baptiste Adamsberg? The casual one? The untidy cop who sniffs things out by intuition.'

The inspector nodded.

'Are you Lanquetot? Captain Yves Lanquetot? Am I right?'

'Where are you from?' asked Lanquetot defensively.

'The Rhine.'

'And that's a toad? A common toad?'

'It's a pleasure to meet someone who knows about toads. Do you have one?'

'Not exactly . . . Well, in the country, near the doorstep, we have one living there.'

'And you talk to him?'

The inspector hesitated.

'Now and then,' he said.

'Nothing wrong with that. Bufo and I have great chats. He's nice. A bit slow but you can't expect him to change the world now, can you?'

Lanquetot sighed. He wasn't sure what to do. If he sent this individual and his toad packing, he was taking a risk, because Louis seemed to know a lot. Keeping him in his office would obviously be pointless, it was Paquelin he wanted to see. And if he didn't get to see him, he might go on causing mayhem and scattering crumbs all over the station. But if he sent him through to Paquelin with his pigs' trotters story, that would be taking a risk too, and a good chance he'd get torn off a strip himself. Unless this guy was aiming to put Paquelin on the spot, in which case it could be worth it, rather pleasing in fact. Lanquetot looked up.

'You're not finishing your sandwich?'

'I'm waiting till I'm with Paquelin, it's a strategic weapon. Obviously you can't use it all the time, you have to be hungry. It's called keeping your powder dry.'

'And your name is? Your real name, I mean.'

Kehlweiler looked appraisingly at the chief inspector. If this man hadn't changed, if he was still as Adamsberg had described him, it was OK to go ahead. But sometimes if the boss is strict, other people get the same way and change their spots. Kehlweiler decided to trust the face.

'Kehlweiler,' he answered. 'Louis Kehlweiler. Here's my ID.'

Lanquetot nodded. Yes, he recognised the name.

'And what do you want with Paquelin?'

'I'm hoping he'll take early retirement. I want to make him an offer which he will refuse. If he accepts, well, that'll be the worse for me. But if he refuses, which I'm counting on, I'll handle it myself. And if this affair gets me anywhere, he'll be in trouble for neglecting to follow up a potential crime lead.'

Lanquetot was still hesitating.

'You needn't be implicated,' said Louis. 'All I'm asking you to do is get me in to see him, and then look blank. If you could be present during our conversation, that would provide a witness, if one should be needed.'

'That's easy. You just have to ask permission to leave for Paquelin to make you stay. But what's this all about?'

'It's just a little something, unusual, perplexing and very interesting. I think Paquelin will chuck me out before he's realised its importance. He doesn't understand about muddle.'

Lanquetot picked up the phone.

'Commissaire? Yes I know, you're very busy. It's just that I've got with me this oddball, who insists he wants to see you in person . . . No, I think it might be wise to see him . . . He has a few tabs on us . . . That, er, tricky business . . . Yes, in the cells . . . He mentioned it. Perhaps he's looking for nits to pick, perhaps he's just boasting, but I'd prefer you made an estimate yourself. It should be all right, he hasn't even got his ID on him. Right, I'll bring him up.'

Lanquetot picked up Kehlweiler's papers and stuffed them in his pocket.

'Here we go. I'll push and shove you a bit, into the office, to give it a bit of realism.'

'Be my guest.'

Lanquetot threw rather than ushered Kehlweiler into the commissaire's office. Louis grimaced, the realism had hurt his leg.

'Here he is, sir. No ID. He changes his name every couple of minutes. Granville, Gravilliers. I'll leave him to you, shall I?'

'Where do you think you're going, Lanquetot?' asked the commissaire. He had a hoarse voice, very bright eyes, a thin and quite handsome face with that detestable mouth which Louis well remembered. Louis had started on his sandwich again, and was dropping crumbs on the floor.

'I'm going to get a coffee, sir, with your permission. I'm exhausted.'

'You'll stay right where you are, Lanquetot.'

'Yes, sir.'

Commissaire Paquelin examined Kehlweiler, without asking him to sit down. Louis put Bufo on the empty chair. The commissaire observed the scene without a word. He wasn't stupid, Commissaire Paquelin, he wasn't going to explode just because of a toad on a chair.

'So, my friend, you've come to stir up a little shit in our offices.'

'Could be.'

'Last name, first name, nationality, occupation.'

'Granville, Louis, French, none.'

'None what?'

'Occupation, I don't have a job any more.'

'So what's your game?'

'I'm not playing games. I just came here because it's the principal police station in our district, that's all.'

'And . . .?'

'I'll allow you to judge. It's about a small object that's bothering me. I thought the correct thing

39

would be to tell you about it. No need to look for any other motives.'

'I'll look for motives where I please. Why didn't you leave this object with one of my staff?'

'They wouldn't have taken it seriously.'

'What is it?'

Louis put his sandwich down on the commissaire's desk and slowly searched his pockets. He brought out the scrap of newspaper, which he carefully unfolded under the policeman's nose.

'Careful,' he warned. 'It stinks.'

Paquelin leaned gingerly over the object.

'What's this bit of filth?'

'Just what I asked myself when I found it.'

'Do you pick up every piece of rubbish you see and take it to the police station?'

'I'm just doing my civic duty, Paquelin.'

'Monsieur le commissaire to you, as you well know. Your provocative behaviour is contemptible and pathetic to see. So what is this rubbish?'

'You can see as well as I can. It's a bone.'

Paquelin leaned over the object more closely. The little thing was gnawed, corroded, pieced with dozens of pinpricks, and slightly brown in colour. He'd seen bones before, but no, this fellow must be having him on.

'That isn't a bone. What are you after?'

'I'm serious, monsieur le commissaire. I think it is a bone, and a human bone, what's more. I agree that it's hard to make out and not very big, but I thought to myself, that is a bone. So I came to see whether it was a matter for the police, whether there had been any reports of missing persons in the *quartier*. I found it on the Place de la Contrescarpe. Because, you see, there may have been a crime, since I've got a bone.'

'My friend, I've seen plenty of bones in my career,' said Paquelin, his voice rising. 'Burnt, crushed, pulverised. And that is not a human bone, I can tell you.'

Paquelin picked up the object in his large hand and shoved it towards Kehlweiler.

'You just have to feel its weight. It's hollow, empty, nothing. A bone would be heavier than that. You can take it away again.'

'I know, I weighed it too. But it might be prudent to check? Get it analysed? A report?'

Paquelin rocked on his feet, ran a hand through his fair hair; it's true that he would have been really good-looking if not for that detestable mean mouth.

'I see,' he said. 'You're trying to trap me, Granville, or whoever you are. You're pushing me to go on a wild goose chase, make me look ridiculous, then plant a newspaper article, it's a little game of fool the cops . . . Well, it won't work, my friend. The stupid attempt at provocation, the toad, the little mystery, the big joke, the silly music-hall act. Find another trick. You aren't the first or the last person who's tried to make a fool of me. And I'm the boss around here, OK?'

'I insist, commissaire. I want to know if anyone's

been reported missing in this *quartier*. Yesterday, day before, recently.'

'You're out of luck, nothing to report.'

'It could be that no one's called you about it yet. Sometimes people wait a long time. I'll have to drop in next week to find out.'

'And then what? You want copies of all our day records?'

'Why not?' asked Kehlweiler, shrugging.

He screwed up the piece of paper and put it back in his pocket.

'So that's a no, is it? Not interested? Still, Paquelin, I think you're being very negligent.'

'That will do!' said Paquelin, standing up.

Kehlweiler smiled. At last, the commissaire was losing his temper.

'Lanquetot, chuck him in the cells,' Paquelin muttered, 'and get him to cough up his identity.'

'Ah, no,' Kehlweiler said, 'not the cells. Impossible, I've got a dinner date.'

'The cells!' Paquelin repeated, with a sharp gesture towards Lanquetot.

Lanquetot had stood up.

'Permit me, please, to phone my wife,' asked Kehlweiler, 'to let her know. That's my right, Paquelin, you know that.'

Without waiting for an answer, he had seized the telephone and dialled a number.

'Extension 229, please, personal and urgent. From Ludwig.'

Half perching on Paquelin's table, Louis looked

42

at the commissaire, who was now standing up as well, with both fists on the table. Good-looking hands, pity about the mouth, really.

'My wife. Busy,' Louis explained. 'Might take a bit of time. Ah, no, there she is. Jean-Jacques? Ludwig here. Listen, I am having a little argument with Commissaire Paquelin in the 5th arrondissement . . . Yes, the very same. He wants to lock me up, because I came with an enquiry about a possible missing person in the quartier . . . Yes, I'll explain . . . Could you sort it please? . . . Very kind of you . . . Hang on, I'll put him on the line.'

Louis held out the receiver to the commissaire with an amiable expression.

'It's for you, commissaire. The Minister of the Interior, Jean-Jacques Sorel, would like a word.'

As Paquelin took the phone, Louis dusted himself down and put Bufo in his pocket. The commissaire listened, answered briefly and hung up, quietly.

'*What* is your name?' he asked again.

'Commissaire, it's your job to know who you're dealing with. I know quite well who you are. So, what's the verdict? You don't want anything to do with my little object? Or to collaborate? Or to let me see the day lists?'

'Nice little scam, isn't it?' said the commissaire. 'With help from high-ups in the Ministry of the Interior . . . And that's all you could come up with, to land me in it up to my neck? Do you really take me for an idiot?'

43

'No.'

'Lanquetot, get this so-and-so out of here before I make him eat his toad.'

'No one touches my toad. They're fragile creatures.'

'Know what I'd like to do with your toad? Or with people like you?'

'I certainly do know. You probably wouldn't want me to say in front of your junior officers, though?'

'Out!'

Lanquetot went back down the stairs behind Kehlweiler.

'I can't give you your papers back now,' Lanquetot whispered. 'He might be watching you.'

'Let's say 8 p.m., metro Place Monge.'

Lanquetot went back up to Paquelin's office, after having made sure Louis Kehlweiler was out on the street. There was a little bead of sweat on the boss's upper lip. He'd take a couple of days to calm down.

'Did you hear that, Lanquetot? Not a word to anyone else here, mind. And how do we know it really was Sorel on the line, after all? We could check, call up the Ministry . . .'

'Yes, we could, sir, but if it really was Sorel, might not be a good idea. He's an irascible man.'

Paquelin sat down heavily.

'You were here before me, Lanquetot, under that lunatic Adamsberg. Have you ever heard of this character before, "Ludwig" or Louis Granville? Does the name ring a bell?'

44

'No, sir, nothing.'

'On your way, Lanquetot. And remember? Not a word to anyone.'

Lanquetot went back to his office, damp with perspiration. To start with, check out any missing persons in the 5th.

CHAPTER 5

Lanquetot arrived on time. Louis Kehlweiler was already there, leaning on the balustrade around the entry to the metro station. He was holding his toad in his hand and gave the impression of being deep in a conversation which Lanquetot dared not interrupt. But Louis had seen him, and turned round and smiled.

'Here are your ID papers, Kehlweiler.'

'Thanks, Lanquetot, it worked perfectly. My apologies to your junior colleagues.'

'I've checked all the missing persons in the 5th arrondissement. I even looked at the 6th and 13th, because they're the adjoining ones. Nothing. Nobody's been reported missing. I'll take a look at the other districts.'

'How far back did you go?'

'The whole of the last month.'

'That should be enough. Unless there's some exceptional circumstance, I think it would have been in the last three or four days, and not too far from the Place de la Contrescarpe. Or maybe somewhere completely different.'

'What makes you so sure?'

'My little piece of bone, Lanquetot. I brought it to your boss quite honestly. And if he hadn't been so aggressive, he'd have had some doubts, thought about it, and done his job properly. I played the game, I don't need to feel guilty, and you're my witness. He didn't do his job. All the better, I get to take it on, with his blessing and a kick up the backside from him. Just what I wanted.'

'So this little thing – it's really a bone?'

'A human bone, my friend. I got it checked at the Natural History Museum just now.'

Lanquetot gnawed at a fingernail.

'I don't get it. It didn't look like anything. What bone is it?'

'The top joint of a big toe. Could be left or right, you can't tell, but probably a woman's. So we need to look for a woman.'

Lanquetot paced around a little, hands behind his back. He needed to think.

'This toe bone,' he said at last, 'could have come from an accident maybe?'

'Improbable.'

'But it's not normal to find a toe bone on the grid round a tree.'

'That's what I think too.'

'So how did it get there? Perhaps it's from a pig?'

'No, Lanquetot, no. It's human, I'm not going to go back on that. If you're still sceptical, we can get it analysed further. But even Bufo agrees, it's a piece of human bone.'

'Well, shit,' said Lanquetot.

47

'You said it, inspector.'

'I said what?'

'You hit on it, how the bone got there.'

'How am I supposed to know that?'

'Wait,' said Kehlweiler, 'I'm going to show you something. Can you just hold Bufo?'

'With pleasure.'

'Right, hold your hand out.'

Louis brought out a bottle of water and sprinkled some on Lanquetot's hand.

'It's for Bufo,' he explained, 'you can't hold him with a dry hand. He gets too hot, he gets upset, it doesn't work. There. Now pick up Bufo with your thumb and index finger, fairly firmly because he doesn't know you. Not too tight though, OK? I'm fond of him. The only being in the world who lets me talk without interrupting me, and never asks for explanations. Now, just take a look.'

'Tell me,' Lanquetot interrupted him, 'was that really Sorel you spoke to at the Ministry?'

'No, not at all, my friend. Sorel is too isolated, he can't afford to cover me too openly. It was a pal acting a part, I'd fixed it in advance.'

'That was a mean trick,' Lanquetot murmured.

'Yes, it was, rather.'

Louis flattened out the screw of paper again and carefully picked up the bone.

'You see, Lanquetot, it's been bitten, gnawed.'

'Yes.'

'And all the little holes, see them?'

'Yes, of course.'

'So now do you understand where this came from?'

The inspector shook his head.

'From the gut of a dog, Lanquetot, from the gut of a dog! This bone has been digested, do you see? It's the acids that make the little holes, quite unmistakable.'

Louis put the bone away, and took his toad back.

'Come on, Bufo, we're going for a little walk, you, me and the inspector. The inspector is a new friend. You've seen him, right? And he didn't hurt you, did he?'

Louis turned to Lanquetot.

'I talk like this to him because he's a bit stupid, as I told you. You have to keep it simple with Bufo, just basic ideas: nice people, nasty people, eating, sex, sleep. He can't cope with anything else. Sometimes I try something a bit harder, a bit of philosophy even, to improve his mind.'

'One lives in hope.'

'He was much more stupid when I first got him. Let's go for a walk, Lanquetot.'

CHAPTER 6

Louis looked in the car park, doorways, cafes. It was night-time by now. Right, the metro. She wouldn't be going far, she didn't like leaving her territory. When he finally saw her on the metro platform at the mainline station, the Gare d'Austerlitz, he felt something relax in his stomach. He looked at her from a distance. Marthe was pretending to be waiting for the last train. And how long would she be able to go on pretending?

Dragging his stiff leg, because he had done too much walking, he hurried along the platform and let himself flop on to the seat next to her.

'So, my old friend, you're not in bed yet?'

'Ah, Ludwig, you've turned up just in time, you wouldn't have a spare ciggie, would you?'

'What the heck are you doing here, Marthe?'

'I'm out and about. I was just leaving.'

Louis lit a cigarette for her.

'Good day?' Marthe asked.

'I got up the noses of four cops, three of them weren't to blame. I'm going to get ahead of them now, with their blessing.'

Marthe sighed.

'All right,' said Louis, 'I was mean, I showed off, I teased them and I humiliated them a bit. But it was fun, you see, just a bit of fun.'

'You played the ancestors' trick?'

'Of course.'

'In another life, you'll have to work things out better. Get your fun without spreading mayhem everywhere.'

'In another life, my dear old Marthe, there will be major works to be done. Rebuild the foundations, large-scale restoration. Do you believe in other lives?'

'No, not at all.'

'I wanted to catch Paquelin out. Had to climb over the others to get to his office.'

OK, Louis said to himself, we're not going to bang on about this all night, he'd had his fun and done very little harm. There wasn't much wriggle room with guys like Paquelin.

'Did it work, anyway?'

'Pretty well.'

'Paquelin, that's the good-looking one, fair hair, skinny, and a real bastard?'

'You got it. He knocks prostitutes about, and the guys he arrests he grabs by the balls.'

'Well, I don't suppose you cut him to bits. What do you want from him?'

'Just that he gets the hell out, that's all I want.'

'Louis, don't forget you're not so well connected these days. Well, it's your funeral. Vincent took a picture of the man from 102 and followed him.'

51

'I know.'

'Can't tell you anything, can we? I like bringing you bits of news.'

'I'm listening. Tell me some news.'

'Well, that's it. Told you everything.'

'And about where you're staying now, you told me everything too?'

'Whose business is that?'

Marthe turned towards Kehlweiler. This man was like a fly strip. All the bits of news stuck on to him, without his having to lift a finger. That's how he was, everyone told him everything. A real pain, in the end.

'Take a fly, for instance,' said Marthe.

'Yes?'

'Oh, drop it.'

Marthe put her chin in her hands. A fly thinks she can flit across a room without being spotted, no problem, and she bumps into Ludwig, so she sticks to him, Ludwig gently extracts all her news and lets her go again. He was such a flypaper for information that he'd made it his profession and couldn't do anything else any more. Fixing a lamp, for instance: no point asking him, he'd be rubbish. No, all he was good at was knowing things. His grand army told him what was going on, from the tiniest details to massive affairs, and once you were in the eye of the storm, it was hard to get out. Well, that was how he'd wanted it.

Ludwig said you shouldn't judge a detail by appearances. You never know, it might be hiding another. And his mission was to chase them up, and it paid off. Why all this energy? Who knew? And Marthe had her own idea about that. Until his dying day, Louis would be chasing exterminators, whether they had exterminated one being or a thousand. But as for where she was lodging, who asked you to poke your nose in? We have our pride. She'd told herself she'd find a solution, and now, not only was there no solution in sight, but Louis knew about it. Who'd been telling him that? Who? Never mind, one of his army of wretched whistle-blowers.

Marthe shrugged. She looked at Louis who was waiting patiently. From a distance, you would think he looked nothing special. But from near to, eighty centimetres say, everything changed. You didn't really have to ask then why everyone came and told him everything. At one metre fifty, or two metres, say, Louis looked like a forbidding scientist, unapproachable, like those pictures of bearded gents in school history books. At one metre, you weren't quite so sure. And the nearer you got, the more you doubted. The index finger he laid lightly on your arm to ask a question, it dragged words out of you on its own. That hadn't worked with Sonia, she must be a fool. She should have stayed with him for life, no, perhaps not for life, because there are times when you absolutely have to eat, earn a living, she knew what she meant. Perhaps Sonia hadn't taken a good look at him, close up. Marthe could see no other explanation. Ludwig himself thought he was ugly;

for twenty years she'd been telling him the opposite, but he did think himself very ugly all the same, and if women were fooled into thinking otherwise, that was his good luck. Too much already, Marthe, who had known hundreds of men and had loved only four of them, knew what she was talking about.

'You're thinking?' Louis asked.

'Do you want a bit of cold chicken? Some left in the bag.'

'I had a meal with Inspector Lanquetot.'

'The chicken will go to waste.'

'Too bad.'

'Even kings don't throw away good cold chicken.'

Marthe had a disconcerting way of suddenly announcing maxims apropos of nothing. Louis liked that. He had a good collection of Marthe-isms and had often used them.

'Right, you're on your way to bed? Shall I see you home?'

'Who said it was your business?'

'Marthe, let's not go round in circles. You are as stubborn as a pig, and I'm as stubborn as a wild boar. Why didn't you tell me?'

'I can manage. I've got my address book. Someone'll find me something. Old Marthe has things up her sleeve, you're not God Almighty.'

'Your address book, your list of ancient toffs . . .' Louis sighed. 'Because you think those toffs will lift a finger to help an old tart who has to sleep in shop doorways in the winter.'

'Yes, that's right, they'll help an old tart. And why not?'

'You know why . . . You tried them? Did you get a result? Not a thing. Am I right?'

'So what?' muttered Marthe.

'Come on, old girl. We're not going to spend all night on this metro platform.'

'Where?'

'To my bunker. And since, as you say, I'm not God Almighty, it isn't paradise on earth.'

Louis hauled Marthe towards the stairs. It was freezing outside. They went quickly through the streets.

'You can fetch your things tomorrow,' said Louis, opening a door on a second-floor landing near the Arènes de Lutèce. 'But don't bring all your stuff, there's not a lot of room.'

Louis switched on the heating, unfolded a narrow sofa bed, and shoved aside some cardboard boxes. Marthe looked around the little room, full of files, books, piles of documents and newspapers on the floor.

'Now don't go poking about, please,' said Louis. 'This is my little annexe of the Ministry. Twenty-five years of records, tons of dodgy scandals of every kind, the less you know, the better for you.'

'OK,' said Marthe, sitting on the little bed. 'I'll try.'

'You all right here? It'll do? We'll try to find something else. We'll rustle up a bit of money.'

'Ludwig, you're very kind,' said Marthe. 'And

when my mother said that to anyone, she always added, "It'll be the ruin of you." And do you know why?'

Louis just smiled.

'Here's a spare set of keys. Make sure you use both the locks when you leave.'

'I'm not stupid,' said Marthe, jerking her chin towards the bookshelves. 'Plenty of names in the files, eh? Don't worry, I'll look after them.'

'Another thing, Marthe. Every morning, there's this guy comes here between ten and twelve. So you need to be up. But you can stay while he works, you can explain.'

'Right. What's he doing?'

'He's filing newpapers, reading, spotting things that look wrong, cutting out and classifying. Then he writes me a summary.'

'Can you trust him? He might go poking about . . .'

Louis took out two beers and passed one to Marthe.

'The key stuff's locked away. And I chose this guy carefully, I think. He's Vandoosler's lad. Remember Vandoosler, the commissaire in the 13th arrondissement? Did he ever pick you up?'

'Several times. He was in the vice squad a long time. Nice man. I went a few rounds with him, we understood each other. He was OK with us girls, have to say that for him.'

'Plenty of other things one can say for him.'

'Was he booted out? He was just the type.'

'Yes. He let a murderer get away.'

'Guess he had his reasons?'

'Yes.'

Louis walked around the room with his beer in hand.

'Why are we talking about this?' asked Marthe.

'Because of Vandoosler. He sent this lad to sort my papers. His nephew, or godson, or something. He wouldn't have sent me just anyone, you know.'

'And what's he like?'

'I don't know. I've only seen him three times in three weeks. He's an unemployed medieval historian. He looks like the kind that asks himself questions all the time, and they pull him in twelve directions at once. So on the question of doubt, he seems very sound, he's unlikely to incline towards inflexible perfection.'

'Should suit you then. What's he look like?'

'A bit odd, very thin, always wears black. Vandoosler's got three of them living with him, he sent me this one. You'll meet him and sort it out yourself. I'm leaving you now, Marthe. I've got a lead to follow up, looks intriguing.'

'Bench 102?'

'Yes, but not what you think. The deputy's nephew I'm leaving to Vincent. He's a big boy now. No, it's something else, a bit of human bone I found near the bench.'

'So what do you think about it?'

'Murder.'

Although Marthe couldn't see the connection,

she trusted Ludwig. At the same time his restless activity worried her. Since he'd been sacked from the Ministry, Ludwig hadn't managed to slow down. She was wondering whether he was beginning to look for anything anywhere, bench to bench, town to town. He could just have given up, after all. But clearly that wasn't on the agenda. Before, he didn't make mistakes, but he'd always been connected, always in charge of a team. Now that he was freelancing, and not in charge of anything, it worried her, she was afraid he'd go crazy. She'd asked him, and Ludwig had snapped at her that he wasn't crazy, but he had no intention of bringing the train to a halt. Then he had put on his German expression, as she called it. So, OK, I give up.

She looked at Louis, now leaning against a bookcase. He seemed calm, as usual and as she had always known him. She knew a thing or two about men, that was something she was proud of, and this man was one of her favourites, apart from the four she had loved, none of whom had been either as gentle or as entertaining as Ludwig. She didn't want him to go crazy, he really was one of her favourites.

'Is there a reason you're thinking it's murder, or are you just inventing a good story?'

Louis pulled a face.

'A murder's not a good story, Marthe, I'm not doing this just to avoid twiddling my thumbs. In the case of 102, I suppose I could be wrong, and

perhaps there's nothing suspicious about this bone.
I hope so. But it bothers me, I'm not sure, so I'm
keeping my eyes open. I'm going to take a stroll
up that way. Sleep well.'

'Shouldn't you get some sleep too? What are you
going to look at?'

'Dogs pissing against trees.'

Marthe sighed. Nothing to be done. Louis was
determined, a runaway train. Slow, but no brakes.

CHAPTER 7

Marc Vandoosler had jumped at it when his godfather had suggested this little job for two thousand francs. By combining it with his part-time work at the local library, starting in January, it would help out. In the ramshackle house where he lived, they had been able to switch on three more radiators.

Of course, he had been suspicious at first. You always felt a bit suspicious about any contact of his godfather who, when he was in the force, had always done things his own way. A very special way. You never knew who might be among the elder Vandoosler's contacts. In this case, the job was to go and classify press cuttings for 'a friend', without touching anything on the shelves. His godfather had said it was confidential, that Louis Kehlweiler had gathered kilos of information and now that he had been sacked from the Ministry of the Interior, he was still collecting stuff. All on his own? Marc had asked. And he manages? No, that's the point, that's why he needs some help.

Marc had said OK, he wouldn't poke about in the files, see if he cared. If they'd been medieval

60

archives, of course, it would have been another story. But crimes, lists, names, networks, trials, no, nothing to interest him there. Perfect, the godfather had said, you can start tomorrow. 'Ten o'clock in his bunker. He'll explain, he might tell you the story; muddle and certainty – that's what he's all about. He'll put it better than I can. I'll go out and call him.'

Because they still hadn't had a telephone installed. It was eight months now, since they'd moved in, the four of them, to this dilapidated house, four men, almost drowned by the 1990s economic recession, with the impossible plan of clubbing together to keep their heads above water. For the moment, the irregular and uncertain resources they managed to contribute allowed them to survive by the skin of their teeth, but without being able to see more than three months ahead. So to make a phone call, they went to a nearby cafe.

And for three weeks now, Marc had been doing his job, conscientiously, Saturdays included, because newspapers were published on Saturdays as well. As he was a fast reader, he quickly finished his daily stack, which was a large one, since Kehlweiler received all the regional papers too. In them, all he had to do was spot echoes of criminal activity of any kind: political, financial, vice, drugs, domestic – and sort them into piles. In the reports, he was asked to pay attention to cold cases rather than recent ones, hard scandals not soft ones, the implacable rather than the crimes of passion.

61

Kehlweiler had kept the sorting instructions short, no point bothering Marc with the stuff about right hand, left hand. Marc had that built in, and could easily make the distinction between efficacity and muddle. So Kehlweiler left him a free hand in cutting up the newspapers. Marc did the necessary connections, classified and indexed by subject, clipped and put the articles into files, and once a week he wrote a general report. Kehlweiler seemed all right to him, but he wasn't sure yet. He had only seen him three times, a tall guy with a stiff leg, good-looking once you got close to him. He was overpowering at times, which was disagreeable, and yet Kehlweiler's manner was always gentle and slow. All the same, Marc wasn't entirely at ease with him. He instinctively felt he had to be on guard, and Marc didn't like having to do that, in fact it pissed him off. If he himself felt like losing his temper, for example, he usually didn't hold back. But Kehlweiler didn't give the impression that he ever lost his temper. Which annoyed Marc, who liked to meet people as nervy as himself, or, ideally, worse.

One of these days, Marc thought, as he used the two keys on the bunker door, he'd try to stop losing his temper. But at thirty-six, he didn't see how he would manage that.

As he crossed the threshold, he gave a start. There was a bed installed behind his desk and an old woman with brightly dyed hair, who put down her book to look at him.

'Come in,' said Marthe, 'and pretend I'm not here. I'm Marthe. You're the one who comes to work for Ludwig? He left a note for you.'

Marc read a few lines, in which Kehlweiler summed up the situation for him. OK, but did he think it was so easy to work, with someone living her little life one metre behind your back? Hell's bells.

Marc nodded a greeting and sat at the table. Best to keep your distance from the start, because this old lady looked as if she was chatty and nosy about everything. You had to think Kehlweiler wasn't worried about leaving her with his files.

He could feel her looking at his back, and that made him tense. He'd picked up a copy of *Le Monde* and found it hard to concentrate.

Marthe was examining the newcomer from behind. Dressed entirely in black: drainpipe trousers, canvas jacket and cowboy boots, black hair too, a smallish man, a bit too thin, the nervous, agile type, didn't look strong. His face was all right, a bit lined, a bit Sioux Indian, but not bad, delicate, attractive. Good. It would be all right. She wouldn't bother him, he looked the jumpy kind who needs to be on his own to work. She had experience of men.

Marthe stood up, and put on her coat. She had some stuff to fetch.

Marc stopped halfway through a line, and turned round.

'Ludwig? Is that his name?'

'Mmm, yes,' said Marthe.

'He isn't called Ludwig.'

'Mmm, yes he is, he's called Louis. Louis, Ludwig, same name, isn't it? Anyway, talking of names, seems you're the nephew of Vandoosler? Armand Vandoosler? When he was commissaire, he was good to us girls.'

'That doesn't surprise me,' said Marc drily.

The older Vandoosler had never been able to restrain himself, he had spent his life seducing with passion, abandoning carelessly, distributing pleasure, excess and also damage, for which Marc, who was rather cautious with women, bitterly reproached him. It was a constant subject of dissension between them.

'He never once hit any of the girls,' Marthe went on. 'When I met your uncle, we'd talk it through. Is he OK? You're a bit like him, now it occurs to me, looking at you. Anyway, I'll let you get on.'

Marc stood up, sharpening a pencil.

'But Kehlweiler, why do you call him Ludwig?' Though really, what did it matter to him?

'What's the problem?' asked Marthe. 'Don't you like Ludwig as a name?'

'Yeah, it's all right.'

'Well, I like it better than Louis. Louis, Louis . . . that's a bit of a posh name in French.' Marthe buttoned up her coat.

'Yes,' said Marc. 'Where's he from, Kehlweiler? Paris?'

Now what, really, did it matter, for heaven's sake?

All he had to do was let the old woman push off, that's all. Marthe seemed to have buttoned herself up, like her coat.

'Paris?' Marc repeated.

'He's from the Cher *département*, in central France. People have the right to be called what they want, haven't they, far as I know?'

Marc nodded, he was missing something here, it seemed.

'Anyway, what sort of name is Vandoosler?' Marthe went on.

'Belgian.'

'Right, well, there you are.'

Marthe went out with a wave of her hand. A wave that also meant 'Put a sock in it', if Marc wasn't mistaken.

Marthe grumbled to herself as she went downstairs. Too nosy and too chatty that guy, like herself. Oh well, if Ludwig trusted him, that was his own business.

Marc sat back down, a little preoccupied. If Kehlweiler had once worked for the Ministry of the Interior, all right. That he went on poking his nose into anything and everything and organising this demented archive, with no rhyme or reason, seemed crazy to him. Big words didn't explain everything. Big words often hide little personal matters, sometimes honest, sometimes sordid. He looked up at the shelves where the box files were all lined up. No. He had always kept his word, he was an honest man, honest to the point of annoying everyone with his honest talk, he wasn't going to poke about. He didn't have so many good qualities that he could afford to sacrifice one of them.

CHAPTER 8

Louis Kehlweiler had spent part of the night in thought.

The previous evening, he had counted the people who had brought a dog to lift its leg against a tree in the little square near bench number 102. At least ten: it was all go, what with bladder-emptying dogs and docile owners. Between ten thirty and midnight, he had looked at the faces and noted details to try and distinguish them, but he didn't see how he was going to trail everybody. It might take days and days. Not counting the legion who had no doubt gone past before ten thirty. An exhausting task, but he was resolute that he could not let this rest. A woman had perhaps been killed. He had always been able to sniff out wrongdoing, and he couldn't simply drop it.

There was no point checking the morning dog walkers – the grid round the tree had been clean when he left the bench at 2 p.m. on Thursday. The dog had come along afterwards. And if there was at least one thing you could count on, it was that dog walkers are regular in their habits. Always at the same time, and one or two possible routes, ending back at the start. As for the dogs' habits, that was trickier. Degenerate creatures that they were, town dogs didn't mark out their territories any more, they did their business on any old spot, but obviously it was on their owner's route.

So there were very good chances the same dog would return to this grid. Dogs like grids, even better than the tyres on cars. But even if he managed to identify twenty-five dog owners, how could he get their names and addresses without spending a whole month on it? Especially since these days he wasn't too good at tailing people. With his stiff leg, he walked more slowly and was more easily spotted. Being so tall didn't help.

He needed someone to give him a hand, but he had no money for that now. It was over, missions with all expenses paid. He was alone, he should really give up. So he'd found a piece of bone on a grid round a tree, he should just get over it.

For a long stretch of the night he'd tried to force himself to forget it. It could just be left to the police. Who couldn't give a toss. As if, every day, dogs swallowed bits of someone's toe which they then excreted here and there. Kehlweiler shrugged. The cops would never mobilise unless they had a body, or a missing person was reported. And a stray little toe joint is not a corpse, it's just an isolated bit of bone. But no, he wasn't going to drop it. He looked at his watch. He just had time to catch Marc Vandoosler in the bunker.

Marc was leaving the office when Kehlweiler

called out to him in the street. He stiffened. What did Kehlweiler have to say to him on a Saturday? He usually dropped by on a Tuesday, to pick up the previous week's report. Had that old Marthe woman said something? Reported the questions he'd asked? Very quickly, Marc, who didn't want to lose this job, concocted in his head a rapid web of defensive lies. He was gifted at this, could do it in a flash. Being fast at defending yourself was a useful skill when you were bad at attacking. When Kehlweiler was close enough for him to see his face, Marc realised that there was no attack to parry, and he relaxed. One day, as the next new year's resolution perhaps, he'd try to stop getting so worked up. Or the year after that – the way things were, there was no hurry.

Marc listened and replied. Yes, he had time, yes, OK, he could go along with him for half an hour, what was it about?

Kehlweiler dragged him to a nearby bench. Marc would have preferred to go to a nice warm cafe, but this big fellow seemed to have an irritating fondness for benches.

'Take a look,' said Kehlweiler, pulling a crumpled ball of newspaper from his pocket. 'Open it carefully and tell me what you think.' He had started to address Marc familiarly as 'tu'.

Though *why* he was asking this question, Louis wondered, since he himself knew perfectly well what he thought about the bone. Probably so that Marc could start at the exact point he had started

69

from himself. The young relation of the elder Vandoosler intrigued him. The summary reports he had provided so far were excellent. And he had solved the Simeonidis affair, two terrible crimes, six months ago. But Vandoosler had warned him: his nephew was only interested in the Middle Ages and unrequited love. St Mark, he called him. Apparently he was very good in his field. But it might transfer to other things, might it not? Louis had learned three days ago that the painter Delacroix was thought to be the son of Talleyrand, and this combination had given him much pleasure. Genius for genius, painting and diplomacy, incompatible itineraries might fit together.

'Well?' Louis asked.

'Where was this found?'

'Paris, grid round tree near bench number 102, the Contrescarpe. What do you think?'

'At first sight, I'd say it's a piece of bone, extracted from some dog shit.'

Kehlweiler gave a start and looked at Marc carefully. Yes, this guy interested him.

'No?' asked Marc. 'Am I way off beam?'

'Not off beam at all. But how did you know? You have a dog?'

'No, but I do have a hunter-gatherer housemate from the palaeolithic period. He's a prehistorian, very into all that, so don't tease him about the subject. And he may be a prehistorian and obsessed, but he's a good friend. I've taken an interest in

70

the kind of remains he digs up, because he's sensitive actually, and I don't want to offend him.'

'Is he the one your uncle calls "St Luke"?'

'No, that's Lucien, he's a historian who specialises in the Great War, he's obsessive about that too. There are four of us in our lodgings, Mathias, Lucien and me, plus my uncle. And the Vandoosler ancestor, who insists on calling us St Matthew, St Mark and St Luke, makes us sound like we're crazies. It wouldn't take much to get the old man calling himself God. Well, that's just my uncle's bullshit. But Mathias's little obsessions are different. In the things he digs up, there are bones like that, with tiny holes in. Mathias tells us they come from the droppings of prehistoric hyenas, and on no account to confuse them with what the hunter-gatherers ate. He used to have this stuff all out on the kitchen table, until Lucien got mad because it was getting too close to his food, and Lucien likes his food. Well, none of that's important, but since there are no prehistoric hyenas prowling round the trees of Paris and their metal grids, I imagine it came from a dog.'

Kehlweiler nodded. He was smiling.

'Only,' Marc went on, 'what of it? Dogs gnaw bones, that's what they do, and they come out looking like that, porous and with holes in. Unless . . .' he added after a silence.

'Unless,' Kehlweiler repeated. 'Because that's a human bone, the top joint of a big toe.'

'Are you sure?'

71

'Certain. I got it confirmed at the Natural History Museum by someone who knows. It's from the toe of a woman, quite an old one.'

'Obviously,' said Marc after another silence, 'that doesn't happen every day.'

'It didn't bother the cops. The local commissaire doesn't believe it's a bone, he's never seen one like this. I realise that this fragment is in an unusual condition, and that I cornered him into making the mistake. He thinks I'm trying to trap him, which is quite true, but not in the way he thinks. Nobody has been reported missing from round here, so they're not going to open an investigation because of a bone covered in dog shit.'

'But what do you think then?'

Marc addressed anyone who called him 'tu' in the same way. Kehlweiler stretched out his long legs and clasped his hands behind his head.

'I think this toe joint belongs to someone, and I'm not sure that the person on the end of it is still alive. I'm ruling out an accident, that's too unlikely. It's true weird things can happen, but still. I think the dog helped itself to a corpse. Dogs are carrion eaters, like hyenas. And we can forget about corpses held legally in a house or a hospital. I don't imagine a dog would be allowed into a laying-out room.'

'What if some old woman died alone in her room, with her dog beside her?'

'How did the dog get out then? No, it's impossible, the corpse must have been in the open air.

A corpse that has been forgotten somewhere, or killed somewhere, a cellar, a building site, a patch of waste ground. That way a dog could have come past. The dog swallows the bone, digests it, excretes it and the torrential rain from the other night gives it a wash.'

'A corpse abandoned on some waste ground somewhere doesn't necessarily mean a murder.'

'But the bone was found in Paris and that's what bothers me. Parisian dogs don't go exploring far from their habitat, and a corpse couldn't remain unnoticed for long in the city. They should have found it by now. I saw Inspector Lanquetot this morning, still nothing, not the slightest hint of a body lying around in the capital. No missing persons reported either. And routine enquiries about the deaths of people living alone haven't shown up anything relevant. I found the bone on Thursday night. No, Marc, it isn't normal.'

Marc wondered why Kehlweiler was telling him all this. He wasn't put out by it, though. It was pleasant to listen to him talking, he had a calm, deep voice, very soothing for the nerves. But as for this dog shit, well, what could he contribute? It was beginning to feel really cold on the bench, but Marc didn't dare say, 'I'm cold, I'm going home.' He pulled his jacket round him.

'You're cold?' asked Louis.

'A bit.'

'Me too, it's November, nothing to be done.'

Yes there is, thought Marc, we could go to a cafe. Though of course it might be a bit tricky to talk about this in a cafe.

'We'll have to wait,' Kehlweiler went on. 'There are some people who'll wait a week before reporting someone missing.'

'Yes,' said Marc, 'but why are you so concerned?'

'I'm concerned because I don't think it's normal, like I told you. Somewhere, some nasty murder has taken place, that's what I think. The bone, the woman, the murder, the nastiness, it's all got inside my head, too late to stop, now I have to know, I have to find out.'

'That's a vice.'

'No, it's an art. It's an irrepressible art and it belongs to me. You don't have something like that?'

Yes, Marc did: but for the Middle Ages, not for a toe joint found at the bottom of a tree.

'It's my art,' repeated Kehlweiler. 'If after a week Paris doesn't come up with anything, the problem will become much more complicated.'

'Yes, of course. Dogs can travel.'

'Precisely.'

Kehlweiler unfolded his long body and got to his feet. Marc looked up at him.

'This dog,' Kehlweiler said, 'could have travelled kilometres that night in a car. It could have eaten a toe in the provinces somewhere and deposited it in Paris. All we can suppose, thanks to this dog, is that there's a woman's body somewhere, but it could be anywhere. France isn't as small as all that, and that's just France. A body somewhere, but nowhere to look.'

'What a lot to come out of a piece of dog shit,' Marc said quietly.

'You didn't see anything in the regional papers, did you? Murders, accidents?'

'No murders. A few accidents as usual. But nothing about a foot, I'm sure of that.'

'Well, keep looking and be vigilant, foot or no foot.'

'OK,' said Marc, standing up.

He'd got the point, his fingers were freezing, he wanted to get away.

'Wait,' said Kehlweiler. 'I need someone to help, someone who can run. I'm slowed down by my leg, I can't follow this bone all on my own. Could you just lend me a hand for a few days? But I can't afford to pay you.'

'To do what?'

'To follow people who walk their dogs near this bench. Note their names, addresses, movements. I don't want to waste too much time, just in case.'

This idea did not appeal to Marc at all. He'd been a lookout man for his uncle once, and that was enough. It wasn't his kind of thing.

'My uncle says you have men all over Paris.'

'They're fixed points, bartenders, newspaper sellers, cops, people who don't move around. They keep their eyes open and alert me when it's necessary, but they're not mobile, do you see? I just need someone who can move about.'

'I don't do running, I just climb trees. I run about after the Middle Ages, but not after people.'

Kehlweiler was going to get upset, it was clear. This guy was even nuttier than his uncle. All artists are nutty. Artists sweating away about paint, the Middle Ages, sculpture, criminology, all mad, he had experience.

But Kehlweiler didn't get upset. He just sat down again on the bench. Slowly.

'All right,' he said. 'Forget it, it doesn't matter.'

He replaced the scrap of newspaper in his pocket.

Good. All Marc had to do was what he'd been wanting, go and get warmed up in a cafe, have a bite to eat, and go back to the shabby lodgings in the rue Chasle. He said goodbye and strode off down the avenue.

CHAPTER 9

Marc Vandoosler had eaten a sandwich in the street, and was back in his room by early afternoon. Nobody was home in the ramshackle house. Lucien was off giving a lecture on some aspect or another of the Great War, Mathias was classifying artefacts from his autumn dig in the basement of a museum, and the elder Vandoosler must have gone for a walk. Marc's godfather always had to be outdoors, and wasn't bothered by the cold.

Pity. Marc would have liked to ask him a few questions about Louis Kehlweiler, his incomprehensible shadowing of various people, and his interchangeable first names. Just a thought. He couldn't really care less, but still, just a thought. It could wait, of course.

Marc was working just now on a bundle of archives from Burgundy, from a place called Saint-Amand-en-Puisaye to be precise. He needed to finish a chapter in his book on the Burgundian economy in the thirteenth century. Marc would continue with his damned Middle Ages until he could make a living out of it, he'd sworn as much to himself. Well, he hadn't exactly sworn, he'd just told himself. At any rate, this was the only thing in his life that gave him wings, or let's say feathers, that and the women with whom he had been in love. All gone, even his wife, who had walked out on him. He must be too nervy, it probably put them off. If he'd been calm, like Kehlweiler, things might have worked out better. Though he suspected Kehlweiler wasn't as calm as he looked. Slow-moving, certainly. But that wasn't right either. From time to time, he turned his head to look at people with amazing rapidity. And he wasn't always calm. His face sometimes tensed up, his eyes focused into the distance, it wasn't as simple as that. Anyway, who'd said it would be simple? No one. This guy who went looking for improbable murderers, because of some dog shit on a pave-ment, couldn't function like everyone else. But he gave the impression of being calm, strong even, and Marc would have liked to be able to do the same. It must make things easier with women. Stop thinking about women. He'd been on his own for months now, and it wasn't worth twisting the knife in the damned wound.

So, back to the accounts of the lord of Saint-Amand. He had reached the income from his barns, columns of figures from 1245 to 1256, with some gaps. It was already pretty good, this snap-shot of a corner of Burgundy to put into the overall picture of the thirteenth century. Come to think of it, Kehlweiler had that strange face, as well as everything else. It makes a difference. Close to, the face was strikingly gentle. A woman might have been better at guessing whether it was the eyes, the lips, the nose, or the combination of all that, but the result was that from close to, he was worth a look. If he'd been a woman, he'd have agreed. Yeah, but he was a man, so that was stupid, and he only fancied women, which was stupid too, because women apparently didn't fancy him above anyone else, in this world.

Shit. Marc stood up, went downstairs into the large kitchen, freezing cold as it was in November, and made himself a cup of tea. With tea to drink, he could concentrate on the seigneur of Puisaye's barns.

Anyway, there was no sign that women made a beeline for Kehlweiler. Because seen from a distance you didn't realise he was good-looking, in fact not at all, he seemed off-putting. And it seemed to Marc that Kehlweiler had the look of a man who was pretty lonely, when it came to it. That would be sad. But it would comfort Marc himself. He wouldn't be the only one not to find anybody, to have disaster after disaster in his love life. Nothing worse than a love affair gone wrong to stop you giving due attention to medieval barns. It really blights your work. All the same, love exists out there, no point denying it. Still, at this moment, he wasn't in love, nor was anyone in love with him, and that way he had a quiet life at least, so it was best to take advantage of it.

Marc went back up to the second floor with his tray. He took a pencil and a magnifying glass, because the archives were very hard to decipher. They were photocopies of course, which didn't help. In 1245, now, they wouldn't have given a toss about a bit of dog shit, even with a bone inside it. Yes, but then again, they might. Justice was taken very seriously in 1245. Yes, in fact, they probably would have taken notice of it, if they'd known it was a human bone, and if they had suspected it came from a murder. Of course they would. They'd have handed the matter over to the customary justice dispensed by Hugues, the lord of Saint-Amand-en-Puisaye. And what would Hugues have done about it?

OK, all very well, but that's not the point. There's no dog shit mentioned in the papers about the lord's barns, don't get everything mixed up. It was raining outside. Perhaps Kehlweiler was still sitting on his bench, since he'd left him there just now. No, he must have changed benches, and gone to sit at observation post 102, by that grid round the tree. He really must ask his godfather some questions about the guy.

Marc transcribed ten lines and drank a mouthful of tea. His bedroom was not very warm, the tea did him good. Soon, he might be able to turn on another radiator, when he got the job in the library. Because as well as everything else, he wouldn't earn any money helping Kehlweiler out. Not a centime, he'd said. And Marc needed money, but not to look as if he would jump at anything. It's true that Kehlweiler would find it hard to follow the dog owners on his own, with his stiff knee as well, but that was his problem. Marc had to keep following the lord of Saint-Amand-en-Puisaye and that's what he would do. In three weeks, he'd made good progress, he'd identified a quarter of the feudal tenants. He'd always been quick at his work. Except when he stopped, of course. And Kehlweiler had noticed it in fact. Oh, the hell with Kehlweiler, and the hell with women, and with this tea that tastes of dust.

True, there might be a murderer around somewhere, a murderer no one would go looking for. But there were plenty of others, and so what? If some guy had killed a woman in a fit of rage, what business was it of his?

Dear God, the steward noting down the Saint-Amand accounts was hard-working, but his handwriting was lousy. If he'd been Hugues, he'd have changed his steward. His o's and a's were interchangeable. Marc picked up the magnifying glass. Kehlweiler's business wasn't the same as the Sophia Simeonidis case. That one he'd had to deal with because he'd been cornered, she was his neighbour, he liked her, and the murder had been a horrible premeditated one. Revolting, he didn't want to think about it any more. Yes, but there might be a crime behind Kehlweiler's bit of bone, and that too might be a horrible premeditated crime. Kehlweiler was thinking about it and wanted to know.

Yes, all right, but that was Kehlweiler's job, not his. If he'd asked Kehlweiler to give him a hand transcribing the accounts of Saint-Amand, what would he have answered? He'd have said no fear, and that would be normal.

Finished, over, impossible to concentrate. All because of this guy, and his story of the dog, the grid, the murder, the bench. If his godfather had been around, he could have told him exactly what he thought of Louis Kehlweiler. He'd been hired for a little filing job, and it had gone haywire, he was being obliged to do something else. Although, to be fair, Kehlweiler hadn't *obliged* him to do anything. He had suggested something, and he hadn't got mad when Marc refused. In fact no one was stopping him carrying on with his study of the barns of Saint-Amand.

No one except the dog. No one except the bone. No one except the idea of a woman at the end of the bone. No one except the idea of a murder. No one except Kehlweiler's face. Something convincing in his eyes, true, clear, sorrowful as well.

Right, but everyone had their cross to bear, and his was well worth Kehlweiler's. To each his cross, his quest and his archives.

True, when he had launched himself into the Simeonidis affair, it hadn't done him any harm. You can mix up your own quest and archives with other people's and not lose your way. Yes, maybe, or definitely, but it wasn't his job. No way. End of story.

Marc knocked his chair over in anger, as he stood up. He flung the magnifying glass on the pile of papers, and grabbed his jacket. Half an hour later, he walked into the bunker with Kehlweiler's archives, and there, as he had hoped, he found Marthe.

'Marthe, do you know where this bench number 102 is?'

'Are you allowed to know that? Because they're not mine, you know, the benches.'

'Good grief!' said Marc. 'I'm Vandoosler's nephew, and Kehlweiler lets me work in his office, of course I get to know the benches.'

'All right, all right, no need to hit the roof,' said Marthe. 'Just kidding.'

She explained where bench number 102 was, in her loud voice. Fifteen minutes later, Marc arrived within sight of the tree and its metal grid. It was already dark, at half past six. From the other end of the Place de la Contrescarpe, he saw Kehlweiler sitting on a bench. He was leaning forward, elbows on knees, smoking a cigarette. Marc stopped for a few minutes, observing him. His gestures were slow and infrequent. Marc was once more un-decided, unsure whether he was the winner or the loser, or whether he should think in those terms at all. He moved back a step. He watched as Kehlweiler stubbed out his cigarette, then ran his hands through his hair, slowly, as if he were holding his head very tightly. He held his head for a few seconds, then both hands fell to his thighs, and he stayed like that, looking down at the ground. This sequence of silent movements made up Marc's mind for him. He walked over to the bench and sat down at the other end, boots stretched out in front of him. Neither spoke for one or two minutes. Kehlweiler hadn't looked up, but Marc was sure he had recognised him.

'You do remember that there's no money in this?' Kehlweiler said finally.

'I remember.'

'You've probably got some other damn thing you'd rather do.'

'True.'

'Me too.'

Another silence. Their breath steamed when they spoke. Hell's teeth, how cold it was!

'You remember it could just be an accident, a set of coincidences?'

'I remember everything about it.'

'Take a look at this list. I've got twelve people already: nine men, three women. I eliminated dogs that were too big or too small. In my view, it came from a medium-sized dog.'

Marc ran his eyes down the list. Brief descriptions, ages, appearance. He reread it several times.

'I'm tired and hungry,' Kehlweiler said. 'Do you think you could spell me for a few hours?'

Marc nodded and gave him back the list.

'Keep it, you'll need it tonight. I've got two beers left – want one?'

They drank their beer in silence.

'See that man coming along, a bit more to the right? No, don't look straight at him, look over his head. See him?'

'Yes. So what?

'This guy is bad news, ex-torturer and more no doubt. Ultranationalist. Know where he's been going for a week now? No, don't for God's sake stare at him, look down into your beer.'

Marc obeyed. He kept his eyes fixed on the mouth of the small glass bottle. He didn't think it obvious why he should look down, and it was dark anyway. He couldn't see anything in fact. He heard Kehlweiler whispering.

'He's going to the second floor of the building opposite. It's where this politician's nephew lives, and he's up to something. And I'd like to know who he's up to something with, and whether the politician knows about it.'

'I thought we were dealing with a story about dog shit,' muttered Marc into the beer bottle.

When you blow into a bottle it makes a fantastic sound. Almost like the wind in the sea.

'This is something different. I'm letting Vincent chase up the politician. He's a journalist, he'll be good at it. Vincent is sitting on the other bench, over there, the guy who looks like he's asleep.'

'Yeah, got him.'

'You can look up now, the fascist has gone inside. But try to look natural. These people look out of their windows.'

'Here comes a dog,' said Marc. 'Medium-sized.'

'Good, make a note. Coming towards us: 18.47, bench 102. Owner a woman about forty, dark complexion, straight hair, mid-length, thin, not very pretty, well dressed, must be well off, blue coat, looks newish, trousers. Coming from the rue Descartes. Stop writing, the dog's coming.'

Marc took a swig of beer, while the dog pottered around the tree. If it had been a bit closer in the darkness, it would have pissed on his feet. No sense of propriety, Parisian dogs. The woman was waiting, with an absent-minded and patient air.

'Make a note,' Kehlweiler went on. 'Return same direction. Medium-sized dog, golden cocker spaniel, old, tired, limping.'

Kehlweiler finished off his beer with a gulp.

'There,' he said, 'that's what you do. I'll come back later. Not too cold, are you? You can go into the cafe from time to time. You can see the street from the counter. But don't come rushing back to the bench in a hurry, do it slowly, as if you're just wanting to digest your beer, or waiting for a woman who hasn't turned up.'

'I get it.'

'In two days, we'll have a complete list of the regulars. After that we'll share out shadowing them, to see where they come from and who they are.'

'OK. What's that in your hand?'

'My toad. I'm just damping him a bit.'

Marc clenched his teeth. Yeah, right, this guy was really nuts. And he'd walked straight into this one.

86

'You don't like toads, I'm guessing? He won't hurt, we talk to each other, that's all. Bufo – that's his name, Bufo – listen carefully. The guy I'm talking to is called Marc. He's a relation of Vandoosler. And Vandoosler's relatives are our relatives. He's going to watch the doggies for us, while we go and have a bite to eat. Understand?'

Kehlweiler looked up at Marc.

'You have to explain everything to him. He's very dumb.'

Kehlweiler smiled and put Bufo back in his pocket.

'Don't look like that. It's very useful, having a toad. You have to make things extremely simple in order to be understood, and that can be quite a relief.'

Kehlweiler smiled again. He had a special kind of smile, very infectious. Marc smiled back. He wasn't going to be thrown by the sight of a toad. What would you look like, if you were scared of a toad? A total idiot, that's what. Marc was scared stiff of touching a toad, yes, but he was also scared stiff of looking a total idiot.

'Can I ask a question in exchange?' Marc said.

'You can ask.'

'Why does Marthe call you Ludwig?'

Kehlweiler took his toad out of his pocket again.

'Bufo,' he said, 'Vandoosler's relative is going to be more of a bloody nuisance than we thought. What do you think?'

'You don't have to answer,' said Mark weakly.

'You're like your uncle, you pretend, but you really want to know everything. Whereas I was told you were quite happy looking after your Middle Ages.'

'Not quite, not always.'

'It did surprise me, I must say. Ludwig is my name. Louis, Ludwig, one or the other, that's the way it is, you can choose. It's always been like that.'

Marc looked at Kehlweiler. He was stroking Bufo's head. How ugly toads are. Gross too.

'What are you wondering now, Marc? How old I am? You're doing the maths?'

'Yes, of course.'

'No need to bother. I'm fifty years old.' Kehlweiler stood up.

'Got it now?' he asked. 'Worked it out?'

'Yes.'

'Born in March 1945, just before the end of the war.'

Marc twisted the little beer bottle in his hands, looking down at the ground.

'Your mother's . . . French?' he asked, in a neutral voice.

At the same time, Marc was thinking, that's enough, leave him alone, what business is it of yours?

'Yes, I've always lived here.'

Marc nodded. He was twisting and turning the bottle in his hands, staring down at the pavement.

'You're from Alsace then? Your father's Alsatian?'

'Marc,' said Kehlweiler with a sigh, 'don't act more stupid than you are. They call me "the

German", OK? And get on with it, another dog's coming.'

Kehlweiler left, and Marc took up the list and the pencil. 'Middle-sized dog, don't know what breed, no idea about that, dogs worry me, black with white patches, mongrel. Man, about sixty, balding, big ears, worn out, looks stupid, no, not stupid, coming from the rue Blainville, no tie, drags his feet, brown coat, black scarf, dog does his business, three metres from the tree grid, I think it's a bitch, going away the other way, no, goes into the cafe, I'll wait and see what he drinks and I'll have the same.'

Marc went up to the counter. The man with the medium-sized dog was drinking a pastis. He was chatting, just about this and that, but Marc noted it anyway. Since he was doing something weird, might as well do it properly. Kehlweiler would be pleased, he'd have all the little details. 'The German', born in 1945, French mother, German father. He'd wanted to know, well, now he knew. Not everything, but he wasn't going to torture Louis by asking whether his father was a Nazi, whether his father had been killed, or gone back across the Rhine, or whether his mother had had her head shaved at the Libération, he would ask no more questions. The hair had grown back, the boy had grown up, he had the soldier's surname, Marc wasn't going to ask why the mother had married a soldier from the German Army of occupation. And since then he'd been running. Marc rubbed his hand with the pencil. It tickled. And what business had he to bother Louis with all that? Everyone must have bothered him about it, and he'd done the same as the rest, no better. Above all, not a word about this to Lucien. Lucien was only doing his research on the *First* World War, but still.

Now he knew, and he didn't know what to do with what he knew. OK, fifty years, it's the past, it's over. For Kehlweiler, of course, nothing would ever be over. That must explain his obsessions, his shadowing, his work, his perpetual movement, his art perhaps.

Marc sat down on the bench again. Oddly, his uncle hadn't breathed a word of all this to him. His uncle was chatty about little things, but discreet over serious matters. He hadn't said Louis was known as 'the German', he'd said he came from nowhere in particular.

Marc picked up his notes on the dog, and crossed out 'mongrel'. That was better. When you didn't pay attention, you wrote a lot of things you shouldn't.

Kehlweiler came back at about eleven thirty. By then Marc had drunk four beers and registered four medium-sized dogs. He saw Kehlweiler first give a shake to the journalist who was dozing on the other bench. Vincent, in charge of the right-wing torturer. Of course it's more prestigious to be keeping watch on a torturer than on dog shit. So Kehlweiler had gone over to Vincent first, and he, Marc, freezing on bench 102, could go hang. He watched them talking for a while. Marc felt put out. Not much, just a little feeling of resentment, which mutated naturally into a nagging irritation. Kehlweiler was checking his benches, registering accounts, just like a lord going round his estate and questioning his serfs. Who did he think he was? Hugues de Saint-Amand-en-Puisaye? His obscure and tragic entry to the world had made him a megalomaniac, that was it. And Marc, who reacted strongly to any kind of servitude, whatever it was and wherever it came from, did not intend to snap to attention in Kehlweiler's grand army. Signing up as a volunteer to be told what to do wasn't for him. Let this child of World War II sort out his own messes.

Then Kehlweiler left Vincent, who went off sleepily through the streets, and started towards bench 102. Marc, who had downed five beers in all, and realised he should take them into account, felt his slight anger fade to a discreet nocturnal sulk, and finally melt into indifference. Kehlweiler sat down beside him and gave him that odd lopsided and communicative smile.

'You've had a lot to drink tonight,' he remarked. 'That's the problem in winter, when you're stuck on a bench.'

What business was it of his? Kehlweiler was playing with Bufo, and was obviously a million miles from thinking, in Marc's view, that Marc now wanted out of it again, and was ready to drop

91

these pathetic enquiries on wooden benches, art or no art.

'Can you hold Bufo for me? I want to get my cigarettes out.'

'No. Your toad gives me the creeps.'

'Don't worry,' Kehlweiler said, addressing Bufo. 'He's just saying that, without thinking. Just stay nice and quiet on the bench while I get my ciggies out. Any more dogs?'

'Total of four. It's all down there. Four dogs, four beers.'

'And now you want out of it?'

Kehlweiler lit a cigarette and passed the packet to Marc.

'You feel trapped? You think you're obeying orders and you don't like doing that? Nor do I. But I didn't give you any orders, did I?'

'No.'

'You came along of your own accord, Vandoosler the younger. And you can leave of your own accord. Show me the list.'

Marc watched as he read the notes, looking serious again. He was in profile, hooked nose, tight-lipped, black hair flopping over his forehead. It was very easy to get irritated with the Kehlweiler profile. Face to face, much less easy.

'Don't bother coming tomorrow,' said Kehlweiler. 'On Sunday, people break their habits, they take their dogs out any old time, or worse, you might see people stroll along who don't even live round about. That would confuse our dog list. We'll begin again Monday afternoon, if you like, and start trailing people Tuesday. Will you be in to do the filing on Monday morning?'

'Nothing's changed.'

'Look out in particular for accidents and murders of all kinds, as well as the rest.'

They parted with a wave of the hand. Marc walked slowly home, a little tired by the beer and the confused zigzag of his decisions and counter-decisions.

This went on until the next Saturday. Bench, beer, dogs to follow, cutting out articles and deciphering the accounts of Saint-Amand. Marc didn't ask himself too many questions about the basis for what he was doing. He'd been drawn into the network surrounding the grid under the tree, and couldn't now see how to escape it. The story interested him and, dog for dog, he wanted to understand too. He tolerated Kehlweiler's hermetic profile, and when he'd had enough of it, made sure to look at him face to face.

On the Tuesday and Thursday, he asked for some help from Mathias who could use his skills as a prehistoric hunter-gatherer to carry out excellent tracker missions. Lucien on the other hand was far too talkative for this kind of work. He always had to express his views on everything in a loud voice and, above all, Marc was worried about bringing him face to face with a Franco-German born from the tragic chaos of World War II. Lucien

would immediately have launched a full-on historical enquiry into Kehlweiler's paternal origins, no
doubt going back to the Great War, and very
quickly it would have become a nightmare.

Marc had asked Mathias on the Thursday night
what he thought of Kehlweiler, because he was still
distrustful of him, and his godfather's recommen-
dation had not reassured him. His uncle had special
views about the sinners on the planet, and some
of his best friends were totally corrupt sinners. His
uncle had once helped a murderer to escape, and
indeed that was why he had been sacked from the
police. But Mathias had nodded three times and
Marc, who greatly respected Mathias's silent appre-
ciations, had been relieved. It was unusual for
St Matthew to be wrong about anyone, as the
elder Vandoosler had commented.

CHAPTER 10

On the Saturday morning, Marc was at work in Kehlweiler's bunker. He had clipped and filed as usual, and had noticed nothing remarkable among the titbits of news, just the usual accidents, and no mention anywhere of a foot. He had archived his findings, he was paid to do that anyway, but frankly, it was time that this trail from bench 102 came to an end, even if it led nowhere. He had grown used to the presence of old Marthe behind him. Sometimes she went out, sometimes she stayed in, reading quietly or racking her brain over crosswords. At about eleven, they made themselves some coffee. And Marthe took advantage of that to break the silence and chat. She too, it seemed, had been a stringer for Ludwig. But she said that nowadays she got benches mixed up, 102 and 107 for instance, she wasn't as efficient as in the past, and that depressed her at times.

'Here comes Ludwig,' said Marthe.

'How do you know?'

'I recognise his step in the courtyard, because of his limp. Ten past eleven, that's not his usual time. It's this business with the dog, he's getting worked up about it. We can't see any rhyme or reason to it, everyone's fed up.'

'We've done complete reports. Twenty-three dog walkers out there, all nice peaceful people, nothing to be said about them. Has he always worked like this? Following up something impossible. Any old bit of dirt?'

'Yes, always,' said Marthe, 'when he's on a case. But I'm telling you, he's got second sight. That's how he made his name, up there in the Ministry. Sniffing out shit, that's Ludwig's vocation, his destiny, the trail he has to follow.'

'Is there anything that stops him pestering people?'

'Yes, of course. Sleep, women, wars. That adds up if you think about it. Say he wants to sleep, or to cook spaghetti, you won't get a peep out of him, he's completely switched off. Same with women. When his love life's not happy, he goes round in circles, he can't be bothered with anything. And I'm surprised he's so hard at work, since things aren't too good in that department just now.'

'Ah,' said Marc with satisfaction. 'And wars?'

'Oh, wars are something else again. That's special. When he starts thinking about wars, it stops him sleeping, eating, loving or working. Not good at all for him, wars.'

Marthe shook her head as she stirred his coffee. Marc was fond of her by now. She was always pulling him up for something, as if he were her little boy – when after all, he was thirty-six years old – or as if she had brought him up. She would say, 'An old hooker like me, you can't pull the wool over my eyes. I know all about men.' She said this all the time. Marc had introduced Mathias to her, and she'd said, nice boy, a bit wild but OK, and she knew about men.

'You're wrong,' said Marc, sitting back down at the desk. 'It wasn't Louis.'

'Shut up, what do you know about it? He's downstairs, talking to the painter, that's all.'

'I know now why you call him Ludwig. I asked him.'

'So, are you any further forward?' Marthe blew out some smoke disapprovingly. 'But don't worry, he'll track them down, you can bank on that,' she added grumpily, shuffling the pages of her newspaper.

Marc didn't insist and it wasn't a subject to tease Marthe about. He had just wanted to tell her he knew, that was all.

Kehlweiler came in, and signalled to Marc to stop filing. He pulled out a stool and sat down opposite him.

'Lanquetot, the local police inspector, gave me an update this morning, on the local district as well as the nineteen other arrondissements. Nothing in Paris. Nor in the suburbs either, he checked. No abandoned corpses, no dead bodies discovered, no missing persons or runaways reported.

Ten days since that dog left us that crap on the grid. So . . .'

Louis broke off, felt the lukewarm coffee pot, and poured himself a cupful.

'So, the dog must have brought it in from outside Paris, further away. It's got to be that. There's a body out there somewhere that corresponds to our bone, and I want to know where, whatever the state of that body is, dead or alive, accident or murder.'

Yes, maybe, thought Marc, but with the whole of the provinces to deal with, and why not the rest of the planet while we're at it, the accounts of the lord of Puisaye are not going to get much further forward. Kehlweiler would pursue this to the bitter end. Marc had a better idea now why Louis took on these kinds of mission, but he had to get out of this one.

'Marc,' Kehlweiler went on, 'among our twenty-three dogs, at least one must have travelled and gone outside Paris. Look at your notes. Who travels about on a weekday, Wednesdays or Thursdays? Have you noticed anyone, man or woman, who moves around?'

Marc looked in the file. Just peaceful people, doing peaceful things. He had Kehlweiler's notes, his own, and Mathias's. He hadn't yet sorted them all out properly.

'Look through them slowly, take your time.'

'Don't you want to take a look yourself?'

'I'm sleepy. I got up at dawn, ten o'clock, to see Lanquetot. I'm good for nothing when I'm sleepy.'

'Drink your coffee,' said Marthe.

'Here's someone,' said Marc, 'a guy the hunter-gatherer noticed.'

'Hunter-gatherer?'

'Mathias,' Marc said. 'You told me he could take a turn.'

'Yeah, right,' said Louis. 'So what did he hunt, your gatherer?'

'As a rule it's the aurochs, but in this case, he's caught a man.'

Marc looked again at the notes.

'There's a man who teaches one day a week at the Arts et Métiers technical school, on Fridays. He comes to Paris on Thursday night, and he leaves again on Saturday morning at dawn. When Mathias says dawn, he means dawn.'

'And where does he go?'

'To the far end of Brittany, place called Port-Nicolas, near Quimper. He lives there.'

Kehlweiler pulled a face, and leaned over to take the note written by Mathias. He read it and reread it, concentrating hard.

'He's making his German face,' Marthe whispered to Marc. 'Watch out for fireworks!'

'Marthe,' said Louis without looking up, 'you'll never manage to whisper in a discreet way.'

He stood up and took from the bookshelf a large card-index box labelled O–P.

'You've got a record for Port-Nicolas?' asked Marc.

'Yes. Tell me, Marc, how did your hunter-gatherer find all this out? Is he a specialist?'

Marc shrugged.

'Mathias is a special person. He hardly says a word. But he says "talk to me", and people talk. I've seen him at work, I'm not kidding. And he doesn't have some kind of trick. I asked.'

'So you think,' remarked Marthe.

'Whatever, it works. But not the other way round, unfortunately. If he says "shut up" to Lucien, for instance, that doesn't work. I suppose he got chatting to this guy while the dog was going about its doggy business.'

'No one else that travels?'

'Yes – another guy spends two days a week in Rouen, second family, I gather.'

'So?'

'So,' said Marc, 'if we look through the last two weeks in the local papers, *Ouest-France* and *Le Courrier de l'Eure*, what do we find?'

Ludwig smiled and helped himself to more coffee. Now he just had to let Marc think out loud.

'Now, what do we find?' Marc repeated.

He took out his files again and looked quickly through the news cuttings for southern Finistère in Brittany, and the area of Normandy around Rouen.

'In the Eure *département*, a lorry driver drove

into a wall one night, eleven days ago, Wednesday, high alcohol level in the blood. In Finistère, an old woman fell over and hit her head on rocks on a beach. No mention of a toe in either case.'

'Pass me the cuttings.'

Marc passed them over and crossed his legs on the table, feeling satisfied. He looked confidently at Marthe. This dog thing was over, they could get on with something else. It was depressing to spend a lot of time talking about a dog's excrement, there are other things in life.

Louis put the cuttings back, and washed out the coffee cups in the little sink. Then he found a clean tea towel to wipe them, and put them back on a shelf between two files. Marthe put away the coffee tin, picked up her book and settled herself on the narrow bed. Louis sat down beside her.

'Well, now, we're getting somewhere,' he said.

'If you like, I can look after Bufo.'

'No, that's kind of you, but I'd prefer to take him with me.'

Marc unfolded his legs quickly and put his booted feet back on the floor. What had Louis said? Take the toad with him? He didn't turn round, he must have been mistaken, he hadn't heard anything.

'Has he ever been to the seaside?' asked Marthe. 'It doesn't agree with everyone.'

'Bufo can adapt to anywhere, don't you worry about him. And what makes you think it's going to be Finistère?'

'A drunk lorry driver in the Eure can't be hiding much. But the old lady on the rocks, that might raise a few questions, and anyway it's a woman. What have you done to your nose?'

'I bumped into something when I got up this morning, didn't see the door, it was early.'

'Lucky you've got a nose, it protects the eyes.'

Good God, were they going to carry on like this for ever? Marc was on edge, saying nothing. Resting his hands on his thighs, hunched over, the reflexes of a man who would like to be forgotten about. Kehlweiler was going off to Brittany, what the fuck was that about? And Marthe seemed to find it completely natural. Had he been doing nothing else all his life? Running off to take a look? At the drop of a hat? Because of a piece of shit?

Marc looked at his watch. Almost midday, it was time. He could leave now, casually, before Kehlweiler signed him up as a runner on this wild goose chase. With someone like him, haunted by futility ever since the Second World War had brought him into the world, and the Ministry had made him redundant, you could spend for ever running all over France in search of some phantom. In the department of lost illusions, Marc considered he had fully paid his dues, and he had no intention of making further contributions on Kehlweiler's behalf.

Louis was examining his nose in the little pocket mirror handed to him by Marthe. Right. Marc discreetly closed the folders, buttoned up his jacket and waved goodbye to everyone. Kehlweiler replied with a smile, and Marc left. Once in the street, he decided he would go and work somewhere else, not back home in the shared house. He preferred to have some time to prepare his negative arguments, before Kehlweiler came calling to recruit him to go running around the far reaches of Brittany. All week, Marc had discovered by experience that it was best to disappear and think up ways of saying no to this guy. So he dropped in briefly to his room at home, to pick up enough work to keep him going in a cafe until the evening. He stuffed an old satchel full of Saint-Amand accounts, and rushed downstairs, just as his uncle was coming quietly up.

'Hello there,' said the elder Vandoosler. 'Anyone would think the cops were after you.'

Was it so obvious? Sometime he must practise not getting so agitated, or if that didn't work, which was predictable, to get agitated without it showing.

'I'm going off to do some work outside. If Kehlweiler gets in touch, you don't know where I am.'

'Reason?'

'The guy's crazy. I've got nothing against him, he has his own reasons, but I'd prefer if he goes chasing rainbows without me. To each his own, I'm not up for pointless expeditions to the ends of the earth.'

'You amaze me,' Vandoosler said simply, and went on climbing to the attic, where he lodged.

Marc found a pleasant cafe quite a distance from the house, and got busy balancing his thirteenth-century books.

Kehlweiler, standing still, tapped on the little cardboard index card he had extracted from his file.

'Bad timing,' he said to Marthe. 'I know too much, I travel too much, I meet too many people. Small world, this country. Much too small.'

'You know someone in this place in Brittany? Tell me.'

'Who do you think? Guess.'

'How many letters?'

'Seven.'

'Man or woman?'

'Woman.'

'Ah. Someone you were in love with, or so-so, or not at all?'

'That I was in love with.'

'That makes it easy then. The second girl? No, she's in Canada. The third? Pauline?'

'Spot on. Funny, eh?'

'Funny? That depends what you're going to do.'

Louis stroked his cheek with the index card.

'No revenge expeditions, Ludwig! People are free agents, they can do what they want. I liked her fine, your little Pauline, except she was a bit too keen on money and that's where you lost out. And as I'm always telling you, I know about women. But how do you know she's there? I thought you'd never heard from her again.'

'Just the once,' said Louis, taking out another card index, 'and it was to tell me about some toxic case. In her village about four years ago. She sent me a press cutting about the guy, with some comments of her own. But no personal message, nothing, not even "take care" or "love from Pauline". Just the information, because she thought this guy was nasty enough for me to keep some record of him. Not even "love", nothing. I replied the same way to acknowledge it, and I filed the man's name away in the big box.'

'Pauline used to provide you with some good tips. Who's the man?'

'Someone called René Blanchet,' said Louis, taking out a card. 'Don't know him.'

He read for a few seconds in silence.

'Quick outline?' said Marthe.

'Real old bastard, is what it looks like. Pauline knew the kind of thing I wanted.'

'And in the four years you've had her address, you haven't been tempted to go and take a look?'

'Yes, Marthe, I have, many times. Go and take a look, examine this Blanchet character, and try to get Pauline back while I'm there. I've been imagining her all alone in a big house by the sea, with the rain beating on the windows.'

'Don't take this the wrong way, but I'd be very surprised. I know about women. Well, anyway, why didn't you give it a try?'

'Because, anyway, as you put it, you've seen what I look like, you can see my leg. I know about women too, Marthe. It's not important, don't worry, I'd have run into Pauline again sometime or another. If you spend your life going around a small country like France, you meet the people you deserve, the ones you try to meet, the ones you want to meet, don't you fret.'

'Still and all,' murmured Marthe, 'no revenge trips, eh, Louis?

'Don't keep repeating yourself. Want a beer?'

CHAPTER 11

Port-Nicolas, Brittany, November 1995

Louis left next morning at about eleven, taking his time. The dog walker really did live at the furthest tip of Brittany, some twenty kilometres from the nearest large town, which was Quimper. That meant seven hours on the road, with a stop for a beer. Louis didn't like rushing when he was driving, and he couldn't go seven hours without a beer. His father was the same way about the beer.

Mathias's notes ran through his head. The dog: 'Medium-sized, beige, short hair, big teeth, could be a pit bull, nasty-looking anyway.' That didn't attract you to its owner. The man: 'Fortyish, light brown hair, brown eyes, receding chinline but otherwise quite nice-looking, bit of a paunch, name . . .' What was the name? Sevran. Lionel Sevran. So the man with the dog had gone back yesterday morning to Brittany, with his dog, and he'd stay there till next Thursday. All he had to do was follow him. Louis drove at a moderate speed, holding the car back a bit. He had thought

about taking someone with him so that the quix-
otic venture would be less lonely and his leg less
stiff, but who? The people who sent him news
from the four Breton *départements* were all resident
there, rooted in their port, their business, their
newspapers, they wouldn't budge. Sonia? No,
Sonia had left, he wasn't going to mope over her
all day. Next time he'd try to be a better lover.
Louis pulled a face. He didn't fall in love easily.
Of all the women he'd had – because when you're
driving along on your own, you're allowed to say
'had' – how many had he really loved? Three, three
and a half. No, it wasn't his strong point. Or
perhaps he wasn't keen to sign up for it any more.
He tried to be moderately in love, not to exag-
gerate, keeping away from wild passions. Because
he was the kind of man who would stay upset for
two years after a love affair had gone wrong, and
brood at length over his regrets before deciding
to move on. And since he didn't rush into half-
hearted affairs either, he was doomed to long
stretches of solitude, which Marthe called his ice
ages. She wasn't in favour. When you're freezing
cold, she would say, where will that get you?

Louis smiled. With his right hand, he felt for a
cigarette and lit it. Look for someone new to love.
Look for someone, look for someone, always the
same old story. Right, that would do, the world
was full of horrors and bloodshed, he'd think about
that later, he was entering one of the ice ages.

He stopped in a service area and closed his eyes.

Ten minutes' rest. Anyway, he was grateful to all the women who had passed through his life, whether he'd loved them or not, simply for passing through. In the end, he loved all women, because when you're on your own in the car you have the right to generalise, all of them, and especially the three and a half. In the end, he felt an indistinct kind of gratitude to them, he admired their ability to love men, something that seemed pretty damn difficult to him, even worse someone with an ugly mug like himself. With his rough-hewn and discouraging features, which he spent as little time as possible looking at in the morning, he should by rights have been alone all his life. And no, he hadn't been. You couldn't make it up, women are the only creatures who could find an ugly man handsome. Frankly, yes, he was grateful. It seemed to him that Marc, too, had a problem with his love life. That nervy character, Vandoosler junior. He could have brought *him* along for the ride, he'd thought of it, they could both have gone searching for women together at the far tip of Finistère. But he had been well aware of how Marc had tensed up at the table when he'd started talking about the trip. For him, this business with the bone had no head nor tail to it – and he was mistaken, because they did have the tail, and were looking precisely for the head. But Marc couldn't see that yet, or was afraid of making a fool of himself, or perhaps the idea of doing something off the wall didn't appeal to Marc Vandoosler

– unless *he'd* thought of it first. That's why he hadn't asked him. And anyway young Vandoosler was better off staying in Paris for now, since there was no need at present for someone who could run. He'd therefore thought it best to leave him in peace. Marc was at once very likely to crumple and very strong – like linen. If we started talking fabric, what was he like himself? Have to ask Marthe.

Louis went to sleep, leaning on the steering wheel, in the service area car park.

He reached Port-Nicolas at seven in the evening. He drove slowly through the streets of the little fishing village to get some idea of it, asking his way once or twice, the place wasn't either very big or very picturesque, and he parked right outside Lionel Sevran's house. That dog must travel hundreds of kilometres to take a piss. Perhaps he only liked pissing in Paris, a snob among dogs.

He rang the bell at the closed front door. A friend had told him that the great difference to ponder between animals and humans was that an animal opened doors, and never closed them after it, while a human did. A great behavioural gulf. Louis smiled as he stood waiting.

A woman opened the door. Instinctively, Louis appraised her carefully, judging, weighing up, wondering yes, no, maybe, just in his head. He did the same to all women, unthinkingly. At the same time, he knew it was a bad habit, but the analysis went on despite himself. In his defence,

Louis might have said he always checked out the face before the figure.

This face was good, but looked very reserved, largish mouth, nice figure, nothing excessive. She replied to his questions politely, made no fuss about letting him in, but didn't put the boat out in the way of hospitality either. Perhaps she was just used to visitors. If he wanted to wait for her husband, yes, all right, he could just sit down in the main room, but it might be a little while.

She was doing a big jigsaw puzzle on a large tray, and went back to work, after having installed him in an armchair and put a glass and some aperitif bottles beside him.

Louis poured himself a drink and watched her do the puzzle. Seen from upside down, it seemed to be of the Tower of London at night. She was working on the sky. He put her age at about forty.

'He's not home yet?' he asked.

'Yes, but he's in the cellar with a new one. Could be half an hour or more, we can't disturb him.'

'Ah.'

'You picked a bad day,' she said with a sigh. 'New ones, always the way, big attraction. Then he gets tired of them and goes off looking for another.'

'OK, yes,' said Louis.

'But this one, she might keep him busy an hour or more. He's been looking out for one like this for ages, looks like he struck lucky. But don't take offence.'

'No, no.'

'Good, you're taking it well.'

Louis helped himself to a second glass. She was the one who seemed to be taking it well. Rather reserved, but you could see why. He felt like helping her, keeping her company until her husband was through. Frankly, he couldn't understand this scenario. Waiting, he'd found a piece of the jigsaw that seemed to fit into the left-hand part of the sky. He leaned forward and pushed it with his finger. She nodded and smiled, yes, that was right.

'You can help me if you like. The sky's always the worst bit in a puzzle, but you've got to do it.'

Louis moved his chair and worked alongside her. He had nothing against jigsaw puzzles from time to time, though you didn't want to overdo it.

'You have to separate the midnight blue from the lighter blue,' he said. 'But why the cellar?'

'That was at my insistence. The cellar or nothing. I don't want all that going on inside the house, there are limits. I made conditions, because if he had his way, he'd have them upstairs. After all, the house is mine as well.'

'Of course. Does this happen often?'

'Fairly. Just depends.'

'Where does he find them?'

'Oh, look, that piece goes on your side. Where does he find them? Ah, yes, of course that would interest you. He just picks them up here and there, he has his regular haunts. He goes prospecting, and when he first brings them home, believe me, they don't look like anything special. Nobody else would give them a second glance, but he's got an eye for them. That's it, and I don't have the right to tell you any more. And then, after the cellar, well, they're real princesses. Alongside them, me? Well, I might as well not exist.'

'Not much fun, eh?' said Louis.

'One gets used to it. Does that bit go there?'

'Yes. It fits on to that one. And you're not offended?'

'At first, yes, I was. But perhaps you would know, it's worse than a weakness, it's a real obsession. When I realised he couldn't do without it, I decided to settle for living with it. I even tried to understand, but to be honest, I don't know what he sees in them, they're all the same really, big lumbering creatures, like cows. But if it keeps him happy. He says I don't understand the first thing about beauty. Maybe I don't.'

She shrugged. Louis wanted to get off the subject, this woman made him ill at ease. She seemed to have lost all her warmth through being forced to live beyond the limits of revolt and lassitude. They went on working on the London sky.

'Getting on,' he said.

'Ah, now we've got some action.'

'This piece?'

'No, it's Lionel, he's coming back up. Must be over for tonight.'

Lionel Sevran came into the room, looking pleased

113

with himself and wiping his hands on a towel. Introductions were made; Mathias had been right, this guy looked healthy and just at that moment like a teenager, delighted with some novelty.

His wife stood up, moved the tray aside. Louis had the feeling that she was not so detached now. But there was something in the air nevertheless. She watched as her husband served himself a drink. The presence of Louis in his house did not seem to surprise him, any more than it had his wife an hour earlier.

'I've told you to leave the towels down there,' she said. 'I don't want them in the kitchen.'

'Sorry, my dear. I'll try to remember.'

'Not bringing her up?'

Sevran frowned. 'Not yet, she isn't ready. But you'll like this one, I promise, very cute, nice shape, curves in the right places, sturdy but manageable. I've locked her in for the night, that's safer.'

'It's damp down there at the moment,' his wife said in a low voice.

'Don't worry, I've given her a nice warm cover.'

He laughed, rubbed his hands, then ran them several times through his hair, like a man waking from sleep, and turned to Louis. Yes, a good head: open, honest-looking face, he looked relaxed as he sat down, one finely shaped hand holding a glass, the opposite of his wife, it seemed hard to believe this business in the cellar. But he did have a rather receding chin and his lips had something a bit thin, determined, economical about them, nothing very sensual at any rate. Yes, he liked the look of the guy, lips excepted, but this cellar business, no, not at all. And the gloomy abandonment of his wife even less.

'So,' asked Lional Sevran, 'you've brought me something?'

'Brought you something? No, it's about your dog.'

Sevran frowned.

'Really? You're not here on business?'

'Business? No, not at all.'

Both Sevran and his wife looked equally surprised at this. They had obviously thought he was a business contact, a salesman perhaps. That was why he had been so casually allowed in.

'My *dog*?' said Sevran again.

'You do have a dog? Medium-sized, short-hair, light-coloured . . . I saw it coming in here, and I took the liberty of calling on you.'

'Yes, that's the one. What's happened? He hasn't been up to his tricks again, has he? Lina, has the dog been up to something? Where is he anyway?'

'In the kitchen, shut in.'

So, she was called Lina. Very dark, matt skin, brown eyes, could be from the south of France.

'If he's done something, I'll pay up,' Lionel Sevran, went on. 'I do keep tabs on him, but this dog is a terrible bolter. Take your eyes off him for a second, leave the door open and he's off. One day I'll find him under a car.'

'With luck,' said Lina.

'Oh, please, Lina, don't be cruel. You see,' said

Sevran, turning to Louis, 'the dog can't stand my wife and vice versa, nothing to be done about it. Apart from that, he's not aggressive, unless he's badly treated of course.'

When people have a dog, thought Louis, they say some ridiculous things. And if their dog bites someone, it's always the person's fault. Whereas with a toad, no problems, that's the advantage.

'You should see what he brings in,' said Lina. 'He eats anything he finds.'

'So he runs away a lot?' asked Louis.

'Yes, but what's he done to you?'

'Nothing. I'm looking for one the same breed. I saw yours and wanted to ask some questions. He's a pit bull?'

'Ye-es,' admitted Sevran, as if it were a reprehensible habit.

'It's for this old friend. She wants a pit bull as a guard dog, her idea. But I'm a bit suspicious of them, I don't want her to get savaged in her bed. So what is he like?'

Lionel Sevran launched into a lecture on the dog's attributes, about which Louis couldn't care less. What interested him was to have learned that the dog ran around a lot and picked up stuff everywhere. Sevran was discoursing on nature and nurture, and ended with the firm conclusion that with proper training a pit bull could turn into a little lamb. Unless you upset it of course, but that's the way with all dogs, not just pit bulls.

'Still, the other day, he attacked Pierre,' said

Lina, 'and Pierre said he hadn't done anything to upset him.'

'Of course he had. Pierre must have annoyed him.'

'Did he bite him badly? Where?'

'On the leg, but it wasn't too serious.'

'Does he often bite?'

'Of course not. He just bares his teeth, that's all. Very rare for him to attack anyone. Unless you upset him, of course. Apart from Pierre, he hadn't bitten anyone for a year. But it's true that when he gets away he can do a lot of damage. He knocks over dustbins, he bites bicycle tyres, he can rip up a mattress. Yes, he's good at all that. But that's not a matter of the breed.'

'You see, I told you,' said Lina. 'He's cost us a fortune in compensation. And when he's not ripping something up, he goes to the beach. He rolls in whatever he finds, preferably rotting seaweed, dead birds, dead fish, and stinks to high heaven when he gets home.'

'Look, darling, all dogs do that, and *you* don't have to bath him. Hold on, I'll fetch him.'

'Does he go far?' Louis asked.

'Not very. Lionel always finds him, on the beach or in the village, or at the rubbish dump.' She leaned towards Louis to whisper: 'He scares me so much that I ask Lionel to take him with him, when he goes to Paris. For your friend, find her a different kind of dog is my advice. A pit bull isn't a nice dog, it's a creature from hell.'

Lionel Sevran came in with the dog, holding it firmly by the collar. Louis saw Lina shrink on her chair and pull her feet up on to the crossbar. What with the cellar and the dog, it didn't look as if this woman led a very relaxing life.

'Come on, Ringo, come on, boy. This gentleman wants a look at you.'

He talked to the dog as stupidly as Louis did to his toad. Louis was glad he'd left Bufo in the car, this mutt would have swallowed him at a gulp. You felt he had too many teeth, that his fangs had swollen his jaws, as they protruded from his misshapen mouth.

Sevran pushed the pit bull towards Louis, who didn't feel too happy about it. The strong-jawed beast was growling softly. They went on chatting about this and that, the dog's age, sex, reproductive habits, appetite, all perfectly tedious subjects. Louis asked them for the address of the local hotel, declined an invitation to dinner, and left them with thanks.

He felt out of sorts and dissatisfied on leaving. Taken by themselves, both husband and wife seemed normal, but together something was wrong. As for the runaway dog that ate any old rubbish, for the moment, that fitted. But tonight Louis had had enough of dogs. He found the village's only hotel, a large new one, which must be of a size to absorb the summer tourists. As far as he could see, Port-Nicolas had no sands, but several shingle beaches interspersed with mud and jagged rocks.

He checked into the hotel, dined quickly and went to his room. On the bedside table were several brochures and folders, useful addresses. The tourist brochure was not large and he forced himself to read it all: local seafoods, the town hall, antique dealers, diving equipment, a seawater health spa, cultural activities, pictures of the church, pictures of the new street lighting. Louis yawned. He had spent his childhood in a village in central France, and while local history did not bore him, brochures did. His eyes halted at a photo of the staff at the health spa. He stood up, examined the picture under the lamp. The woman in the middle, the owner's wife. Shit.

He lay on the bed, hands behind his head. He smiled. Oh well, if that was who she'd married, if she'd left him for that, it wasn't worth it. OK, he was no oil painting himself. But that man, with his low brow, his black hair in a crew cut, his ugly mug staring out from the centre of a group photo, frankly no, bad exchange. Yes, but what would be worse, to find her in the bed of someone with film-star looks or with a money-grubbing ape? Worth discussing.

Louis picked up the phone and called the bunker.

'Marthe, old lady, did I wake you up?'

'No fear. Doing my crossword.'

'Me too. Pauline has married the big cheese around here, director of a health spa. She must be really hard up! I'll send you the photo of the couple. It'll amuse you.'

119

'A health what?'

'A spa. Official name "Thassalotherapy Centre". What it is, it's a machine for making money by covering people in seaweed, fish sauce, soup with iodine and other nonsense. Like sea-bathing cures, but a hundred times more expensive.'

'Ah, not stupid then. What about your dog?'

'Found it. Horrible dog, mouthful of teeth; its master seems OK, except he has some kind of obsessive sex thing going in his cellar, need to find out about that. The wife's a bit disturbing. Polite but frozen, or rather drained of vitality. She seems to be repressing something, she represses herself all the time.'

'While I've got you on the line: "Flows through Russia", two letters.'

'The Ob, Marthe! For heaven's sake, it's the Ob!' sighed Louis. 'Get it tattooed on your hand so there's an end of it.'

'Thanks, Ludwig, you're a pal. Have you eaten? Yes, well, love and kisses and don't hesitate to ask me for contacts. You know I know all about men, don't you . . .? And also—'

'Will do, Marthe. Just write down "Ob" and sweet dreams, but keep an eye on the archives.'

Louis hung up and decided on the spur of the moment to go and take a look at Lionel Sevran's cellar. There was an outside door, he'd noted that when he left, and locks rarely bothered Louis except those blasted multi-locks which required time, tools and tranquillity.

A quarter of an hour later, he was standing at the door. It was after eleven: everything was dark, the world was asleep. The cellar was protected by a lock and a bolt, and it took him some time. He worked silently because of the dog. If there really was a woman under the blanket, she was sleeping soundly. But Louis was beginning to doubt there was a woman. Maybe he understood nothing about women, or about this one in the cellar, or the wife upstairs, and perhaps he had better give up the job of being a man right away? Yes, but what else could he do? The Sevrans seemed to have been speaking quite openly about her. But there was something grotesque about it all, and Louis was always suspicious of the grotesque.

The door yielded. Louis went down a few steps and closed it behind him softly. In the middle of an indescribable chaos stood a large workbench, and on top, under a quilted blanket, a bulky dark shape. He felt it, lifted it up, looked, and nodded. Some misunderstanding, eh? He hated ambiguity, word games, useless and malevolent pastimes, and wondered to what extent Lina Sevran had been deliberately misleading him.

The only thing under the blanket was a huge ancient typewriter, from the early twentieth century, if he judged correctly. And yes, as Lina had said, it was big and lumbering like a cow, and in need of a good clean. Louis ran his torch across Lionel Sevran's obsession. On the shelves and on the ground, everywhere, there were dozens of ancient typewriters, but also gramophone parts, horns, old telephones, clothes horses, ventilators, heaps of metal objects, screws, levers, pistons, fragments of Bakelite, anything you like. Louis returned to the machine on the table, now unveiled. So this was 'the new one' Sevran had 'picked up'. And he himself had evidently been taken for another collector of machines, since he had been so calmly received. The couple must be used to frequent visits from addicts. Sevran must be well connected to the market network, if people came to visit him in this remote spot of Brittany.

Louis fingered his three-day stubble. Sometimes he shaved, sometimes he didn't, to cover up his jaw which was rather too prominent. He resisted the temptation to hide behind a real beard, and opted for this half-hearted solution to soften the offensive chin which he didn't like. So enough, the world was full of horrors and bloodshed, he wasn't going to worry about his chin all night, there are limits. That Lina Sevran had taken him for one of the scores of collectors she must see all the time, yes, it was quite possible. But it also seemed she had been playing games with him, and had perhaps been amused to see him looking ill at ease. Perversity perhaps? If you're bored, you might pass the time with jigsaw puzzles, or if it takes you that way, with perversity. As for the husband, well, *now* there was nothing much to be said about him. Louis returned to his initial favourable opinion, except for the dog. It looked like an exception to the usual rule, many times observed: like master, like dog. In this case, the master and the dog were not at all alike, and that was odd, because they seemed to be attached to each other. He must remember this exception, because it is always reassuring in human existence to see a rule being broken.

He replaced the cover on the typewriter, as a gesture of kindness to protect it from the damp, not to conceal traces of his entry, since he had in any case removed the screws holding the bolt. He went out into the night, pulling the door shut after him. Tomorrow, Sevran would discover the break-in and react. Tomorrow, he would go and see the local mayor to find out more about the old woman who had been found dead on the beach. Tomorrow, he would also go to the seawater spa to see his little Pauline. He might tell himself she had married the man with the low brow for his money, but he couldn't be sure. It wouldn't be the first time he had been dropped for someone he wouldn't have wanted to touch with a bargepole. But all the same, since Pauline was the third woman he had really loved, it hit him hard in the guts. What had Marthe said? This wasn't supposed to be a revenge expedition. No, of course not, he wasn't such a bastard. But it would be difficult. Because he had really suffered when she left. He had downed unimaginable quantities of beer. He had put on weight and wallowed in endless memories. Then it had taken months to recover, first the inside of his head, then the rest of his body, which was too tall but normally solid and in good shape. Yes, it would be difficult.

CHAPTER 12

Kehlweiler got up too late for breakfast at the hotel. He gave himself a near-complete shave and went out into the fine rain falling on the village. Village wasn't really the right word. Scattered locality, he would have called it. Port-Nicolas must originally have been a small medieval port, and there were still some narrow alleyways which might have interested someone like Marc Vandoosler, but not Louis. Thinking of Marc, he found his way up to the church with its *calvaire*, which was unquestionably very fine, a calvary crawling with sculpted monsters and other horrors fit to inspire terror into religious souls. Twenty metres away, a partly demolished granite fountain emitted a thin stream of water.

Under the now heavier rain, Louis leaned over, one leg bent, the other stiff, to trail his hand in the fountain. Thousands of people must have come to dip their hands into this water, telling it their sorrows, praying for help, or for lost love, for children, or for vengeance. Centuries on, that makes the water full of meaning. Louis had always liked miraculous springs. He briefly considered plunging his knee into it. True, there was no evidence this fountain could work miracles. But in Brittany, right alongside a *calvaire*, it must be able to, people aren't stupid, any fool could tell a miraculous spring when he saw one. It was a beautiful spot and he liked it. Up here, he could look down and see part of the modern settlement. Port-Nicolas had spread itself. Now it looked like a scatter of dispersed villas, built several hundred metres away from each other, with an industrial zone in the distance.

Of the original village centre, all that now remained after the ravages of time were a central square, with a large stone cross, the hotel, the cafe, the town hall and a handful of run-down houses. All the other buildings were ranged throughout the landscape in no particular order: a garage, a few villas, a supermarket, the spa – an unlovely structure – and the rest, thrown down like a game of dominoes and linked by a series of roads and roundabouts.

Louis preferred the miraculous fountain, in which he was still trailing his hand, and the worn granite demons on the *calvaire*. He sat there in the rain, on a rock protruding from the mown grass. Small figures were moving about down below, one around the villas, and another in front of the town hall. Perhaps it was the mayor, Michel Chevalier, of uncertain allegiance, officially listed under 'N' for 'non-aligned'. Non-aligned politicians had always bothered him. They were often rather weak people, as if they had somehow shrunk in the wash of life and preferred to shelter on some vague central ground, people whose decisions were unpredictable. Louis couldn't get much purchase on these floating politicians. Perhaps the mayor wondered every day whether his hair was dark or fair, whether he was a man or a woman, perhaps he would hesitate when faced with the simplest questions. But then, after all, Louis himself hesitated when people asked where he was from. Don't know, it doesn't matter, son of the Rhine. Men had spent much time trying to grasp the Rhine, they had even cut it in two. Cutting a river in two, what lunacy, only mankind could come up with something so idiotic. But the Rhine is nowhere and belongs to no one, and he was a son of the Rhine, that was what his father had told him, indefinite nationality, the world was full of horrors and bloodshed, he wasn't going to think about that all day.

That said, the advantage of belonging nowhere was that you could be from anywhere. If he chose, and he often did, he could be Turkish, Chinese, Berber, why not, Indonesian, Malian, or from Tierra del Fuego, hands up if you object, Sicilian, Irish, or of course French or German. And the practical thing about that was that you could then lay claim to a whole gallery of ancestors, heroes or villains.

Louis took his hand out of the water and looked at it. Wiping it on his wet trousers, he thought for the thousandth time that he'd lived for fifty years in France, and for fifty years people had been calling him 'the German'. People didn't forget, nor did he. Standing upright again, he thought he ought to call his father. It was a month since he had heard from him. Over there, in Lörrach, across the Rhine, the old man would be amused to know what he was chasing now. From the fountain, Louis surveyed the whole of Port-Nicolas. He knew why he was hesitating. Should he start with Pauline or, less upsettingly, with the mayor?

CHAPTER 13

Arriving at the bunker at ten in the morning, Marc had prepared all possible responses to any future requests by Louis Kehlweiler. So he went in calmly, kissed Marthe hello, and was surprised not to find a note on the desk. Surely Louis would have left a message, asking him to go haring off to the other end of the country. Or perhaps Marthe was supposed to act as go-between. But Marthe wasn't saying anything. Ah, right, everyone was keeping quiet. Just as well.

Marc had never managed to hold to a resolution, good or bad, for more than about ten minutes. Impatience always made him lower his guard and his most ferocious sulks could be ruined in a few moments by the need to rouse himself and deal with something that was hanging fire. If there was one thing he couldn't tolerate, it was letting something hang fire. He wriggled on his chair before finally asking Marthe if she had any messages for him.

'No messages,' said Marthe.

'No matter,' said Marc, resolving again to keep his mouth shut. 'But you know what?' he began again. 'Louis wants me to be a runner for him. Well, no, Marthe, I'm not cut out for that. Not that I can't run, that's not it. I can run very fast if I have to, well, fairly fast, and I'm especially good at climbing. Not mountains, no, too depressing, I get fed up, but walls, trees, fences. You wouldn't think so to look at me, would you? Well, actually, I'm very gymnastic, Marthe, not strong, but gymnastic. You don't just need strong men on earth, do you? You know something, my wife left me for this guy, a big hunk. Yeah, a hunk, but he couldn't have balanced on a stool, and what's more—'

'*You* were *married*?'

'Why not? But it's all over now, don't talk to me about it, please.'

'It was you brought it up.'

'Yes, OK, you're right. What I'm saying, Marthe, is I'm not cut out to be in anyone's army, even Kehlweiler's, and he recruits you very subtly and gently. I just can't fucking well obey orders, they drive me mad, my nerves can't take it. And this criminal case, I can't be bothered, no idea who to suspect. Understanding, studying, deducing, OK, but suspecting living people, can't do that. On the other hand, I can suspect *dead* people, that's my job. I suspect the lord of Puisaye's steward of cheating in his records of the tithe barns. He must have been fleecing him over the number of sheepskins. But he's long dead, you see? Big difference. In real life, I don't suspect anyone much, I believe what people tell me, I trust them. Oh shit, I don't know why I'm rabbiting on like this, I do it all the time, I spend my life going over what I've done, it's exhausting for me, and it bores everyone else. All that to tell you that as a soldier, or a snooper, I'm completely useless, that's all. Useless as a strong man, or a suspicious man, or a powerful man, or any other kind of superman such as your Ludwig seems to be. Kehlweiler or no Kehlweiler, I'm not going off to Brittany to be a dog that runs after another dog. It distracts me from my work.'

'You're hysterical this morning,' said Marthe with a shrug.

'Ah, you can see something's wrong too.'

'You talk too much for a man, it damages your image. Listen to my advice, because I know about men.'

'I couldn't care less about my image.'

'You couldn't care less, because you don't know what to do about it.'

'Maybe. But what difference does it make?'

'I'll explain to you one day how not to tie yourself in knots by chattering. You go too far. Look, next time you want to choose a woman, show her to me first, because I know about women. I'll tell you if she's the right one for you, then if you were going too far or getting in too deep, no harm will be done.'

Oddly enough, this idea was not displeasing to Marc.

131

'What should she be like?'

'Oh, there aren't any rules, don't imagine things. We can discuss it when you bring one along. Apart from that, I can't see why you're so worked up this morning. You've been talking about yourself for a quarter of an hour, God knows why.'

'I told you. I don't intend to go off with Louis.'

'Don't you think the job's worth it?'

'Good grief, Marthe, of course I do! And I've already done a job like that before.'

'Ludwig said you did it well.'

'I wasn't alone. Anyway, that's not the point. I'm surrounded by corrupt ex-cops and would-be prosecutors, and I don't want to be dragged around with a ring through my nose, I've done it all week, that's enough.'

'Well, naturally, when you're only thinking about yourself, you won't understand anything about other people.'

'I know. That's a problem.'

'Let's see your nose.'

Without thinking, Marc leaned towards Marthe.

'No room for a ring, it's too thin. Believe me, I know about men. Anyway, having you hanging about him all day can't be much fun either.'

'Ah, you see.'

'And nobody's asking you to go with Ludwig.'

'Not in so many words. He's tempting me with this piece of crap, yes, effective, and subtle, and then he'll drag me away to Brittany because he knows I can't give up on something once I've started. It's like a bottle of beer. Once you open it, you've had it, you've got to drink the lot.'

'This isn't beer, it's a crime.'

'I know what I mean.'

'Ludwig went yesterday. *Without* you, young Vandoosler. He very respectfully left you to carry on with your studying.'

Marthe smiled at him, and Marc had nothing left to say. He felt hot, he'd talked too much. On New Year's Day, he'd make a resolution. He asked in a calm voice if it wasn't perhaps time for some coffee.

They made their usual little cup of coffee without a word. Then Marthe asked him for some help with her crossword. Exceptionally, because he was feeling rather weak, Marc agreed to put aside his work. They both sat on the sofa bed, now a sofa. Marc put a cushion behind his back and fetched one for Marthe, got up to look for an eraser, you can't do a crossword without one, fiddled about with the cushions again, took off his boots, and wondered about 6 across: 'Form of art' 10 letters.

'Plenty of choice,' said Marthe.

'Don't talk, think.'

CHAPTER 14

Before tackling the town hall, Louis went for breakfast at the Market Cafe facing him on the other side of the square. He was waiting for his jacket to dry off a bit. At a glance, Louis had judged the cafe to be the kind he liked: untouched for forty years. It had an original pinball machine, and a billiard table with a notice on a dirty scrap of cardboard: 'Caution, new cloth'. Hitting one ball in order to pocket another was a system whose subtlety had always pleased him. Calculating the cushions, the angles, the rebounds, aiming left to catch the right. Very clever. The games room was large and dark. They must only put the lights on when people were playing, and this Monday morning at eleven thirty, it was too early. The feet of the little players on the table football game were worn away with use. Feet, ah yes, feet again. He would have to see about this big toe, and not let himself be drawn into a catechism class with the pinball machine holding out its arms towards him.

'Would I be able to see the mayor today?' Louis asked the old lady dressed in black and grey who was behind the bar.

She thought about it, then leaned her thin hands on the counter.

'If he's in his office, no reason why not. But if he's not there . . .'

'Yes?' said Louis.

'Tell you what, he usually comes in for his aperitif at about twelve thirty. If he's out on a site, he won't come. But if he isn't, he will.'

Louis thanked her, paid, picked up his still damp jacket and went across the square. Inside the little town hall, he was asked if he had an appointment because monsieur le maire was working in his office.

'Can you tell him I'm passing through and would like to see him? Kehlweiler, Louis Kehlweiler.'

Louis had never had any visiting cards made, it didn't suit him.

The young man spoke on the phone, then told him he could go up to the first floor, the door at the end of the corridor. There was only one more floor in the building anyway.

Louis had no memory of this mayor, who was also a member of the French Senate, apart from his name and label of 'non-aligned'. The man who received him was rather heavily built, but flabby, with one of those faces you have to concentrate hard to remember, always in motion. He bounced a little when he walked, and without making them crack, he had a disturbing habit of twisting the fingers of one hand with the other. As Louis was

135

watching this movement, the mayor put his hand in his pocket, and asked him to sit down.

'Louis Kehlweiler? To what do I owe the honour?'

Michel Chevalier was smiling, but not all that much. Louis was used to this. An unexpected visit by an emissary from the Ministry of the Interior never put elected politicians at their ease, whoever they were. Apparently Chevalier wasn't aware that Louis'd been dismissed, or else his dismissal was not enough to reassure him.

'Nothing to worry about.'

'I'd like to believe you. You couldn't hide a pin in Port-Nicolas. Too small.'

The mayor sighed. He must be bored stiff in his office here. Nothing to hide and not much to get involved in.

'Well, then?' the mayor went on.

'Port-Nicolas may be small, but it scatters its belongings. I've brought you something that might come from down here, something I found in Paris.'

Chevalier had large blue eyes which he couldn't narrow, but that's what he was trying to do.

'I'll show you,' said Louis.

He fumbled in the pocket of his jacket, and his hand encountered the bumpy skin of Bufo, who was snoozing there. Shit. He had brought him out for a walk this morning to the *calvaire* and had forgotten to drop him off at the hotel. It certainly wasn't the moment to bring Bufo out, since the mayor's sagging face was already looking anxious. He found the screw of newspaper under Bufo's belly: his toad had no respect for exhibits in a case, and had snuggled down on top of it.

'It's this little thing,' said Louis finally, putting the fragile piece of bone on Chevalier's wooden table. 'It bothers me enough to have brought me all the way to you. But I hope it may be a big fuss about nothing.'

The mayor leaned forward, looked at the object and slowly shook his head. A patient, plastic type, thought Louis, he operates in slow motion, nothing panics him and he's not stupid, in spite of those big eyes.

'It's a human bone,' Louis went on, 'the top joint of a big toe, which I had the bad luck to find on the Place de la Contrescarpe, on the grid round a tree, and you'll have to pardon my being explicit, monsieur le maire, but it was in the excrement of a dog.'

'So you go poking around in the excrements of dogs?' said Chevalier calmly, and without irony.

'There'd been a torrential rainstorm in Paris. The organic matter was washed away, leaving this bone sitting on the grid.'

'I see. And the connection with my little municipality?'

'I thought it unusual and worrying. So I paid attention to it. It was quite possible that it came from an accident, or in an extreme case, a dog could have got inside where a body had been laid out. But one couldn't rule out the possibility that this bone came from a murder.'

Chevalier didn't budge. He listened, without intervening.

'And the connection with this place?' he asked again.

'I'm getting there. I waited in Paris. And nothing happened. You must know that you can't hide a corpse for long in the capital. Nothing turned up in the suburbs either, and there've been no reports of missing persons for twelve days. So I checked the movements of dogs in the area, found two that lived outside, but had left their excrement on a Paris street. I'm following the trail of Lionel Sevran's pit bull.'

'Go on,' said the mayor.

He remained his usual flaccid self, but his concentration was progressively increasing. Louis leaned one elbow on the table, but put the other hand in his pocket, because his blessed toad didn't want to go back to sleep and was wriggling around.

'At Port-Nicolas,' he said, 'there was an accident down by the shore.'

'Ah, now we're getting somewhere.'

'Yes. I've come to check it really was an accident.'

'Oh yes,' Chevalier interrupted him. 'It was an accident all right. The old lady slipped on the rocks, and fractured her skull. It was in the papers. All the necessary statements were taken by the gendarmes from Fouesnant. There's no doubt about it being an accident. Old Marie always went to the same spot, rain or shine, all weathers. It was her special place for gathering winkles, she collected bags full of them. Nobody else would have gone to look for winkles there, because it was her patch. She must have gone out as usual, but it was raining that Thursday, the seaweed was slippery, and she fell over, alone, in the dark. I knew her well, and nobody would have wished her any harm.'

The mayor's face clouded. He stood up with his back to the wall behind the desk, listlessly, fiddling once more with his fingers. In his eyes, this interview was coming to an end.

'They only found her on Sunday,' he added.

'That's very late.'

'Nobody missed her on the Friday because it was her day off. By Saturday midday, she hadn't been seen in the cafe, so someone went to her house, and to the people she worked for. Nothing. So it was four o'clock before they started to look for her, a bit amateurishly, people weren't seriously concerned. Nobody thought to go along to Vauban Cove. It had been such bad weather for three days that they didn't think she would have gone gathering winkles. Finally, they called in the Fouesnant gendarmes at eight that night. And they found her next morning when they extended the search. Vauban Cove isn't that near the village, it's along at the point. That's all. As I said, the necessary formalities were gone through. An accident. So?'

'So, art begins where the necessary formalities leave off. Did anyone notice anything about her foot?'

Chevalier sat back down with apparent docility, glancing briefly at Kehlweiler. It wouldn't be easy to throw Kehlweiler out of his office, and he was not a man to throw people out without taking precautions.

'Well, look now,' said Chevalier. 'You could have spared yourself a lot of trouble and kilometres if you'd just telephoned me. And I'd have said, Marie Lacasta slipped over, and there was no injury to her feet.'

Louis looked down and thought.

'Really? Nothing? You're sure?'

'Nothing.'

'Would it be indiscreet of me to ask you for the report?'

'Would it be indiscreet of me to ask you if you're here officially?'

'I'm not working at the Interior any more,' said Louis with a smile. 'And you knew that, didn't you?'

'I merely suspected it. So you're here unofficially.'

'That's right, you have no obligation to answer me.'

'You might have told me that at the start.'

'You didn't ask me.'

'True. All right, go and take a look at the report, if it sets your mind at rest. Ask my secretary for it, and please consult it without taking it out of the office.'

Once more, Louis wrapped up his piece of bone,

which obviously nobody else wanted to be bothered with, as if it was a matter of little moment that a woman's toe should be found on the grid round a tree in Paris. He read the gendarmes' report attentively. It had been prepared that Sunday evening. Nothing about the feet, quite true. He thanked the secretary and returned to the mayor's office. But Chevalier had now gone for his aperitif at the cafe over the road, the young man in reception explained.

The mayor was playing an energetic game of billiards, surrounded by a dozen of his constituents. Louis waited until he had missed a shot before going up to him.

'You didn't tell me Marie worked for the Sevrans,' he whispered from behind his ear.

'What does that matter?' the mayor whispered back, his eyes on his opponent.

'Well, for heaven's sake, the pit bull! It belongs to the Sevrans.'

The mayor had a word with his neighbour, passed him his cue and took Louis into a corner of the games room.

'Monsieur Kehlweiler,' he said, 'I don't know exactly what it is you want, but you can't twist reality. In the Senate, my colleague Deschamps had spoken well of you to me. And I find you here chasing after some local incident, tragic, no question, but not at all the kind of thing to interest a man like you. You come six hundred kilometres to try and fit together two elements that have nothing to do with each other. I've been told it's hard to shake you off, which may not be a desirable quality, but when you come up against the evidence, what do you do?'

A little criticism, a little flattery, Louis registered. No politician had ever liked seeing him turn up in their constituency.

'In the Senate,' Chevalier went on, 'they say a man would rather find a bedbug in his sheets than "the German" looking through his papers. Forgive me if that sounds rude, but it's what they say.'

'I know.'

'They go on to say the only way to get rid of him is like you do for bedbugs: burn the furniture.'

Chevalier gave a little laugh and threw a satisfied glance at the man who had replaced him at billiards.

'In my case,' he continued, 'I have nothing to burn and nothing to show you, because you are not here officially any more. I don't know if it's because you're at a loose end that you're being so obstinate. Yes, the pit bull belongs to the Sevrans, and so did Marie, if one can say that. She'd been Lina Sevran's nanny, always with her. But Marie had a fall on the beach, and her feet hadn't been touched. Do I have to say it again? Sevran is a public-spirited man, does a lot of good in the village. I won't say the same for his dog, just between ourselves, mind you. But you have no reason and no right to come harassing him.

142

Because his dog, you need to know this for your own good, spends its life running away, prowling the countryside and snouting around in dustbins. You could be ten years trying to find where the dog picked up that bone – that's if it was him.'

'Shall we finish the game?' said Louis, pointing to the billiard table. 'Your opponent seems to have given up.'

'Very well,' said Chevalier.

They each chalked their cues, and Louis, played first, surrounded by a dozen spectators who passed comments or maintained an appreciative silence. Some left, others arrived, there was a lot of coming and going in this cafe. Louis ordered a beer, in the middle of the game, which seemed to please the mayor, who ordered a Muscadet and ended up winning. Chevalier had been down in Brittany about twelve years, that makes four thousand games of billiards, that adds up. Evidently feeling expansive, the mayor invited Louis to lunch. Louis discovered behind the games room a huge dining saloon with about fifteen tables. The walls were bare granite, blackened by smoke from the open fire. This old cafe with its sequences of rooms pleased Louis more and more. He would willingly have installed his bed in a corner by the fire, but what was the point, since Marie Lacasta had died on the rocks with both feet intact? The thought depressed him. He wasn't going to find out what was at the end of the piece of bone he had recuperated so carefully, and yet, damn it all, he didn't have the sense that he was dealing with an incident of no importance.

Sitting at table, Louis remembered Marthe's advice. When you're faced with someone who is trying to decide whether to accept you or reject you, sit facing him. Seen in profile, you're intolerable, just get that into your head, but face to face, you have every chance of winning him over, if you make an effort not to put your German expression on. If it's a woman, the same but closer to. Louis sat down facing the mayor. They talked about billiards, then the cafe, then how things were going in the town hall, business and politics. Chevalier wasn't a native of the region, he had arrived there as a candidate for his Senate seat. He'd found it tough being exiled to the far end of Brittany, but he'd grown to like the place. Louis dropped a few confidential bits of information which he knew would please him. The whole lunch operation seemed to work, and the mayor's wary limpness had relaxed into cordial and benevolent limpness, with a few whispered confidences. Louis was a past master at creating an entirely artificial complicity. Marthe thought this disgusting, but useful, of course, it was always useful. Towards the end of the meal, a fat little man came over to talk. Low of brow, heavy of jowl, Louis immediately recognised the director of the health spa, the husband of his little Pauline, in other words the bastard who had claimed Pauline. He was talking about figures and water courses with Chevalier, and they agreed to meet later that week.

This last encounter had unsettled Louis. After leaving the mayor on a note of insincere *entente cordiale*, he took a walk round the harbour then along the deserted streets of houses with closed shutters, allowing Bufo to take the air. The toad had not suffered too much inside his damp pocket: Bufo was an easy-going creature. Perhaps the mayor was too. The mayor was well content that Louis would be leaving Port-Nicolas and Louis chewed over his disappointment and his discreet dismissal. He called a taxi from the hotel, and had himself driven to the gendarmerie in Fouesnant.

CHAPTER 15

Marc stepped down from the train at Quimper in the early evening. It was too easy by half. Kehlweiler made him go charging around after a carrion-gobbling dog for days, and then he went off to wrap up the mystery all on his own. No, it was just too easy. Kehlweiler wasn't the only person who liked to see things through, even nasty businesses. He, Marc, had never left an enquiry unfinished, never, because he hated leaving anything unfinished. His investigations might all be medieval ones, but they were still investigations. He had always followed his archive trails through to the bitter end, even the most difficult. The big study on village economy in the eleventh century had cost him blood, sweat and tears, but hell's bells, he had finished it. This was obviously something else, a nasty murder, Louis suggested, but Louis didn't have exclusive rights to nastiness. And now this son of World War II – yes, he must stop calling him that, one day he was going to blurt it out by accident – this son of World War II was off all alone in pursuit of the dog, a dog identified by Mathias, what was more. And Mathias had agreed, yes, follow the dog. That was probably what, more than anything else, had decided Marc. He had hastily packed a rucksack, which Lucien, the historian of World War I, had immediately emptied, telling him he had no idea how to fold shirts properly. Oh God, with friends like that . . .

'Shit, you'll make me miss my train!' Marc had shouted.

'No, you won't, trains always wait for brave soldiers, it's written up for all time at the Gare de l'Est. Women weep, but alas, trains depart, for the Western Front in that case.'

'I'm not going to the Gare de l'Est!'

'Doesn't matter. And in fact you've forgotten the crucial thing.'

Lucien, while folding up shirts into tidy squares, nodded in the direction of the lord of Puisaye's accounts.

And indeed, Marc had felt reassured to be able to sleep with his head resting on Hugues's registers. The Middle Ages, his salvation. You can't get fed up anywhere if you carry ten centuries around with you. The genius of the Middle Ages, Marc had explained to Lucien, was that you would never get to the end of it, you could go on digging around for thousands of years, and it was far more comforting than to work as he did on the Great War, which he would eventually know day by day. Massive error, Lucien had replied. The Great War is a chasm, a black hole in humanity, a seismic shift in which the key to all catastrophes lies. History isn't meant to reassure you, it's meant to alert you. Marc had gone to sleep between Lorient and Quimper.

A taxi had taken him to Port-Nicolas, and Marc had quickly left the neglected harbour, and the scattered settlement of which only the tiny village centre survived, to go and wander on the shingle at the shore. Night was falling, but half an hour later here than in the capital, and he lost his footing several times, stumbling on the slippery rocks. The tide was coming in. Marc walked along the water's edge feeling calm and satisfied, rain dripping from his hair and down his neck. If he hadn't been a medievalist, he'd have been a sailor. But boats these days didn't make him want to clamber aboard. Still less submarines. He had visited the French Navy's submarine *Swordfish* once, underwater in Saint-Nazaire, and had had a panic attack in the torpedo chamber. So, a sailor in the olden days then. Not that the big warships or whalers really tempted him either. So perhaps a sailor way back in the late fifteenth century, setting off for one destination, getting it wrong and arriving in another? In fact, even as a sailor, he found himself back in the Middle Ages, no escaping your destiny. This conclusion made Marc gloomy. He didn't like to feel himself trapped, closed in and predestined, even for the Middle Ages. Ten centuries can seem as narrow as ten square metres in a cell. That must be the other reason drawing him here to land's end, the Finis Terrae, the very furthest point, Finistère.

CHAPTER 16

Late that evening, Louis roused the mayor at his home address.

Standing on the doorstep, Chevalier stared at him with his wide blue eyes, moving his fine disenchanted lips soundlessly. He appeared to be mouthing 'shit' to himself, in a resigned way.

'Chevalier, I need to talk to you some more.'

Should he just kick Kehlweiler out? Pointless, he'd be back in the morning, he knew that. So he let him in, explained that his wife was already in bed, without saying why, and Louis sat down in the armchair indicated to him, in silence. The chair was as slack-looking as its owner, as was the dog lying on the floor. Here, at least, the rule certainly applied. It was a fat male French bulldog, tired after chasing female bulldogs perhaps, and it evidently thought it had done enough today to prove it was a dog, so don't count on it now to start howling just because there's a stranger in the house.

'That looks like a dog that's come to terms with life,' said Louis.

'If it interests you,' said Chevalier, settling himself

on the couch, 'he's never bitten anyone, or eaten any feet either.'

'Never bitten *anyone*?'

'Maybe once or twice when he was a pup, and only because he'd been teased,' Chevalier admitted.

'Yeah, sure,' said Louis.

'Cigarette?'

'Thanks, yes.'

The two men remained without speaking for a moment. There was no animosity between them, Louis noted. A sort of understanding, born of resignation and mutual acceptance. The mayor was not a bad guy to be with, very restful, Vandoosler the younger would have said. Chevalier waited for the other person to speak, he wasn't one to take the initiative.

'I went to the gendarmerie at Fouesnant,' said Louis. 'Marie Lacasta died by fracturing her skull on the rocks.'

'Yes, we've already established that.'

'But she was missing the top joint of her left big toe.'

Chevalier did not jump, he tapped out his cigarette, and said 'shit', this time out loud.

'Impossible,' he muttered, 'it's not in the report. What on earth is all this?'

'I'm really sorry, Chevalier, but it *is* in the report. Not the one you showed me, the other, the next one, written on the Monday by the pathologist, and they posted out a copy to you on the Tuesday, marked "Confidential". I know

I'm not here officially, but why didn't you tell me?'

'But I haven't seen that report! Wait a minute, let me think. It must have arrived Wednesday or Thursday. Wednesday, I went to Marie Lacasta's funeral, then I went straight to Paris. Meetings in the Senate until Saturday. I got back on Sunday, and this morning I was in the town hall . . .'

'And you didn't open last week's post? When I came to see you, it was almost midday.'

The mayor spread his arms and twisted his fingers.

'Good Lord, I'd only got there at eleven, I hadn't had time to check the post, I wasn't expecting anything urgent. But there was a burst main at Penfoul Bay, and I wanted to deal with that before I had all the residents on my back. It's a pain in the backside that bay, I should never have let them build there, and for God's sake don't you go poking your nose in.'

'Don't worry, I'm on to something different from local flooding. But I thought your office hours started at nine.'

'My office hours, as you call them, are held in the cafe at aperitif time as everyone knows. You think I read the report and didn't tell you? No, Kehlweiler. At ten o'clock I was still asleep, like it or not. I'm no good in the morning,' said the mayor with a frown.

Louis leaned across and put his finger on the mayor's arm.

'I was asleep myself.'

The mayor took out two glasses and poured them each a cognac. Louis's morning lie-in seemed to have sent him up in his estimation.

'Worse,' Louis went on, 'I take a siesta. In the Ministry, I would close my door, and lie down on the floor with my head on some big law book. Half an hour sometimes. I would forget about the book on the floor, no one ever knew why I was consulting points of law on the carpet.'

'Well?' asked the mayor. 'What's in this second report?'

'The gendarmes did the first appraisal on Sunday, as you know. The body had been rolled about by five successive tides, it was battered and covered in mud and seaweed. The head wound was clear to see, but not the damage to the foot. All the same, Marie Lacasta was barefoot. Apparently she always wore short rubber boots belonging to her husband when she went to the beach, and they were too big for her.'

'That's right. She would put them on without socks to go out after shellfish.'

'So the waves must have washed the boots off.'

'Yes, she was barefoot, it said that in the first report. They found one of the boots about ten metres away on the rocks.'

'And the other?'

'The other was missing. It must be halfway to New York by now.'

'In his first examination, done late that first

night, the local doctor at Fouesnant looked at the head in particular, where the fracture was obvious, and the foot, covered in mud, didn't engage his attention. No blood to be seen. He made his diagnosis, which was correct, that she had died of a fractured skull, the front of her forehead was caved in, from falling against a rock. And that was the preliminary report which reached you. The police pathologist only came along next day, because he'd been called to an accident on the main road on the Sunday evening. His conclusions about the blow to the head were the same as his colleague's. About the foot, this is what he wrote.'

Louis felt in his trouser pocket and brought out a crumpled piece of paper.

'I'll summarise. Joint 2 missing on left toe 1. The toe had not been *cut* off, but torn off, so the pathologist ruled out any human intervention. From the context, he suggested seagulls. So, accidental death, followed by some carnivorous creature. The time of death couldn't be given with any precision, but at latest Friday morning. Marie had been seen on Thursday at about four o'clock, so she died between, say, four thirty Thursday and midday Friday. Did she ever go out to get winkles in the early morning?'

'She might have done. She was free from Friday to Monday. But still, the pathologist agreed it was an accidental death, in spite of the nasty detail about the toe. So where does that get you? The seagull theory is a bit dodgy, but why not? – there are thousands of them around, they're savage and they might flock round a wound.'

'Chevalier, you're forgetting that I didn't find this bone in the stomach of a seagull.'

'True, I forgot.'

Louis leaned back in his chair, his stiff leg stretched out in front of him. The cognac was good, the mayor was obviously changing his attitude, and he waited for thoughts to arrange themselves inside the politician's head. But he would like to know whether or not Chevalier really had seen the second report, whether he had been surprised this evening, or whether he had been lying this morning, hoping that Louis wouldn't pursue the matter any further. With a man like this, it was impossible to be sure. His shapeless features and relaxed body language covered up any trace of his actual thoughts. It was as if the thoughts were drowning until they came to the surface and reached the light. Everything about him was submerged, floating, between two tides. A very fishy character. Which made Louis realise that those round, wide-open eyes, which had seemed somehow familiar, were ones he had seen before – on the fishmonger's slab. Louis glanced at the old dog to see if he had eyes like a fish too, but the bulldog was asleep, slobbering on the tiles.

'Look,' said Chevalier suddenly. 'Yes, the facts are on your side, Sevran's pit bull could well have bitten off Marie's toe, it's revolting, and doesn't surprise me, coming from that dog, I've often warned Sevran about it. But again, so what? Marie falls over, dies as a result, the dog comes along in his usual horrible carrion-eating way – though all dogs are a bit that way inclined, it's their nature – finds itself on the beach and bites off her toe. Well, it still doesn't *prove* anything. You can't take a dog to court for mutilating a corpse, can you?'

'No.'

'Right you are, perfect, that's an end to it. You've found what you were looking for, and there's no more to be said.'

The mayor refilled the two glasses.

'There is just one little thing,' said Louis. 'I found the bone on Friday morning, after the rain on Thursday night. But it was already there on the grid at about 1 a.m. Sevran's dog must have gone past between two in the afternoon on Thursday, when the grid was clean, and 1 a.m., when I noticed it had done its business there.'

'You have a funny way of spending your time. Working for the Ministry of the Interior must make you a bit crazy . . . you might call it obsessional behaviour.'

'Never mind, the dog still passed that way before 1 a.m. on the night from Thursday to Friday.'

'But for crying out loud, of course it did! Sevran drives to Paris every Thursday evening! He gives classes at Arts et Métiers on Friday. He leaves at six, arrives at midnight. He always takes the dog, because Lina is afraid to be alone with it, and just between ourselves, she's quite right.'

Chevalier overused the expression 'just between ourselves', which didn't fit his character. He wasn't the kind of man to confide to you what was going on under the surface.

'So,' the mayor concluded, drinking off his cognac, 'when Sevran arrived in Paris, he let the dog out at once – with a creature like that it's normal. But that said, I'll go and have more words with him about his dog. Savaging corpses is totally unacceptable. He'll have to tie him up, or I'll take action.'

'It's not against the dog that there'll need to be some action.'

'Oh, come on, Kelhweiler, you don't mean the engineer's responsible for this barbarism?'

'The engineer?'

'Sevran, that's what he's known as round here.'

'Well, not necessarily Sevran, but somebody, yes.'

'Somebody? Somebody who cut off Marie's toe to give it to the dog to eat? Don't you think you're pushing this story for your own amusement? The pathologist said the toe hadn't been cut. Can you imagine a human being attacking a corpse with his teeth? Kehlweiler, you must be off your trolley.'

'Monsieur le maire, pour us out another cognac, and go and get the tide tables please.'

Chevalier gave a slight start. It was rare for anyone to order him about, and in a jokey tone what was more. A quick thought about how to react, but no, he'd been warned, pointless to kick the German out if you had the bad luck to find him sitting in your armchair. He sighed and moved towards his desk.

'Pour out the cognac yourself, make yourself at home, why don't you?' he said grumpily.

Louis smiled and refilled the glasses. Chevalier came back on his bouncing footsteps and held out the tide table.

'Thanks, but I've already seen it. It was for you.'

'I know the tide tables by heart.'

'Oh, really? And if you know that, you haven't noticed something very obvious?'

'No I haven't, so hurry up and get to the point, I'm very tired.'

'Well, look, Chevalier, can you imagine a dog, or even a seagull, pulling the boots off a corpse, in order to go and eat its feet? Why didn't the pit bull just bite a bit of a hand, or an ear?'

'Jesus Christ, you read the reports, she was *bare-foot*, her boots were off. The dog attacked a foot by pure chance. Of course it didn't take her boot off first, do you really take me for an idiot?'

'Not at all, that's why I'm asking you this question: if the dog attacked Marie when her feet were bare, and if the dog didn't pull her boots off, who did?'

'Well, the sea of course, dammit. It's in the report. Between ourselves, you're losing the plot, Kehlweiler.'

'Not the sea, the *tide*, let's be precise.'

'The tide then, same thing.'

'And what time was high tide that evening?'

'About one in the morning.'

This time, Chevalier did give a start. Not a real one, but a wobble, as he put his cognac down on a coffee table.

'You see?' said Louis, spreading his hands. 'Marie's boots can't have been pulled off by the tide on Thursday night, because the tide was going *out*, and it only reached her again at seven o'clock in the morning at the earliest. But the pit bull excreted this bone in Paris before 1 a.m.'

'Well, I don't understand any more. Could the dog have pulled off her boot? It doesn't make sense.'

'For the sake of absolute completeness, I asked to see the one boot they still had at Fouesnant. We were lucky – it was the left one.'

'How come they had the right to show you that?' asked Chevalier indignantly. 'Since when do the gendarmes get out their crime scene exhibits for a retired civilian?'

'I know a friend of the captain at Fouesnant.'

'Congratulations.'

'I just examined this one boot, and with a magnifying glass. No trace of a dog's jaws, not the least little scratch. The dog hadn't touched it. She already had her boot off, when the pit bull arrived, round about six o'clock.'

'There must be some explanation. For instance . . . let's see . . . she could have taken off her boot because she had a pebble in it, and then, balancing on one foot, she fell over, and hit her head.'

'I don't think so. This Marie was an old lady. She'd have sat on a rock to take her boot off. You don't go balancing on one leg at her age. Was she an athletic, fit sort of person?'

'Well, no. Timid, fragile, careful.'

'So, it wasn't the tide, and it wasn't Marie, and it wasn't the dog.'

'What was it then?'

'Who, you mean.'

'Who?'

'Chevalier, someone killed Marie, and you're going to have to deal with that.'

'All right, what's your version?' asked the mayor quietly, after a short silence.

'I went to the spot. At about five or six o'clock, the light is fading, but it's not quite dark. If you were going to kill Marie, the beach, although it's deserted at this time of year, isn't the best place, because it's too exposed. Imagine, then, that someone killed her let's say in the clump of pines above the beach, or in the cabin nearby, by hitting her on the head with a rock. Then they carried her down by the little path that leads to the cove. The murderer carries Marie on his shoulders, she doesn't weigh much presumably.'

'No, a featherweight. Go on.'

'On his shoulders then, down to the beach, where he lays her, face down, on the rocks. On the steep path, might there be a good chance that one of her boots worked loose and fell off?'

'All right.'

'Then the murderer, as he puts the body down, notices the boot is missing. He absolutely has to find it, because it has to look like an accident. He wasn't to know that the sea would wash both the boots off anyway. He goes back up the path, to the cabin, or to the pinewood, looking around, in the failing light. It's full of bracken and gorse, and then the trees. Let's say that he, or *she* even, spends four minutes going back up the path, four minutes to find the boot, which is black, and another three to come back down. That leaves a gap of eleven minutes, during which Sevran's dog, mooching about the beach as usual, has plenty of time to bite off a toe. You've seen its jaws, very powerful. As night falls, the murderer hurriedly replaces the boot, without noticing that the toe has been amputated. Let's have another cognac.'

Chevalier obeyed, without a word.

'If they'd found Marie at once, with her boots on, they'd have noticed the amputation straight away, when they took off the boots for the post-mortem, and the murder would have been obvious. A dead person doesn't bother putting her boots back on when her toe's been bitten off.'

'Go on.'

'But the tide, and this is a lucky break for the murderer, washes her boots away, deposits one on the pebbles and carries the other off to America. So they find her barefoot, but there are seagulls all around, they can easily be blamed, even if it's a bit unlikely. Only . . .'

'Only Sevran's dog had passed by . . . and had deposited the bone even before the tide came up.'

'I couldn't put it better myself.'

'All right, you win, she was killed. Someone killed Marie. But Sevran took his dog with him, as usual at six o'clock.'

'The dog had had time to find Marie sometime before six. We'll have to ask Sevran if the dog was loose before he left.'

'Ye-es, of course.'

'We don't have any choice now, Chevalier. We'll have to alert Quimper tomorrow. Murder, and premeditated, whether someone followed Marie to the beach, or lured her there to fake an accident.'

'Sevran, do you think? The engineer? It's impossible! He's a really nice man, talented, polite. Marie had been with them for years.'

'I didn't say Sevran. His dog runs about all over the place. Sevran and his pit bull operate independently. Everyone knew where Marie went winkling, didn't they? – you said so.'

Chevalier nodded and rubbed his big eyes.

'Let's sleep on it,' said Louis. 'We can't do anything tonight. You'll have to notify your constituents here. If one of them has anything to report, they'd better do so discreetly. A murderer can strike twice.'

'A murderer . . . That's all we need. Not to mention a burglary I've got to deal with.'

'Oh, really?' said Louis.

'Yes – and it's the engineer's cellar in fact, where he stores his old machines. The door was forced last night. It might be a collector, you know they come from all over to see him, and the machines are valuable.'

'Any damage?'

'No, oddly enough. Just entered, but nothing touched. But it's still a nuisance.'

'Yes.'

Louis felt no urge to say more on the subject, and bade the mayor goodnight. As he walked through the dark streets, he could feel the effects of the cognac. He couldn't lean hard on his stiff leg to balance the other one. He stopped under a tree swaying in the west wind which had suddenly blown up. Sometimes this gammy knee really got him down. He had always thought Pauline had left him because of it. She had made her mind up six months after his accident. For a few seconds, Louis remembered the fierce fire in Antibes, where his knee joint had been shattered. He had trapped those men, after a chase lasting almost two years, but he had trapped his knee as well. Marthe, to cheer him up, had said it was distinguished to limp, it was like wearing a monocle, and he should be pleased to be like Talleyrand, since he was his ancestor. The fact that Talleyrand limped (and was known as 'the Lame Devil') was the only thing Marthe knew about this famous figure in French history. But Louis knew that limping was not actually a big turn-on. He felt vaguely inclined to get weepy about his knee. That was how you could tell a good cognac, and that you'd had too much of it. The world was full of horrors and bloodshed. He'd discovered the woman whose tragic remains had been found on the grid round the tree, he was right, she'd been killed, someone had killed an old lady, just a frail elderly resident, with a savage blow from a rock, there was a murderer in Port-Nicolas, the dog had given the game away at bench 102, for once he was going to forgive the dog. That would do about the knee, he was going to bed now, he wasn't going to cry all night about limping, after all Talleyrand didn't, well, he did after a fashion.

If someone had told him he'd drunk too much cognac, Louis wouldn't have disputed it, it was the truth. He'd be in bad shape tomorrow to meet the cops from Quimper for the start of the investigation. He really needed to find out whether Chevalier had known about the second report or not, but to break into the town hall to check the envelope seemed out of the question. The municipal offices couldn't be opened like a sardine tin, or like Sevran's cellar. He set off again, dragging his leg, and crossed the dark square where the wind was now blowing as hard as it could. The town hall was a small building and well secured. And yet. Louis looked up. On the first floor, a small window was open, its white square visible against the night sky. A little window, probably the toilets, it couldn't be an office. What negligence, and what a temptation for someone like him. But a pointless temptation. There was a drainpipe one could hold on to, and there were hollow gaps between the granite blocks to make footholds, but with his knee, it was no use even thinking about it. Anyway, the window was too small for someone his size, even if you weren't a Lame Devil. Too bad for the town hall then, and too bad about Chevalier, he'd have to fish out the secrets of this man some other way. Louis slipped into the hotel with the image of Marie going through his head. The photo of her he had seen in the report showed a little old lady who wouldn't hurt a fly. Or a toad. A featherweight, the mayor had said. Whoever had bashed her brains out with a stone, Louis would make him sweat out his vileness and arrogance. That was a promise. He thought about his father, far away across the Rhine. Yes, he promised his father, he'd wipe that murderer's self-satisfaction off his face.

He had a bit of difficulty putting his key into the lock. That's the problem with cognac. You get sentimental about your knee, about Marie, and the Rhine, then you can't fit the key in the lock. And yet he'd switched on the feeble light in the corridor.

'Need a bit of help?' said a voice behind him.

Louis turned round slowly. Leaning against the opposite wall, Marc was smiling, arms folded, legs crossed. Louis looked at him for a moment, thought that Vandoosler junior was a pain in the arse, and handed him the key.

'Lucky you turned up,' he said, 'and not just for the key.'

Marc opened the door without a word, switched on the light and watched as Louis lay down full length on the bed.

'Five cognacs all in a row,' he said, pulling a face. 'Good stuff too, very good. The mayor is a great host, we've fallen on our feet here. Sit down. Did you know that Marthe calls me "the Lame Devil" like Talleyrand?'

'Is that an honour?'

'She thinks so. I don't, it's a pain. But you don't limp, you're small and thin, and you're just the person I need.'

'Depends what for.'

'To climb in the toilet window: perfect.'

'Sounds fun. What's it about?'

'What did you say you could do? Apart from your fucking Middle Ages of course.'

'What can I do? Apart from that?'

Marc thought a bit. He didn't find it an easy question.

'I can climb,' he said.

Louis sat bolt upright.

'Off you go then. Look.'

He pulled Marc towards his bedroom window.

'See the house opposite. It's the town hall. On the left, the toilet window's open. There's a drain-pipe, plenty of footholds, all you need. Not that easy, but a piece of cake for a man like you if you haven't been spinning me a yarn. You've blown in on the west wind, young Vandoosler. But I'd better find you some different shoes. You can't climb in those cowboy boots.'

'I've only ever climbed in my boots,' said Marc, reacting, 'and I'm not going to wear any other shoes.'

'Why not?'

'They comfort me, they make me feel safe if you want to know.'

'All right,' said Louis, 'to each his crutches, and after all, you're the one doing the climbing.'

'And inside, what do I do? Take a piss and come out again?'

'Sit down and I'll explain.'

Twenty minutes later, Marc was slipping stealthily over to the town hall, approaching from the left. He smiled as he climbed, fitting the toecaps of his boots into the cracks between the stones. Foothold after foothold, he made quick progress, helping himself by holding on to the rough surface of the drainpipe. Marc had large, very strong hands, and tonight he took pleasure in the agility of his body, too thin of course, but therefore gravity-defying.

Louis watched from his bedroom window. In his black clothes, Marc hardly showed up at all against the wall of the building in shadow. He saw him steady himself at the level of the window, then go inside and disappear. He rubbed his hands and waited, without anxiety. If there was a problem,

166

Marc would be able to handle it. As Marthe would say, he knew about men, and Vandoosler junior, with his nervousness, his excessive frankness, his volatile emotions, his knowledge from wrestling with historical records, his boyish curiosity, his tenacity as a thinking reed, all mixed up together, made him special. Louis had felt real relief when the medievalist had suddenly appeared in the hotel corridor, and hadn't been surprised. In a way he had been expecting him, they'd started this hare together, and Marc knew the background as well as he did. For very different reasons from his own, Marc Vandoosler always finished what he'd started.

He watched Marc emerge from the window another twenty minutes later, climb down the facade without haste, land on the ground and cross the square with long strides. Louis went down to open the front door and in a few minutes Marc was inside and drinking water from the basin in the little bathroom.

'Ah, shit,' he said as he came out, 'you put your toad in the bathroom.'

'He chose it. He likes sitting under the basin.'

Marc rubbed at his tight trousers which were covered in dirt from his climb, and readjusted his silver belt. Austere but showy, the elder Vandoosler had said of him, and it was true.

'Not uncomfortable in those leg-huggers?'

'No,' said Marc.

'Good for you then. OK, tell me.'

'You were right, the toilets were next to the

mayor's office. I looked in the in-tray. The big envelope from the Fouesnant gendarmerie was marked "Confidential". But it was open, Louis, I checked. Like you said, it was the second report, and it gives the detail about the missing toe.'

'Ah!' said Louis. 'So he *was* lying. Believe it or not, he's a man who lies all the time without it showing. He's like the surface of a pond covered in weed, you can't see the fish underneath. Just a vague movement or a few shadows, and that's all.'

'A clean pond or a dirty one?'

'Ah, if I knew that . . .'

'But why did he lie? You don't think it was the mayor that bashed in the old woman's head?'

'You can think anything you like, we don't know any of the people here. There could be a quite simple explanation for him covering up. You could think he hadn't imagined any link between the missing toe and a murder, since he couldn't possibly have known that the toe had travelled all the way to the Place de la Contrescarpe, or that I would find the dog shit before the tide came in.'

'All right, but don't go so fast, it makes me jumpy.'

'You want me to speak more slowly?'

'No, that makes me jumpy too.'

'What doesn't?'

'No idea.'

'Well, keep up at the back then. All the mayor could have known this morning was that one of his local residents had died on the rocks, and that seagulls had probably pecked off one of her toes. Note that he doesn't tell that bit to the press, and why? Because Brittany lives off tourism and Port-Nicolas is a modest little place as you can no doubt see. He has no wish to draw attention to the greedy seagulls in his village. And as well –'

'I'm thirsty, I need some water.'

'God, you're annoying. Go and get something to drink, you don't need my permission.'

'What if your toad leaps out at me? I saw him move just now.'

'You go and burgle the town hall like Robin Hood and you're scared of Bufo?'

'Too right I am.'

Louis got up and went to fetch a glass of water from the basin.

'And as well,' he went on, holding out the glass, 'this guy turns up in his office and brings out old Marie's missing toe. It isn't the toe that bothers him, although it does intrigue him, it's the guy. No politician, and especially a senator, however blameless his record, likes to see me prowling around his patch. These people have friends, and friends of friends, agreements, pacts, and they prefer not to meet "the German". That's what he said to me in the bubbles that came up to the surface of his pond.' Louis pulled a face.

'He called you that?' asked Marc. 'He knows you?'

'Knows what they call me, yes. I could do with a beer now, what about you?'

'Yes,' said Marc, who had noticed that Louis would suddenly say 'I could do with a beer' at regular intervals.

'In short, Chevalier could have been lying to stop me hanging about any longer in his little port,' said Louis, opening two bottles.

'Thanks. And he might have opened the post without reading it. You open a letter, glance over what's inside, leave it for later, go on to the next. I do that. The pages weren't crumpled.'

'That's possible too.'

'So what do we do now?'

'Tomorrow the cops will arrive, and open the murder investigation.'

'So that's it? We go home? We can follow what happens by reading the papers?'

Louis didn't reply.

'What?' said Marc. 'We're not going to stay here and watch, are we? You can't keep an eye on all the cases in France, can you? You've made your point, they're going to investigate it. So what's keeping you?'

'There's this woman I know here.'

'Oh shit,' said Marc, opening his arms wide.

'As you say. I'm just going to say hello, and then I'm off.'

'Say hello? And you never know where that will end, don't count on me to wait for you, hanging around on my own, what's more, like some poor sod who hasn't got anyone to say hello to. No thanks.'

Marc drank a few mouthfuls from the bottle.

'She means a lot to you, this woman?' he went on. 'What did she do to you?'

'None of your business.'

'All women are my business, let me tell you. I observe other people, that's how I get my education.'

'Nothing to educate you with here. She left me after I did my leg in, and I find her here with a fat husband who runs a health spa, "thalasso-therapy" if you please. I want to take a look. And say hello.'

'And then what? Say hello, talk to her, get her back? Push the husband into the mud bath? You know that won't work. You turn up like a long-lost nobleman, and you'll get chucked into the moat like a peasant.'

Louis shrugged.

'All I said was I wanted to say hello.'

'Would that just be "hello" or "hello, whatever possessed you to marry this bloke?"? It'll end in tears, Louis,' said Marc, standing up. 'When you've lost a woman, my motto is brace up and run away, or brace up and have a good cry, or if you prefer, brace up and commit suicide. Or you can try and love someone else. Or indeed back to square one, run away, whereas here you are, going in there to stir it up, and I'm taking the train home tomorrow night.'

Louis smiled.

'What?' said Marc. 'That makes you laugh?

171

Perhaps you weren't as keen on her as all that. You look as cool as a cucumber.'

'It's because you're getting worked up enough for two. The more anxious you get, the calmer I become. You're very good for me, St Mark.'

'Don't push it. You've already used my right leg without asking, as if it was your own, that will do. You can find plenty of nice people who'll lend you their legs for nothing. So if you're trying to exploit my natural anxiety, just for your own advantage, well, it's disgusting. Unless,' he added after a silence and few more mouthfuls of beer, 'you feel like passing on your advantage to me afterwards, we could discuss that.'

'Pauline Darnas,' said Louis, walking round Marc, 'that's her name, she was very sporty, she used to run the four hundred metres.'

'See if I care.'

'She's thirty-seven now, too old, so she does the sports reports for the local paper. She goes into the paper two or three times a week, she knows a lot about the people round here.'

'Stupid excuse.'

'No doubt. You have to have some stupid excuse to hide a wicked thought. And then I want to take a look at the guy as well.'

Marc shrugged and risked looking through the neck of his empty bottle. Incredible what you can see if you press an empty bottle to your eye.

172

CHAPTER 17

Louis managed to get up at about nine o'clock. He wanted to hurry, say hello, get it over, the sooner the better, because he couldn't resist doing it. Marc was right, he should have avoided it, never see her face again, not take a closer look at the husband, but it was no use, he had never been wise enough to let things lie, he always wanted to stir it up. So long as he didn't start a row, one of those compressed rows that drive people to distraction, things would be fine. So long as he didn't act like a sarcastic bastard. It would all depend on the expression on her face. The whole thing would in any case be sad and depressing. Pauline had always been interested in money, she'd have got worse over the years, and it would be a sorry sight. But that was exactly what he wanted to see: a sorry sight, Pauline vegetating among her banknotes and fishy sauces, sleeping with that little man, eyes tight shut, Pauline unglamorous, unmysterious, caught in the toils of her worst failings. And when he'd set eyes on that, he wouldn't have to give it any more thought, one box ticked. Marc was wrong, he didn't want to sleep with her, but to be able to judge how much he *didn't* want to sleep with her.

But watch out, he said to himself as he left the hotel, no cold-hearted picking of a quarrel, no vindictive sarcasm, too easy, too crude, get a grip, behave properly. He was surprised not to see any police car in front of the town hall. The mayor must still be asleep, and would in his dozy way be calling the cops during the morning, which would give more breathing space to the murderer. The face of the old woman on the rocks, of the sleeping mayor, of Pauline in bed with that guy, the face of a town full of no-hopers. Watch it, Louis, no picking quarrels.

He went up to reception in the thalassotherapy centre, pulling himself up to his full one metre ninety, conscious of standing very straight, and asked to see Pauline Darnas, her new name. No, he wasn't a customer, he wanted to see Pauline Darnas. She didn't see people in the morning? Right, would you have the goodness to tell her that Louis Kehlweiler would like to have a word?

The secretary passed on the message, and Louis sat down in a nauseating yellow armchair. He was pleased with himself. He'd done things politely, conventionally. He would say hello, and go away with the newly tarnished image of the woman he had once loved. The cops would soon be at Port-Nicolas, he wasn't going to spend the night here, in this luxurious entrance hall where there was nothing of any beauty. Hello and goodbye, he had other things to do.

Ten minutes passed and the secretary came over. Madame Darnas couldn't see him, and asked him to excuse her, and to call some other time. Louis felt all his good manners evaporating. He got up too fast, almost falling over because of his damned leg, and headed for the door where the notice 'Private' had been annoying him for some time. The secretary ran to her office to telephone, and Louis went into the forbidden private apartment. He stopped on the threshold of a large room where Monsieur and Madame Darnas were finishing their breakfast.

They both looked up, but Pauline immediately dropped her gaze. At thirty-seven, you couldn't count on a woman having completely lost her looks, and Pauline hadn't. She wore her dark hair cut short now, which was the only difference Louis had time to register. The man stood up, and Louis found him quite as ugly as he had hoped when he had seen him briefly at lunch-time. He was short, fat, though less so than in the photo, his skin was very pale, almost green, his brow was low, his cheeks and chin shapeless, his nose nondescript, his eyebrows enormous, above his rather lively brown eyes. These were his only striking features, but those eyes were narrowed right now. Darnas was also hesitating, looking at the man who had burst into his apartment.

'I suppose,' he said, 'that you have very good reasons for ignoring my secretary's message.'

'Yes, I do have reasons. But I doubt whether they are very good.'

'Well, well, now,' said the little man, inviting him to sit down. 'It's Monsieur . . .?'

'Louis Kehlweiler, an old friend of Pauline's.'

'Well, well, now,' said Darnas again, sitting down in turn. 'Would you like some coffee?'

'Yes, please.'

Darnas leaned back comfortably in his large chair and looked at Louis, with an air of being highly amused.

'Since we obviously have similar tastes,' he said, 'let's skip the formalities and cut to the chase, the reason for your intrusion, what do you think?'

To tell the truth, Louis was far from expecting this. He was used to taking the initiative, and Darnas was getting a clear advantage. This did not altogether displease him.

'That will be easy,' said Louis, looking up at Pauline, who was still sitting tensely on her chair, but was now prepared to meet his eye. 'As your wife's former boyfriend, former lover, I should make it clear, in all humility, a lover who was abandoned after eight years, I'm telling you this while keeping my temper, and having found out she lived here, I wanted to see how she was doing, what her husband was like, and why and for whom she had let me nurse my sorrows these past years, just ordinary questions anyone would ask.'

176

Pauline stood up and left the room without a word. Darnas twitched his big eyebrows.

'Of course,' said Darnas, pouring a second cup of coffee for Louis, 'I hear what you're saying, and I quite understand that Pauline's refusal has upset you, that is perfectly legitimate. You can consider those questions between yourselves, you will be more comfortable without me. Please excuse her, your arrival must have been a surprise, and you know her, a very sensitive nature. In my view, she's not as keen as all that to show me off to her former boyfriends.'

Darnas had a very girlish, high-pitched voice, and he appeared to be as naturally calm as Louis, without affectation or effort. From time to time, he would slowly shake his large hands as if he'd burnt himself, or got them wet and was shaking water off them, or as if he wanted to shake his fingers into place, an odd gesture that Louis found strange and interesting. He always watched what people did with their hands.

'But why did you suddenly decide to turn up here in mid-November? Was there some other reason?'

'I was going to tell you. That is the second reason for my visit, the more respectable one, the first one naturally being more vile and vindictive, as you have noticed.'

'Of course. But I do hope that you intend no harm to Pauline, and as for any harm you might do me, we'll see about that in due course, if necessary.'

'Yes, of course. So here's the second reason. You're one of the wealthiest men around here, your spa attracts plenty of people of both sexes, and lots of gossip, you've been here almost fifteen years, and what's more, Pauline works on the local paper. You might therefore have something of interest for me. I've been following a little object all the way from Paris, and it's led me to the death of Marie Lacasta on the rocks in Vauban Cove, about twelve days ago. Officially described as an accident.'

'And according to you?'

'Murder.'

'Well, well, now,' said Darnas, shaking his hands. 'Tell me about it.'

'Marie Lacasta can't have meant much to you, can she?'

'You're wrong. What makes you think that? I liked the woman, on the contrary, she was quite sweet, and not stupid. She came to our garden every week. She didn't have a garden herself, you see, and she missed it. So I let her have a little allotment inside our grounds. She could grow her spuds or peas or whatever. It didn't bother me, I don't have time to do any gardening, and the customers at the spa aren't going to go and hoe vegetables when they come out of the pool, no way, they're not the type. We saw her often, she brought Pauline vegetables for soup.'

'Pauline? Makes soup?'

Darnas shook his head.

'No, I do the cooking.'

'And does she still run? Four hundred metres?'

'Let's keep things in separate compartments,' said Darnas in his girlish voice. 'You can have your tête-à-tête with Pauline to talk about that, and you can tell *me* about this murder. You're right, I know everyone here, obviously. So tell me what's going on.'

Louis wasn't bothering to keep it secret. Since the murderer had taken care to disguise the murder as an accident, it would be better to overthrow the whole structure at once, quickly, put it about, make a big fuss. Force the murderer to take a different direction from the course he was on, the only hope of getting something to appear: pure common sense, as solid as an old bench. Louis explained how things now stood to Darnas, who still looked as ugly as ever, thank goodness, but whose company pleased him greatly, after all, why bother hiding the chain of events that had brought him to Port-Nicolas? The toe, the dog, Paris, the rubber boots, the tide, his talk with the mayor, the opening of an investigation. Darnas shook his fat fingers two or three times during this recital, but didn't interrupt at all, not even to say 'well, well, now'.

'I see,' Darnas said. 'I suppose now we'll get a police inspector sent from Quimper. If it's the tall dark one, it'll be a disaster, but if it's the little weedy-looking one, it might be better. The little thin one, I had dealings with him – four years ago, we had an accident here, a woman died in the shower, a tragedy, yes, but a pure accident, don't get ideas – anyway, the little inspector, Guerrec, is very sharp. He is also very suspicious, he doesn't trust anyone, which slows him up. You have to choose people to count on, otherwise you get bogged down. And another thing, he has an examining magistrate hovering over him, who's haunted by the idea of failure. The magistrate orders people into custody at the drop of a hat, he grabs the first suspect that comes along, because he's afraid of missing the real culprit. Being in too much of a hurry is bad too. Well, you'll see. Although I presume you're not going to stick around for the investigation? Your part in all this is over?'

'I just want to see how Quimper plans to handle it. It's kind of my baby, so I want to know who I'm handing it over to.'

'Like for Pauline.'

'We said to keep things separate.'

'Right, let's do that. What can I tell you that would help? In the first place, Kehlweiler, I like you.'

Louis looked at Darnas in stupefaction.

'Yes, Kehlweiler, I like you. And while we'll have to wait and see what damage you're going to do me concerning Pauline, whom I love, as anyone who has known her well will perfectly understand, and while waiting for the traditional kind of rivalry to send us head to head – and indeed I feel sadly that I won't have the upper hand, since as you have noted, I'm ugly, which you are not – waiting then for the possible moment which may shake the foundations of my life, I find totally intolerable the idea that someone bashed old Marie over the head. Yes, Kehlweiler, intolerable. And don't count too much on the mayor to dish the dirt about his constituents, either to you or to the cops. He nurses every vote, and spends his life trying to avoid trouble, I don't blame him, but he is – how shall I put it? – rather flaccid.'

'On the surface or all the way through?'

Darnas pursed his lips.

'Well, well, now, you've seen him. Nobody knows what's underneath the surface with the mayor. He's had two terms of office here, since coming down from Paris, and even after all this time, it's impossible to find anything firm about him. Perhaps that's the secret if you want to get elected. The best thing to do, if you want to be able to turn in any direction without seeming to, is to be smooth-edged, don't you agree? Well, Chevalier is like something round, slippery and glossy, like a conger eel, a masterpiece in some ways. He'll very rarely give you a straight answer, even if they seem straight to you.'

'And what about yourself?'

'I'm as capable of lying as the next man, naturally. Only a fool would deny that. But apart from the garden, I can't see any connection between Marie and me.'

'From the garden, she might easily get into the house.'

'She did indeed, as I said. With the vegetables.'

'And inside a house, you might find out a lot of things. Was she inquisitive?'

'Ah, yes! Very! Like many people who live alone. She had Lina of course, and Lina's children, whom she brought up, but the children are big now, both of them, and away at high school in Quimper. So she was around a lot on her own, especially after her husband disappeared, Diego, about five years ago I think, yes, about that. Two old folk who'd married late in life, and were very fond of each other, it was touching, you should have seen them. Yes, Kehlweiler, Marie was indeed a very inquisitive person. Which is why she accepted the rather sleazy job the mayor offered her.'

'Do you mind if I take my toad out of my pocket? I didn't mean to stay as long as this and I'm afraid he's getting too hot.'

'Well, well, now, go ahead,' said Darnas, who was as little perturbed to see Bufo on his marble floor as if he had been a packet of cigarettes.

'I'm listening,' said Louis, picking up the kettle, now cool, and sprinkling a few drops on Bufo.

'Why don't we go and talk about that in the grounds? There are a lot of staff here, and as you found out this morning, anyone can just walk in. Your pet will be better off outside too. I like you, Kehlweiler, at least for the time being, and I will tell you about Marie and the dustbins, just between ourselves. Pauline is the only other person who knows about it. Other people may have found out though, Marie was less discreet than she thought. It'll interest you.'

Louis stood up, sat back down to pick up Bufo and got up again.

'You can't bend your leg?' asked Darnas. 'The left one? I saw you were limping when you came in.'

'Yes. I did my knee in during a particularly nasty investigation. It was after that that Pauline left.'

'And you think that was the reason?'

'I thought so. But now I'm not sure.'

'Because when you set eyes on me, you told yourself that Pauline doesn't set too much store on physical appearances? Well, well, now, you could be right. But let's keep things separate, like we said.'

Louis moistened his hand, picked Bufo up, and both men went out into the grounds.

'You really are rolling in it, aren't you?' said Louis, looking at the size of the pine forest.

'Yes, I am. But look, this is what I wanted to talk about. About five years ago, this man came to live in our village. He bought a big villa, an ugly one, as ugly as this spa building, which is saying something. Nobody knows where his money comes from, he works at home. Nothing out of the ordinary at first sight, seems sociable enough, plays cards, talks loudly. You can't miss him at the Market Cafe, he's there every day, for a game, a big solid chap, all of a piece. Blanchet, his name is, René Blanchet, pushing seventy perhaps. Not very interesting then, I'd have nothing particular to do with him, except that he's got it into his head that he wants to be our next mayor.'

'Ah.'

'He's got time, another five years before the election, anything could happen. People like him. He's a sort of local anti-immigrant campaigner. Port-Nicolas for the Port-Nicolas residents and no one else, which is a bit odd, considering he's an incomer himself. But it goes down all right with some folk round here, as you can imagine.'

'And you don't like him?'

'He bad-mouths me. René Blanchet mutters during his card games that the thalassotherapy centre brings foreigners into Port-Nicolas: Dutch, Germans, and worse, Spanish, other Latins, and worst of all, rich Arabs. Getting the picture now?'

'Yes, indeed.'

'And you are German yourself?'

'Partly.'

'Well, he'll nose that out before long. He's a dab hand at sniffing out foreigners.'

'I'm not a foreigner, it's just that my father is German,' Louis said, smiling.

'Well, for René Blanchet, you'll be German all right, you'll see. I could find ways to get him out of town, I have the means. But it's not my style, Kehlweiler, believe it or not. I'm waiting to see what he's up to, and I keep my eyes open, because things wouldn't be nice in Port-Nicolas with him in charge. Better by far to have the smooth conger.

And it was because I was keeping an eye on him that I discovered our dear old Marie was doing the same thing. That is to say, she was going through his dustbin after dark.'

'On behalf of the mayor?'

'Well, well, now. Here we put the bins out once a week, on Tuesday nights. And for the last seven or eight months, Marie was taking René Blanchet's dustbin bags home, looking through them, then putting them back, tied up again, nobody the wiser. And next day, Marie would trot off to the town hall.'

Louis stopped and leaned against a tree trunk. He stroked Bufo automatically with one finger.

'And the mayor's afraid Blanchet is looking for some way to discredit him, before his term of office is up? Has Blanchet got something on him?'

'Possibly, but you might also think the opposite. The mayor could be trying to find out more about Blanchet – what he's up to, where he's from – and hoping to pick up enough from the dustbin to sabotage him as a candidate when the time comes.'

'Right. And if Marie was surprised by René Blanchet while she was going through his rubbish, he might have killed her?'

'And if Marie had learned too much about the mayor from Blanchet's dustbin, *he* might have killed her?'

The two men fell silent.

'Dirty business,' said Louis at last.

'Dustbins are never very glorious.'

'What about the Sevrans? What do you think of them?'

'Apart from their ghastly pit bull, I have nothing but good to say about them. She's impressive, beautiful rather than pretty, you probably noticed, and very reserved, except when her children are home, she changes completely then, much more fun. I think she's bored to death here, frankly. Sevran is a pleasant enough companion, he's intelligent, amusing, open, but there's a big problem with his wretched machines. He's mad about levers, pistons, gears, he goes all over the place finding his blessed typewriters, but then he does make his living from them. He's a genuine collector, and he does good business with them, he deals, buys and sells, and that's what they live off, believe me. He's one of the big specialists in the country, European reputation, people come from all over. Lina has no interest in the machines, and he loves them too much. So, naturally, she's going to be fed up. I'm just throwing that out, because in my case, I'd prefer it if Pauline was interested in machines for instance, rather than in you.'

'Let's keep things separate.'

Darnas looked up and scrutinised Louis's face.

'You're examining me? Something wrong?'

'I'm getting an idea, estimating the degree of risk.'

Darnas screwed up his small eyes and looked hard at Louis without moving. Finally he nodded and stirred the pine needles on the ground with his foot.

'Well?' asked Louis.

'The danger is not negligible. I'll have to think.'

'So will I.'

'Right, goodbye for now, Kehlweiler,' said Darnas, holding out his hand. 'Rest assured that I shall be following you closely, both on this case and regarding Pauline. If I can help you with the former and hinder you in the latter, it will be with the greatest pleasure. You can count on me.'

'Thanks. And you have no idea what Marie might have found in the bins?'

'Alas, no. I saw her doing it, that's all. The mayor will be the only other person who knows, or possibly Lina Sevran. Marie was her nanny too. But before you get any information from either of them, you'd need to spend a number of hours in the cafe.'

'Does Lina Sevran go to the cafe?'

'Everyone does. Lina's often there, watching her husband playing billiards or meeting her friends. It's the only place to go for a chat in winter.'

'Thanks,' Louis said again.

He went towards the gates, dragging his leg, and could feel Darnas observing him from behind his back: he must be wondering whether or not this man with a limp was in with a chance. At any rate that was the question Louis was asking himself. He shouldn't have seen Pauline again, that was clear. She hadn't changed, except for place and surname, and now a slight sorrow was chasing round inside his head. And she had run away from him. Not surprisingly, considering he had behaved like a clumsy oaf. The most annoying thing about it was that he liked Darnas as well. If only *he* had killed Marie, that would be very convenient, of course. Darnas had been pretty keen to provide him with avenues to explore, useful ones in fact. A fine rain began to fall, which pleased Bufo. Louis did not hurry. He almost never did. He breathed in the scent of the pine trees, brought out by the moisture in the air. The smell of pines was very good, he wasn't going to think about Pauline all day. He could do with a beer.

CHAPTER 18

The health spa was quite a distance from the Market Cafe, and Louis was walking slowly along the empty narrow road, as a cold shower began to drench the grass verges. His knee hurt. Seeing a milestone, he sat down on it with Bufo for a few moments. For once, he was trying not to think. He wiped the moisture off his forehead with his hand, and then looked up to see Pauline standing in front of him. Her expression did not look conciliatory. He struggled to get to his feet.

'Stay sitting down, Ludwig,' said Pauline. 'You were the one who played silly buggers, so you can just stay where you are.'

'OK. But I don't want to talk.'

'No? Then what the fuck were you doing in my place this morning? Coming in like that, talking like that. Who the hell do you think you are?'

Louis watched the grass grow wetter. Best to let Pauline have her say when she was angry, simplest way for it to settle down. In any case, she was completely in the right. And Pauline did have her say, for five long minutes, tearing strips off him with the energy she could put into a four hundred metres race. But at the end of the race, you have to stop.

'Have you finished?' asked Louis, looking up. 'Fine, OK, I absolutely agree, you're right in every respect, no need to say any more. I just wanted to call on you, no serious intention, and it wasn't necessary to shut your door on me. Just a call, nothing else. Now it's over, all right, no point shouting for hours about it, I don't intend to bother you any more, I give you my word of honour as a German. And Darnas isn't a bad chap. Not bad at all, and in fact better than that.'

Louis stood up. His knee hated damp weather.

'Are you in pain?' Pauline asked sharply.

'It's just the rain.'

'You haven't been able to get your leg fixed?'

'No, spare me the sympathy, it stayed this way after you left.'

'Loser!'

And off she went. Honestly, said Louis to himself, it wasn't worth her while to have come after him. Still, if she'd shouted at him, she had good reason. He could do with a beer.

Marc appeared in the distance, on a bike.

'I hired this for the day,' he said, as he came to a stop by Louis. 'I like cycling. It's all over with the woman?'

'Totally,' said Louis. 'Our relations are strained to the point of non-existence. The husband's very interesting, I'll tell you about him.'

190

'Where are you going?'

'To get a beer. See what the cops are up to in the cafe.'

'Get on,' said Marc, pointing to his luggage rack.

Louis thought for a nanosecond. He used to be able to ride a bike. He'd never been carried before. But Marc was already turning the bike round in the right direction, and there was clearly no hurtfully condescending purpose in his proposal. He was just offering to help, that was all. Marc wasn't like him, he never hurt anyone.

Marc braked five minutes later in front of the cafe. On the way he had had time to shout through the wind and rain, telling Louis that after abandoning the lord of Puisaye for a while, he'd hired a bike to take a look round the village, and opposite the supermarket he'd found a fantastic thing. A machine about four metres high, an immense and magnificent mass of iron and copper, very intricate with levers, discs, cogwheels, pistons, and all for absolutely no purpose. And as he was standing looking amazed at this strange machine, a local man came past and showed him how it worked. You turned a handle at the bottom, and the big machine went into action, every single part moving, all the way up and all the way down again, and for what? 'You'll never guess,' Marc had shouted over his shoulder. 'All that for a lever to come down on a roll of paper and print off: "*That's quite possible. Souvenir from Port-Nicolas.*" And this chap said, "You can take the paper, it's for you, it's free, and there are about a hundred and one other mottos."' After that, Marc had turned the handle several times, made the big machine shudder from head to foot, and been rewarded with many maxims and souvenirs of Port-Nicolas. Things like *'You're getting warm. Souvenir from Port-Nicolas'* or *'Don't overdo it. Souvenir from Port-Nicolas'*, *'Why not? Souvenir from Port-Nicolas'*, *'Good idea. Souvenir from Port-Nicolas'*, *'Why so much hatred? Souvenir from Port-Nicolas'*, *'No, getting colder'*, and various others he couldn't remember. It was a unique machine. By the time of his last try, Marc had grasped the point of it: you had to make up a question in your head, then consult the oracle. He had hesitated between 'Will I get my medieval accounts finished in time?' which he found too footling, and 'Is there a woman somewhere who will fall in love with me?', but he didn't want to know if the answer to that was no, so he had finally opted for a question which didn't commit him to anything: 'Does God exist?' 'Know what it replied?' Marc added, as he came to a stop outside the cafe, still astride the bicycle. *'"Rephrase the question. Souvenir from Port-Nicolas."* And guess what! This marvellous and pointless machine was constructed by Sevran, four years ago. It's got his name on it: *L. Sevran 1991.* I'd love to have created something like that, an enormous and totally futile object that gives vague answers to silly or formulaic questions. Ah, look, wishful thinking, eh? The cops are here.'

'Right, let's wait for them. Or no, never mind

the beer, let's go over to Sevran's. Since you mentioned him, and since the cops are slow off the mark, let's go and talk to both the Sevrans before they get there. Off we go, on your bike.'

CHAPTER 19

The Sevrans were just sitting down to lunch. When Lina saw the two men arriving, soaked to the skin and apparently determined to stay, she had no choice but to set out two extra plates. Louis introduced Marc, who suddenly had but one thought in his head: keep out of the way of the pit bull if it came into the room. He could think straight in front of ordinary dogs, but a pit bull, and one that ate the toes of corpses, made him go weak at the knees.

'So,' said Sevran, sitting down, 'it's still about the dog, is it? You want an address? You're going to get one for your friend?'

'I've made up my mind. But I wanted to talk to you before . . .'

'Before what?' asked Sevran, serving each of them with a ladleful of mussels.

Marc hated mussels.

'Before the police get here. You didn't see them in front of the town hall this morning?'

'What did I say?' said Lina. 'I told you that dog would get us into trouble.'

'I haven't seen anyone,' said Sevran. 'I've been

working on my latest typewriter, an 1896 Lambert in very good condition. Are the cops after Ringo? This is taking things a bit far, isn't it? Has he done something to you, or what?'

'He's made it possible to reconstruct something very important. It was thanks to him that we know now that Marie didn't simply fall, down on the rocks. She was murdered there. That's why the cops are here. I'm sorry, this must be unhappy news for you both.'

Lina looked unwell. She glanced at Kehlweiler while gripping the table, as if she didn't want to faint in front of everyone.

'Murdered?' she said. *'Murdered?* And it was the dog –'

'No, no, the dog didn't kill her,' said Louis quickly. 'But, and I'm afraid this is not easy to say . . . he must have been on the beach right after the murder, and I'm really sorry – he bit off one of her toes.'

Lina didn't cry out, but Sevran jumped up and went to clasp his wife's shoulders, standing behind her chair.

'Calm down, Lina, calm down,' he said. 'Can you explain please, Monsieur . . . sorry, I've forgotten your name.'

'Kehlweiler.'

'Please explain yourself, Monsieur Kehlweiler, but be quick, Marie's death was a terrible shock for us, she helped bring up my wife and the children, so you will understand that it's upsetting for Lina to talk about her. What's this all about? Where does the dog come into it . . .?'

'I'll be as quick as I can. Marie was found down on the beach, barefoot, you know that, the tide had washed away her boots. And, something that wasn't in the papers was that her left big toe was missing. They thought it might have been the seagulls. But the toe had been lost *before* the tide came up. So somebody must have killed her on the Thursday night, and one of her boots slipped off. The murderer finished the job on the rocks and went back to find the missing boot. But in that time, the dog must have come along and bitten her foot. The murderer can't have noticed, because it was getting dark, put the boot back on the foot and it was another three nights before Marie was found.'

'But how do you know all that?' asked Sevran. 'Are there some witnesses?'

He was still gripping Lina by the shoulders. The meal was forgotten by everyone.

'No, no witnesses, just your dog.'

'*My* dog? Why him? He's not the only dog running around the village, for heaven's sake.'

'No, but he's the only one who excreted the bone, on Thursday night, before 1 a.m., on the Place de la Contrescarpe, in Paris.'

'I can't make head nor tail of this,' said Sevran.

'I found it there, and followed the trail down here. I'm sorry but it *was* your dog. As it happens, he was very useful. If it hadn't been for him, nobody would have suspected a murder.'

Suddenly, Lina gave a cry, wrenched herself free from her husband, and ran out of the room. They heard a loud clatter outside, and Sevran rushed out in turn.

'Quick, quick,' he cried to them. 'She adored Marie!'

They caught up with Lina fifteen seconds later. She was in the courtyard behind the house, facing the growling pit bull. Lina was holding a rifle. She leaned back, shouldered the gun and took aim.

'Lina, no!' cried Sevran, running towards her.

But his wife didn't even turn round. Teeth clenched, she fired two shots and the dog convulsed and fell bleeding to the ground. She threw the gun down on the dog's corpse without a word, her jaw trembling, and went back inside, not deigning to glance at the three men standing round.

Louis followed her, leaving Marc with Sevran. Lina had taken her place at the table again. Her hands were shaking, and her face was so contorted that she was no longer beautiful. Her features were so frozen that, for all the trembling of her body, nobody could have felt sympathy for her. Louis poured her some wine, pushed the glass towards her, and handed her a lit cigarette. She accepted both. She looked at him, breathed deeply, and her face relaxed into a milder expression.

'He paid for it,' she said, taking breaths between

each word, 'that damned dog from hell. I knew it would hurt us one day, me or my children.'

Marc came back inside.

'What's he doing?' Louis asked.

'Burying the dog.'

'Good,' said Lina. 'Good riddance to bad rubbish. I've taken revenge for Marie.'

'No, you haven't.'

'I know, I'm not stupid. But I couldn't spend another minute in the same house as that piece of filth.'

She looked at them in turn.

'What? Are you shocked? Are you going to mope over that filthy dog? I've done everyone a good turn by shooting it.'

'You're a cool customer,' said Louis. 'You didn't miss.'

'Just as well. But it's not being cool, to kill a dog that scares you. That dog has always scared me. When Martin was younger – Martin's my son – the dog bit him on the face. He's still got the scar on his chin. Nice dog, eh? I begged Lionel to get rid of it then, he didn't want to know, he promised to train it properly, he said it would settle down as it got older, and Martin had been teasing it. Never the dog's fault, always someone else's.'

'Why did your husband keep Ringo?'

'Why? Because he found the creature half dead in a ditch. He took it in, he coddled it and the dog recovered. Lionel is capable of getting senti-mental over some clapped-out old typewriter when

it gets back in working order, so I'll let you imagine
how he was when this puppy leapt into his arms.
He's always had dogs. I didn't have the heart to
object. But this was the last straw, Marie, my dear
old Marie, no.'

'What will Lionel say now?'

'He'll be very upset. I'll get him another dog,
something gentler.'

Just then Sevran came into the room. He leaned
a muddy shovel against the wall, and sat down at
the table, though not in his place. He ran his hands
over his face and hair, transferring more earth to
them, before going out again to wash his hands.
Then he went and held on to his wife's shoulder,
as he had before.

'I should thank you all the same for getting here
before the police,' he said. 'Better have that happen
in front of you than in front of them.'

Louis and Marc rose to leave and Lina gave
them a pale smile. Sevran joined them at the door.

'Can I ask you,' he said, 'if it's possible . . .?'

'Not to mention this to the police?'

'Yes. Of course. What would they think if they
knew my wife had fired a gun? At the dog, yes,
but you know what the police are like.'

'So what will you tell them if they ask to see the
dog?'

'That he ran away, that I don't know where he
is. We'll say he never came back. Poor dog. Don't
judge Lina too hastily. Marie was her nanny,
they've known each other for thirty-eight years,

and she was due to be moving in with us. Since
Diego disappeared, that's her husband, Marie had
been a bit of a lost soul in her house, and Lina
had decided she'd better come and live here.
Everything was ready. So Marie's death gave her
an awful shock. Bad enough that it was an accident, but if it was a murder, even worse, and then
the dog . . . she lost control. You have to understand her, Kehlweiler, she'd always been scared of
my dog, especially for the children.'

'It bit Martin.'

'Yes, yes, three years ago, he was still a very
young dog and Martin had provoked him. So?
What will you tell the police?'

'Nothing. They can find things out for themselves, that's their job.'

'Thank you. If I can help you at all, about Marie.'

'Have a think, both of you, when you've got
over the business about the dog between you.
What time did you leave the house that Thursday
night?'

'What time? I always leave at about six o'clock.'

'With the dog?'

'Yes, it's true, that night he wasn't around the
house. He'd got out again. One time too many,
you'll think. I was furious, because I don't like
getting to Paris too late, I need to sleep before
lecturing in the morning. I took the car and
drove around a bit. I found him much nearer
here than Vauban Cove – he was running into
the village. I caught him, gave him a row and

put him in the car. I couldn't have guessed . . . what he'd been up to, could I?'

'As I said before, Sevran, your pit bull did us a good turn. If it wasn't for him, nobody would know Marie had been murdered.'

'That's true, one should try and see things in that light. He did a good turn. But look, you haven't had any lunch.'

'It's fine,' Marc interposed quickly, 'we'll manage.'

'I'm going back to Lina then. She's probably already regretting it, and thinking of getting a puppy for me, I know what she's like.'

Marc said goodbye, telling himself now wasn't the time to ask him questions about the fabulous and pointless machine, and took hold of the bike. He pushed it along slowly, while Louis walked beside him.

'Did you see her face when she shot the dog?' Marc asked.

'Yeah, a sight to see.'

'Weird how someone so good-looking can become horrible. And then she went back to normal.'

'What do you think of her? Would you want to go to bed with her if she asked?'

'You're a funny guy. I'd never have asked myself that.'

'Never asked yourself that? What the hell do you do with your life? You should always ask yourself that, Marc.'

'Oh, I didn't know that. So *you* asked yourself? And was it yes or no?'

'Ah, well, it depends. With her, it would depend on the circumstances.'

'So what's the point of asking the question, if you can't give a better answer than that?'

Louis smiled. They walked on in silence for a while.

'I could do with a beer,' said Louis suddenly.

CHAPTER 20

Louis and Marc had lunch at the counter of the Market Cafe. The room smelt of damp clothes, cigarette smoke and wine. Marc loved the smell, it made him want to sit straight down with his work in a corner, but he had left the lord of Puisaye's accounts on the bedside table in the hotel.

It was on the late side for lunch, and the back room would only be opened up if the mayor decided to come, but he had not yet left his office. Everyone now knew that the police were up there talking to him, and that Marie Lacasta had been murdered. The mayor's secretary had spread the word. And everyone also knew that it was the big tall guy over there, the one with the limp, who had brought the case from Paris, though no one knew exactly how. People were hanging about in the cafe, waiting for the mayor, going up to the counter at intervals to take a look at the two men from Paris. And while they waited, they drank and played billiards. For the occasion, the proprietress of the cafe, the tiny grey-haired woman dressed in black, had taken the covers – placed there in winter – off the second table, which was set up for pool, American-style. Be careful, the baize is new, she'd said.

'Look, the third table along by the window, see?' said Louis. 'No, don't turn round, look in the mirror over the bar. The fat little man with bushy eyebrows, see him? Well, that's Pauline's husband. What do you think of him?'

'Is this the same question as just now? To go to bed with?'

'No, you imbecile. But what do you think of him?'

'To be avoided if necessary.'

'That's what's so clever. Darnas is a man of superior intelligence, but you wouldn't know that from the way he looks.'

'And the woman with him? Is that the one you wanted to go and say hello to?'

'His wife, yes.'

'I see. Right, I agree, I'd certainly like to sleep with her.'

'Nobody asked your opinion.'

'You said one should always ask oneself that question. I'm following instructions.'

'I'll tell you when to follow them. And anyway, shit, Vandoosler, don't start getting up my nose, we've plenty to get on with.'

'Who else do you know here?' asked Marc, examining the smoke-filled room from the reflection in the bar mirror.

'No one. According to the electoral register,

there are 315 voters in Port-Nicolas. That's not many, but as suspects in a murder case, it's a lot.'

'The victim died on Thursday after four o'clock and before six. That's a very small window, and the cops shouldn't find it too hard to establish alibis.'

'It may be a small window, but this is a big open space. Nobody goes wandering around Vauban Cove in November in the rain for fun. Between there and the centre of the village there are just quiet roads and empty houses. A wet, deserted landscape. That Thursday, the weather was dreadful. And on top of that, between five and six, half the local people are coming back from Quimper if they're in work, and driving home from work has never been much use as an alibi. Some of the others will have been out fishing, and there's nothing so vague as a fisherman or as mobile as a boat. If they manage to rule out forty people, they'll be lucky. Only 275 left. Take out the old people and it's maybe 230.'

'So better to start with Marie then.'

'The Sevrans weren't the only people in Marie's life. There's her husband Diego, and I haven't managed to find out if he died, or just went away. There was her little allotment in Darnas's grounds, which brings in the Darnas couple and the staff at his seawater centre, fourteen in the off season. There's her job searching René Blanchet's dustbins, her regular visits to the mayor, and everything we don't know yet. Marie had links with a lot of people – that's the trouble if someone is nosy by nature. The owner here, the little woman they call Antoinette, says that Marie would come in here for a sit-down twice a day – except when she didn't.'

'And what did she drink? Did you ask that? You should always ask that.'

'Hot toddies in winter, cider in summer and a little white wine any time of year. Marie used to go for walks either by Vauban Cove, where nobody else dared compete with her over her precious winkles, or down by the harbour where there's always something going on. People arriving, people leaving, discussions about whether the weather's going to turn nasty, men repairing tackle on the quayside, others sorting out their lobster pots. Have you seen the harbour?'

'Is there really much fishing here?'

'If you'd kept your eyes open, you'd have seen two big trawlers anchored in the distance. They go as far afield as Ireland. Most of the men in here are connected to the harbour, the ones who aren't here work in offices in town. See that guy coming in? No, for God's sake, stop turning round every time I want to show you someone!'

'That's how I am, a creature of instinct, I have reactions.'

'Well, learn how to react without batting an eyelid. Right, he's the handyman who cleans the church, that's all he does. I saw him the other day up by the *calvaire*, a sort of sidekick to the parish priest. What do you think of him?'

Marc bent down a little to look in the bar mirror.

'Well, I wouldn't want to sleep with him either.'

'Shut up, Darnas is coming over.'

Darnas sat down alongside Louis and shook hands with Marc.

'Vandoosler,' Marc said.

'Well, well, now,' said Darnas in his high-pitched voice, 'what are the police up to?'

Marc wouldn't have thought that such a high-pitched sound could have come from that bull neck.

'Still closeted with the mayor,' said Louis. 'It's going to be tough establishing alibis. Have you got one yourself?'

'I thought about what I did on Thursday afternoon. The beginning's fine, I was two hours at the garage, taking delivery of a BMW.'

'Congratulations.'

'My pleasure. I test-drove it for a bit, but the weather was terrible. So I parked it and worked in my office, alone. Pauline came to fetch me at dinner time.'

'No good at all,' said Louis.

'Correct.'

'And Pauline?'

'Just as bad. She worked at the newspaper in the morning, got back from Quimper about three, went for a run.'

'In the pouring rain?'

'Pauline runs all the time.'

'So, it's going to be tough,' Louis said again. 'All these people sitting behind us, who are they?'

Darnas glanced quickly round the room and turned back to Louis.

'In the corner, on the left, Antoine, Guillaume and their father Loïc, they're all fishermen, and Bernard, he's the man from the garage, very reliable. Next to them, the very young man, Gaël, is an inveterate dreamer, and opposite him a man about forty, looks a bit fragile, that's Jean, he looks after the church, he cleans it out, he oils the locks, he fixes the stonework, he's a bit, you know, and totally devoted to the priest. Then Pauline Darnas, my wife, whom you have the honour of knowing, I won't introduce you, let's keep things separate. Table behind her, Lefloch, the toughest fisherman round here, goes out in all weathers, owns the trawler *Belle de Nuit*, and opposite him his wife and the future lover of his wife, Lefloch doesn't know that yet. With them, the skipper of the other trawler, the *Atalante*. Right-hand corner, that's the manageress of the supermarket, with her daughter Nathalie, currently being courted by Guillaume from the left corner, and Pierre-Yves who is also keen on Nathalie, but she's not interested. Standing in the corner . . . Now look out, Kehlweiler, there he is, the Port-Nicolas fundamentalist, the candidate for the town hall.'

'René Blanchet,' Louis whispered to Marc, 'the man with the dustbin, and *don't* turn round.'

Louis was staring at the mirror, over his glass, and Marc did the same, as they watched a burly grey-haired man come in and make a lot of commotion taking off his waterproofs and stamping his boots. Outside, the weather wasn't improving, the west wind was bringing in squall after squall. Louis followed Blanchet's movements as he shook hands with men, kissed women, nodded to Pauline, and came to lean against the counter. Louis moved Marc aside to see better. The Sevrans also came into the cafe at that moment, and sat down. Marc decided to go and sit with them, since Louis kept shoving him, which was annoying. Now there was an open space between Louis and René Blanchet. Louis noted the red face, the brown eyes, the bulbous nose, the cracked lips, just then clamped round an unlit cigar, the small ears with finely tapering lobes, the nape of the neck in a straight line with the head, and a rather deeply lined face. Antoinette served Blanchet a drink. Loïc, the older fisherman, had come to join him.

'Have you heard?' Loïc was saying. 'Seems someone did Marie in, wasn't no accident.'

'So I gather,' said Blanchet. 'Poor old dear.'

'The cops are here – see them? It's Guerrec looking into it.'

'Guerrec, he'll have everyone under lock and key before you can turn round.'

'I'll be the only one out fishing then. Mayor's been with them three hours up there at the offices.'

'At least when he's doing his job, he's not asleep.'

'Do you believe it, though? That someone pushed her? Looks like it's true.'

'I believe what I see, Loïc, and I think what I think.'

Darnas raised his eyebrows to Kehlweiler, with a sigh. But Kehlweiler was on edge. He was gripping his glass and glancing frequently to his right. From the table where he was sitting with the Sevrans, alongside Lina, Marc watched him. Louis stood motionless, his body quite rigid except for those brief movements of the head.

'Looks like it, sure enough,' Loïc said again.

'Depends who tells you,' said Blanchet. 'It seems that it was you, monsieur?'

Blanchet had turned to look at Louis.

'Yes, I came down specially,' said Louis in a polite tone.

'To tell us what exactly?'

'What you were just told. That Marie Lacasta was murdered.'

'And on what basis are you making this accusation?'

'Just my simple citizen's duty. A certain dog was good enough to deposit the truth at my feet. I used it and I've shared it.'

'The people round here are law-abiding folk,' Blanchet went on in a loud voice. 'You're bringing unwanted trouble to Port-Nicolas. Accusing us of killing that old woman, and the mayor hasn't denied it. But I will. The people of Port-Nicolas are not murderers. But in spite of that and thanks to you, they'll all come under completely unjustifiable suspicion.'

Various voices rose, and a murmur of approval followed Blanchet's words. Darnas pulled a face.

Those who were not yet on Blanchet's side might change their minds. Blanchet had seized the opportunity and was exploiting it quickly.

'Want my opinion?' Blanchet went on. 'This business about Marie is some kind of a trick, the mayor's in on it, and I'll get to the bottom of it. You'll have me to deal with, to defend these honest people, monsieur . . . Sorry I didn't catch your name, it sounded hard to pronounce.'

'Look out,' Sevran said quietly to Marc. 'Blanchet's looking for trouble. Kehlweiler may have to watch himself, he's not from round here, he won't have many people on his side. They *are* all good law-abiding people, except when they're not.'

'Don't worry,' Marc whispered. 'Louis is armed.'

'Armed?'

'With his tongue.'

'Blanchet can talk too,' murmured Sevran, shaking his head. 'He's the local loudmouth. Terrible man, always coming out with this stuff, and he's got plenty of dramatic tricks up his sleeve. He's cleverer than he looks.'

Louis had also turned slightly towards Blanchet, and Marc noted with satisfaction that he was easily the taller. He had drawn himself to his full height, so that, alongside him, Blanchet looked squat. An advantage without real merit, but an advantage all the same. Louis was staring at the other man, and his profile, at that moment severe and vaguely scornful, was not at all attractive.

A buzz arose in the room. Some people stood up, others came out of the games room, craning to see what was going on at the counter.

'Not everyone has a simple name, Monsieur Blanchet,' said Louis slowly, and Marc detected a whole gamut of dangerous politeness in his tone. 'But I'm sure that with a little effort, intelligent as you seem to be, you will manage to pronounce it. It only has three syllables.'

'Kehlweiler,' Blanchet said, exaggerating his lip movements.

'My compliments, you are gifted for foreign languages.'

'In France we were given a lot of practice, and some people remember, even after fifty years.'

'So I see that you took the opportunity to get an education.'

Blanchet gritted his teeth, hesitated and drank some of his white wine.

'Will you be staying long with us?' he asked. 'Or have you done enough damage to these people who didn't ask you for anything?'

'Since you suggest it, it's possible I might stay around. Indeed, I feel I may not yet have done enough for Marie Lacasta, who didn't ask for anything either, and who was battered to death with a rock. To be honest, you provide plenty of distraction and it's very pleasant in this cafe. It would be amusing to get to know you better. Madame Antoinette, could you give me another beer please?'

Louis had remained outwardly calm, but René Blanchet was making no effort to keep his composure, indeed the opposite.

'He's going to pounce,' said Sevran. 'That's how he works.'

Antoinette put a beer on the counter, and Blanchet grabbed Louis's lapels, making a sign towards the skipper of the *Atalante*. But the trawlerman hesitated.

'Monsieur Blanchet,' said Louis, detaching the fingers which were holding his jacket, 'some manners, please. We hardly know each other. I'm willing to come and see you, of course. The big white house after the town hall, isn't it? A bit further down on the right.'

'I'll be the one who chooses my guests, Monsieur Kehlweiler. My door is not open to you.'

'A door – what's that? Just a symbol really. But as you like, at your place or somewhere else, but now, may I ask that you let me drink my beer in peace, you're warming it up.'

Marc smiled and at last, apart from some indifferent faces, the audience had stopped taking sides and were enjoying the show.

'That's right,' Antoinette intervened suddenly, since she was very sensitive to any slight on the service at the Market Cafe. 'Don't warm the gentleman's beer. Give it a rest, René. And for the love of God, what are you complaining about? If Marie really was murdered, then this gentleman better do whatever he's got to do, nothing wrong with that. If there's some monster in Port-Nicolas, best we find out. People here are no better than anywhere else. You're getting on our tits.'

Marc looked at Sevran in astonishment.

'She always talks like that,' said Sevran with a smile. 'Wouldn't think it to look at her, would you?'

'Antoinette,' said Louis, 'you are a woman of good sense.'

'I've sold fish on the marketplace in Concarneau, and I know what people can be like. A rotten fish can turn up in any harbour, in Port-Nicolas like any other place.'

'Antoinette,' said Blanchet, 'you don't –'

'That'll do, René, go and do your shouting outside, if you must, I've got my customers to see to.'

'And you'll let any riff-raff in as a customer?'

'I let in any man who's thirsty, what's wrong with that? Nobody's going to say Antoinette didn't serve a man with a thirst on him, never mind where he comes from, hear what I'm saying? Never mind *where* he comes from.'

'I have a thirst on me,' said Louis. 'Antoinette, can I have another draught beer.'

Blanchet shrugged his shoulders, and Marc saw him change tactics. He gave Antoinette a warm pat on the arm with a sigh, acting like a man who's been beaten at dice, but is prepared to let things lie, without making a fuss, because he's a good guy at heart. He took his glass over to the fishermen's table and sat himself down. Antoinette went to open a window to air the smoke-filled room. Marc admired the little woman, with her black dress and puckered face.

'Here comes the dozy bastard,' Blanchet was saying to Guillaume.

The mayor came into the cafe. It was three o'clock. He waved a vague greeting, and with tired steps, headed for the back room, gathering Louis up on his way through. Louis motioned to Marc to follow him aside.

'Just a minute, Chevalier, I've got something I need to say urgently to Vandoosler.'

Marc found that Louis was looking unusually strained. He tried to fathom the reason for such tension, since he could detect neither anger nor exasperation, nor even worry. It was as if Louis's face had been stripped down into a rigid state, removing the shadows and soft tissue, leaving only the bone structure. All his habitual charm, kindness, nuance and vagueness had gone. Marc wondered whether it was the face of someone who has been badly hurt.

'Marc, I need someone to fetch me something from Paris.'

'Me?'

'No, I need you here to run.'

'Something from the bunker? What about Marthe?'

'No, not Marthe, she'd fall over in the train, she'd lose the stuff, anything could happen.'

'Vincent?'

'Vincent is guarding bench 102 and he won't leave it. I don't have anyone who can get around. What's he called, your friend, not the talkative one, the other one?'

'Mathias.'

'Is he free?'

'At the moment, yes.'

'Is he reliable, really reliable?'

'The hunter-gatherer is as solid as an aurochs. And much cleverer. But it depends whether the subject interests him.'

'He'd have to bring me a packet of papers clipped together in a yellow folder marked "M", and not lose it whatever happens.'

'We can always ask him.'

'Marc, the less you know about this folder the better, tell him.'

'OK. How will he find it?'

Louis took Marc into a corner, and Marc registered his instructions with a series of nods.

'Go now,' said Louis. 'If Mathias can do it, and as soon as possible, tell him thank you. Warn Marthe he'll be coming round. Hurry.'

Marc didn't try to understand. Too much secrecy, it was pointless to protest, better wait for it all to become clear. He found an isolated phone box and called the cafe in the rue Chasle in Paris, which was their way of sending messages. He waited five minutes and got his uncle on the line.

'I need Mathias,' said Marc. 'What are you doing on the phone?'

'Finding out what it's about. Tell me.'

Marc sighed and explained briefly.

'A file marked "M", you say, in the bunker? What's that got to do with anything?'

'Must be about the murderer, what do you think? I think Louis must be on to something, he looks gaunt.'

'I'll fetch St Matthew for you,' said Vandoosler the elder, 'but don't get yourself too mixed up in all this.'

'I already am.'

'Let Kehlweiler go chasing after his own hares.'

'I can't,' said Marc. 'I'm his right leg. And I think there's only one hare.'

Vandoosler muttered something and put the phone down. After a wait of ten minutes, Marc had Mathias on the line. And since the hunter-gatherer was quick on the uptake and a man of few words, the call ended in three minutes.

CHAPTER 21

So that wretched busybody has poked his nose in. And all because of the damned dog. And now the cops are here. Not that it matters, I don't care, plan B all ready to go in case there was a hitch. I'm no fool. That grumpy little inspector, Guerrec, will go wherever he's pointed. He may look like a man who does what he wants. But he's like everyone else, really, that's just on the surface. With a bit of help, he'll go where he's directed, like an ant. He's no exception. People talk a lot of nonsense about ants being intelligent. They're blind slaves to instinct, nothing else. You just have to put your finger in their path, and off they go in another direction. Until the light changes. Foreseeable result: the ant has no idea how to get home, it's lost, it dies. Done it plenty of times. Guerrec's the same. All you have to do is put a finger in his path, send him off on a trail. Not that everyone would be clever enough. An ordinary murderer, one who panics the moment the cops arrive, who's never thought about the ant and the sun, they'll get caught in a couple of days.

No, I'm not stupid. And as for that guy from Paris with his story about dogs and dog shit, he'll find that out to his cost, if he doesn't lay off. Though he doesn't want to lay off. He wants to be everywhere, see everything, find everything, be in charge. Who does he think he is, pathetic meddler? All the same, he's less pathetic than the others, keep an eye on him. Still, never mind, I know the type. Thinks he's so clever, with his intellectual airs, they can be the blindest of the lot. If he tries to start a forest fire to smoke out the rat, he'll get a quick blast from the extinguisher. Fast and deadly. He'll disappear into the landscape, and never know what hit him. I'm in control here. First better deal with the little squirt of a cop, then the poet. Big deal. In fact if I'd never done anything else in my life, I'd have made a good murderer. Well, I am one already, yes, but I could have made a career of murder. I'm a genius at it. And killing makes me feel so good inside. But careful, don't let it show. Do what you have to do now, and then look concerned, interested. But make sure to relax all over, eyes, cheeks, hands, everything.

CHAPTER 22

While Marc was torn between going to fetch the lord of Puisaye's accounts from his bedside table and having another go at the big Port-Nicolas machine – the question he'd prepared was '*How do we get the earth out of the solar system when the sun explodes in five billion years?*' – the mayor had shut the door leading to the back room in the Market Cafe and was telling Louis about his session with Guerrec, the inspector from Quimper. Guerrec had worn the mayor out with questions about Marie Lacasta, he'd taken the electoral register away with him, and he wanted to find out what Kehlweiler had to say, and to take possession of the bone.

'They're at the Fouesnant gendarmerie now. Then he'll start questioning people generally.'

'And why are you telling me all this?' asked Louis.

'Guerrec asked me to. He wants to question you before nightfall. I'm just passing on the message.'

'Does he have a theory, a plan?'

'Guerrec can only see one thing that's significant in Marie's life: the disappearance of her husband Diego Lacasta, five years ago.'

'He's dead?'

'We don't know, he was never seen again, dead or alive. His gun was found abandoned on the quayside, and a boat was missing. What's certain is that Marie avoided talking about his disappearance, and that she was still waiting for him to come back. She didn't touch a single thing in his den.'

'They'd married late in life?'

'Yes, both over sixty.'

'Did he meet her here then?'

The mayor gave an impatient little twitch. It's so tedious to have to repeat these stories that everyone knows by heart. But Guerrec had told him not to annoy Kehlweiler, they might need him. He'd heard of the man by reputation, and he was wary of him.

'He met Marie at Lina's house of course, when she still lived in Paris. In the days of Lina's first husband. Marie worked for them, she looked after the children, simple as that.'

'What was he called, the first husband?'

'Marcel Thomas – his name won't mean anything to you. He was a physics teacher.'

'So Diego knew Lina then?'

'No, no, give me a break, Diego worked for *Sevran*, that was the connection.'

'So what was the link with Lina?'

The mayor sat down and asked himself how this man could have done all the things he was supposed to have done without being capable of understanding how Diego had met Marie, for fuck's sake.

'Sevran,' the mayor said, articulating clearly, 'was an old friend of the couple, well, of Marcel Thomas. They both collected those old typewriters, and the engineer always called on them when he was in Paris, and visited his friend's collection. Diego worked for Sevran. So, he would accompany him to Lina's. So, Diego got to know Marie.'

'What did Diego do for Sevran then?'

'He went all over France for him, searching out machines. Sevran had found Diego in some dead-end job in the antiques trade, and he hired him. So, to cut a long story short, Diego married Marie, two months after Sevran married Lina. And they all came back here to live.'

Louis now sat down in turn, patiently. He was wondering how anyone could be so bad at telling a story. Chevalier really did have a woolly mind.

'So Lina divorced her husband to marry Sevran?'

'No! Give me a break. It was after the accident. Her husband fell from their balcony, vertigo. She was a widow.'

'Ah. Tell me about that then.'

'She was a widow, like I said. Her husband had fallen from their terrace. I only got the story from Marie because Lina doesn't like anyone to talk about it. She and Marie were inside with the children, Lina was reading in bed, and Marcel Thomas was having a final cigarette on the terrace. Lina still blames herself for letting him go out there, because he had drunk a lot that night. But that's stupid, how could she have foreseen?'

'And that was where in Paris, do you know?'

'In the 15th, rue de l'Abbé Groult, and don't ask me the number for God's sake, because I don't know it.'

'Don't blow a fuse, Chevalier, I'm just trying to get it clear in my head, not to annoy you. So Lina was a widow with her two children, and Marie. So what next?'

'A year later she turned to the family friend Sevran, and married him.'

'Right.'

'She had the kids to bring up, no job, no money. All her husband had left her were the machines, beautiful ones, but she had no idea what to do with them. So she married again. I suppose she must have been in love with the engineer, in fact I'm almost sure of that. At any rate he certainly rescued her. So be that as it may, everyone got married. And Sevran settled them all here. And now Guerrec is interested in this Diego, about whom we know nothing, any more than Sevran did, he'd just found him selling junk in some provincial antiques fair. I told Guerrec I thought well of Diego, a reliable chap, a bit sentimental but steady, strong, he got up every morning at six. He was missed by everyone when he disappeared. And as for Marie, two weeks ago she was still waiting for him to come back.'

'Sad.'

'Very, and just between ourselves, a nuisance for the local authority.'

'Where does Guerrec want to start?'

'With you, then Sevran, then everyone else. He and his sidekick will have the devil's own job sorting out alibis, and they won't add up to anything. People are always on the move round here.'

'Did they ask you for yours?'

'Why would they?'

'*Did* they ask you?'

'No, of course not, come on.'

'Well, they will.'

'Right, you want to land me in the shit now? That's your idea of fun?'

'And don't you think *you* may have landed Marie in the shit? What about René Blanchet? You got her to poke about in his dustbins. That was your idea of fun?'

The mayor pouted a little, bent back his fingers without cracking them, but didn't shift on his chair. This man was incredible, just like a fish pond or a pool of water. Louis had always been intrigued by the liquid element. You pour it into a cup and the surface is flat. You tilt the cup and the liquid tips too, but the surface is still as flat as before. Even when you turn it in every direction, the water stays flat. The mayor was like that. You would have had to cool him down to freezing point to get hold of him. But Louis was sure that even if you deep-froze the mayor, he would manage to frost over his surface and stop you seeing inside.

'Is it cold here in winter?' he asked.

'Not often,' Chevalier replied, on automatic pilot. 'It's exceptional for it to freeze.'

'Pity.'

'How do you know about Marie and Blanchet's dustbins, anyway? Did you look in a crystal ball, or perhaps in some dog shit?'

'You did get her to do her spying then?'

'Yes, I did. But I didn't force her to do it, and I paid her.'

'What were you after?'

'It was Blanchet who was after *me*, so don't get the wrong end of the stick. He's bent on getting to be mayor instead of me. I'm well established here, but knowing the man, I'm sure he wouldn't shrink from dirty tricks. I wanted to know what he was planning for me.'

'And did you find anything out from the dustbin?'

'I found out that he eats chicken twice a week, and a lot of tinned ravioli. That no one knows where he really comes from. No family, no party, no known political contacts, nothing. His past is buried in the mist.'

Chevalier frowned.

'He burns all his papers. It was when I noticed that that I got the idea of getting Marie to look in the bin, in case some scraps escaped. Because a man who burns his papers? Eh? A man who refuses to have anyone come in to clean his house?

But Blanchet is meticulous, he cleans all the meat off his chicken bones and he scrapes out his ravioli tins, he smokes his cigars down to his fingers, not one escapes. His rubbish bins are a quintessence of rubbish, no body or soul, just ash, nothing but ash. And if you think that's normal, I don't.'

'Where's he from? Do we know that at least?'

'Northern France somewhere, near Calais.'

'Are you sure about that?'

'It's what he says.'

Louis frowned in turn.

'So, to get back to Marie,' he started again.

'Yes, I know,' said the mayor. 'If he *did* catch her poking in the bin . . . Then if he killed her . . . It would be my fault, I don't need you to tell me. But I can't believe that someone in Port-Nicolas would be a murderer, not even him.'

'Chevalier, get this into your head, somebody *did* kill her. And did Marie find out anything about you? Something Blanchet might have used to attack you?'

'If I knew that, Kehlweiler, I wouldn't have gone looking.'

'How do you imagine he might do it?'

'How do I know? He could invent anything. Embezzling money, cheating, having half a dozen mistresses, a secret life, forty illegitimate children . . . Plenty of things. Anyway, Kehlweiler, when are you planning on leaving? When you've seen Guerrec?'

'Logically, yes.'

It was impossible to tell whether Chevalier was looking relieved or not.

'But in fact, no,' Louis went on.

'Don't you think he can handle it? Guerrec's pretty good. What would keep you here?'

'Three things. I could do with a beer.'

Chevalier shrugged. He went back into the bar with Louis. The place was still full, this was a special day, the cops were in town. People were differently distributed now, as they moved around chatting. Marc had returned and was sitting between Lina and Pauline. He was hesitating. If he had been Pauline, he would have married Sevran rather than Darnas – but each to his own – although Sevran had rather low-slung buttocks and sloping shoulders, a body more womanly in a way, which was uncommon, and which, according to Marc, should be taken into account. But still, let's be generous, you hardly noticed, and Sevran was showing signs of anxiety, which in Marc's view gained him some bonus points out of solidarity. The engineer was coming and going between the counter and tables, bringing drinks over, picking up glasses, doing Antoinette's job, interrupting now and again his disquisition on the history of the Remington typewriter company, his fair-skinned but lined face alternating between open happy smiles and fleeting anxious frowns whenever he looked at Lina. Paradoxically, Darnas, who looked rather like a turtle made of boiled sugar that had stuck to the bottom of the saucepan in places, seemed far more virile than the engineer. He was smiling peacefully, as he listened to Sevran, his big hands resting on his thighs, and he shook them now and again as if to get rid of something – melted sugar, Marc thought – while casually noting, with his bright brown eyes, every movement in the cafe and of all those who had taken refuge there. Lina, tall and indeed rather beautiful, with shapely, sometimes startling lips, who certainly worried Marc more than somewhat, was exchanging occasional remarks with Pauline across his shoulders. Marc had to lean forward to let them talk. He drank a mouthful to compensate for his silence. In half an hour, he hadn't managed to exchange a single word with Pauline and felt cornered. Marthe would have said that it was plain silly to sit between two women, you can't talk to one without turning your back on the other, ridiculous, you should sit opposite them. Louis motioned to him to come over.

'So. What's the answer?' Louis asked in a low voice.

'I've thought it over. I'd prefer to sleep with Pauline, but she's not interested in me.'

'Marc, don't start pissing me off. St Matthew, I mean.'

'He'll be here tonight. Twenty-one minutes past ten, Quimper station.'

Louis gave a brief grin.

'Excellent. Go back to your chat, and listen to everything they say while I'm with Guerrec.'

'I don't know how to chat. I'm hemmed in.'

'Sit facing them, that's what Marthe would say. Sevran,' Louis said out loud, 'fancy a game of billiards?'

Smiling, Sevran accepted at once. The two men went towards the back of the room.

'French or American?' asked Sevran.

'American. I can't concentrate enough for three balls. I've got forty thousand balls running around in my head, it'll be good for me.'

'Me too,' said Sevran. 'To be honest, I was beginning to feel fed up. I didn't want Lina to be left alone after what happened at lunchtime, and the best thing was to bring her here. But I've got my blessed machine waiting for me, I'd have preferred to be dealing with that, to help me forget about my dog. Still, it wasn't the right moment. Lina looks as if she's feeling better already; your friend is distracting her. What does he do for a living?'

'He's a historian. He just does the Middle Ages.'

'No kidding?'

'No kidding.'

'I wouldn't have thought medieval historians looked like that.'

'I think he feels the same. He can't reconcile his two halves.'

'Oh, so what does he do in the middle?'

'He goes crazy, he makes sparks, or he laughs.'

'Ah. Tiring, I should think. You start, Kehlweiler. Go first.'

Louis aimed and pocketed the 6 ball. With one ear he listened to what was being said at the bar.

'Right,' Guillaume was saying, 'why are we all so puzzled? We don't know who killed Marie? So you could just ask the big machine, couldn't you, engineer?'

'And you know what it'll tell you?' called someone from the other end of the room.

'Hear them?' said Sevran, laughing. 'They're on about my big machine, that big monstrosity I built near the campsite. Have you seen it? It gives out little messages. I would never have thought they'd take to it. I was hoping for a little local scandal, but after a few months' distrust, they really got fond of it. My machine can answer any question you like. People come a long way to consult it – worse than a goddess. If I'd made it so you had to pay to turn the handle, we'd have made a fortune in Port-Nicolas, I'm not joking.'

'Yes,' said Louis, watching Sevran's shots – the other man was as good a player as himself. 'Marc told me about it, he's already asked it any number of questions.'

'Your turn. But the machine nearly caused big trouble. One night,' he said, lowering his voice, 'this guy asked it if his wife was cheating on him and the stupid machine thought it was funny to say yes. He took the message for holy writ, and he nearly wiped out his supposed rival.'

'And what if the machine was right?'

'No, it wasn't,' said Sevran, laughing again. 'The

230

poor wife had to go through hell to get the machine to change its mind. Oh, we had a drama on our hands, I'm telling you. And not the only one. Some people have become real addicts. Any little problem, and off they go, to turn the handle. My machine has got beyond my control now, I'm not joking.'

'What did you want then, when you made it?'

'Just to build something, to construct something useless. I wanted to construct a monument to the glory of machinery. And to celebrate the pure beauty of machinery. I wanted it to serve no useful purpose, the only point of it would be that it functioned, that it worked, and you could say when you looked at it: "It's working!" Glory to pure function, the ridiculous and the pointless. Glory to the lever that pushes, the wheel that turns, the piston that slides, the roller that rolls. What for? Just to push, turn, slide and roll.'

'And then in the end, the useless machine turned out to be useful for something, didn't it?'

Louis, distracted by the engineer's conversation, was relaxing and potting ball after ball. Sevran, leaning on his cue, was smiling and forgetting about the death of his dog.

'Exactly! A factory of unsatisfied questions. I assure you, people come from two hundred kilometres away to consult it. Not to look at it, Kehlweiler, but to consult it.'

Louis won the first frame. Sevran asked for a return match, after they'd had a quick drink. The customers at the bar had gradually gathered round the pool table to watch. People were coming and going, making comments, and asking the engineer about the machine, and what it would answer now. It was still raining hard outside. At about five o'clock, Louis just had the 7 ball to pot.

'He's stuck on the 7,' said a voice.

'Always the last one,' said another. 'That's the trouble with pool. At first you've got balls everywhere, you have to be cack-handed not to get them in. And then afterwards it gets harder, and you find out it's worse than you thought. But with French billiards, you know from the start if you're useless.'

'French billiards is harder, but it's more straightforward,' said another voice. Louis smiled. He had just missed the 7 for the third time.

'What did I say, the 7 won't listen to him,' said the first voice.

Sevran aimed and pocketed the 7 after a double cushion.

'Well played,' said Kehlweiler. 'It's almost five. Do you have time for the decider?'

Lina had come to join the spectators sitting on a bench near the billiard table. Sevran glanced at her.

'I'm going back to Lina,' he said. 'I'll pass the game on to whoever wants to play.'

Sevran sat down by Lina and put his arm round her shoulders, scrutinised by Marc, who always watched how other men dealt with women. He thought he wouldn't have put his arm there, but *there*, more comfortable. Darnas wasn't holding on to Pauline at all. Pauline could take care of herself, it seemed. Louis now took on the skipper of the *Belle de Nuit*, Lefloch. He was an easier opponent. The big trawlerman could hold his own, but better against a nor'wester than on the new green baize. Antoinette reminded him to watch out for it, and not to put glasses on the edge, for the love of God.

'The cops are here,' said Marc suddenly.

'Carry on,' said Louis to the trawlerman. 'Don't look round.'

'Is it you they want to talk to?' asked Lefloch.

'Apparently,' said Louis, leaning across the table, one eye half shut.

'Well, you brought it on yourself now. What René said back then makes sense, doesn't it? Sow the storm and reap the whirlwind, see.'

'If that's true, it'll be a good year.'

'Aye, maybe, but Port-Nicolas is none of your business, is it?'

'You go out into the Irish Sea, don't you, Lefloch?'

'That's different. I'm a deep-sea fisherman, got no choice.'

'Right, then, it's the same for me, it's a kind of deep-sea fishing. We do the same job, I've got no choice either, I follow the fish.'

'That so?'

'If he says so,' Sevran intervened.

'Well, OK then,' admitted Lefloch, scratching his

cheek with his cue. 'If it's all the same thing, I'll not argue. Your turn.'

Inspector Guerrec had come into the games room and was watching the match with no show of impatience. Lefloch's cheek was blue with chalk where he had rubbed it, and Louis, who had now been playing for an hour and a half, had damp locks of hair falling over his forehead, his shirt had come untucked from his trousers, and his shirt-sleeves were pushed up to the elbow. Seated or standing, glasses of Muscadet in their hands, cigarettes in their mouths, a dozen or so locals, men and women, were still surrounding the billiard table, but began turning their attention from the game to the police from Quimper. Inspector Guerrec was a very small man, thin-faced with sharp features and hooded eyes, fading blond hair, cut short and receding. Louis put the cue down across the table and shook hands with him.

'Louis Kehlweiler, pleased to meet you. Do you mind if we finish the game? I've already lost one.'

'Go ahead,' said Guerrec, without smiling.

'Forgive me, one of my ancestors was a gambling man, it's in my blood.'

Ah, thought Louis, this cop is clever. He's not flinging his authority about, he's waiting, he goes round obstacles, he doesn't allow himself to get irritated by trifles.

Ten minutes later, Louis had beaten Lefloch, promised him a return match, put on his sweater and jacket, and followed the policeman outside.

Guerrec took him over to the town hall. Louis realised that he was sorry to leave the steam-filled cafe, with its smell of sweat and cigarette smoke. The place had got under his skin and among the huge number of cafes strung out in his memory, this one had inexplicably taken its place among the very closest to his heart.

CHAPTER 23

It was while he was talking to the police inspector, who was a prudent man, not unpleasant, but not wildly amusing either, that Louis found the screw of paper in his left-hand jacket pocket. Guerrec was explaining to him that Diego, Diego Lacasta Rivas, was Spanish: of his life before the age of fifty, when he had started to work for Sevran, nothing was known. They were going to have to alert the Spanish authorities, which did not please him greatly. But to disappear without leaving any traces, Diego must have had some good reason, no doubt shared with Marie, who had continued to expect him back. Who knows whether he might indeed have come back? And even killed Marie? As he listened, Louis had put his hand in his pocket and found the paper, screwed into a ball, something that shouldn't have been there, because he had passed the twist of newspaper with the bone in it over to Guerrec. He unfolded it, without interrupting the inspector.

'Kehlweiler,' said Guerrec, 'are you listening to me or not?'

'Read this, inspector, but try not to get your fingerprints on it, it's already covered with mine.'

Kehlweiler passed Guerrec a small piece of crumpled paper, torn along the edge. The short lines had been typed.

> *There was a couple*
> *in the Vauban cabin,*
> *but nobody's letting on.*
> *What are you waiting for*
> *wasting your time*
> *missing the 7?*

'Where did this poem come from?' asked Guerrec.

'From my pocket.'

'Go on.'

'I can't tell you any more. Someone must have slipped it into my jacket just now at the cafe. It wasn't there when I went into the bar at three o'clock.'

'And where was your jacket?'

'Near the billiard table, hanging on a chair to dry.'

'And this paper was crumpled up?'

'Yes.'

'What's all that about missing the 7?'

'It's a billiard ball, number 7. I tried to pot it three times towards the end of the game, without succeeding.'

'It's not very well written.'

'But clear enough.'

'A couple,' Guerrec muttered. 'If there was some clandestine couple that night in the cabin, Marie might have surprised them, and one of them might have killed her. It's possible, we already had a case like that in Lorient, four years ago, recent as that. But . . . why this anonymous note? And why doesn't the writer name the couple? Why send it to you? And why in the cafe? Why this business with the 7 ball? What's that all about?'

'A dog in a game of skittles,' said Louis softly.

'A whole lot of pointless questions,' said Guerrec as if talking to himself, and shrugging his shoulders. 'This takes us into the twisted world of anonymous letter writers, their weird motives, their roundabout methods, against all logic . . . Greed, cowardice, violence, weakness. Same thing, six years ago in Pont-L'Abbé, recent as that. Still, the tip-off could be about something real.'

'The Vauban Cove cabin would be well chosen for an assignation. It's got a roof, it's remote, the risk of being seen is minimal.'

'Even if you knew that Marie Lacasta regularly went gathering shellfish in the bay?'

'She would surely have been unlikely to go into the cabin, because of its reputation. Those old stone huts, people only use them to take a leak or to meet someone secretly, everyone knows that. They were doing it four thousand years ago, recent as that, everywhere in the world. But perhaps, that Thursday, Marie, for once, took a look inside. And then one thing led to another.'

238

'But what about whoever wrote this note? He was there too?'

'That would make a lot of people on a murder scene the same evening. I don't believe in that kind of coincidence. But he might know that a couple met regularly in the cabin. When he heard about the murder, he might have put two and two together, and suggested it to us. He's not speaking openly, because he's frightened. You saw what it said: "nobody's letting on". Either the writer is exaggerating, or one of the couple is dangerous, or possibly just an influential person you wouldn't want to cross. So nobody does let on.'

'Why was it sent to *you*?'

'My jacket was accessible and it was a good way to reach you.'

'A couple,' Guerrec murmured again. 'A couple. What kind of tip-off is that? The world's full of them. Setting a watch on the cabin wouldn't work, they won't go back there. Questioning people won't get us anywhere, just spread panic and we'd learn nothing. What we need is the writer of the note. Fingerprints . . .?'

'He wouldn't have risked leaving any. That's why he, or she, screwed up the paper.'

'Oh yes?'

'You couldn't keep gloves on in the cafe without people noticing. To slip the paper into my jacket, the simplest thing was to screw it into a ball, and hold it in a handkerchief or a closed fist and let it drop into the pocket. It's very small. You could

239

easily hold it in your hand, just letting your arm swing casually.'

'He saw you losing on the 7, so he must have gone out after that. When was that?'

'Right at the end of my game with Sevran, before five o'clock.'

'Then he comes back in, the note already typed, swinging his arm casually. Who did you see coming and going then?'

'I can't possibly give you a rundown of all their coming and going. I was concentrating on my game with Lefloch, and I don't know many of the locals yet. There were plenty of people in the bar and around the billiard table. They were waiting for you to appear. People went out, hung about, came back.'

'What about the typewriter, could we trace it through that?'

'Well, you've got a specialist on the spot, might as well use him.'

CHAPTER 24

Sevran had stared hard for several minutes at the note which the inspector had unfolded in front of him, using tweezers. Looking puzzled, and concentrating, it was as if he were trying to identify someone's face in a photograph.

'Yes, I do know this,' he said in a low voice. 'This is a slow, soft, smooth action. And if I'm not much mistaken, the machine is one of mine. Come along.'

The two men followed him into a large room upstairs in the main house, full of typewriters: ranged around on tables and shelves were as many as two hundred black machines of unusual shapes. Sevran made his way unhesitatingly between the tables, and sat down in front of a black-and-gold typewriter with a dial.

'Put these on,' said Guerrec, passing him some gloves, 'and type gently.'

Sevran nodded, pulled on the gloves and put a sheet of paper into the carriage.

'This is the Geniatus 1920,' he said. 'What is the wording I should type?'

'*There was a couple*, new line, *in the Vauban cabin*, new line, *but nobody's letting on*,' Guerrec recited. Sevran typed a few words, took out the sheet and examined it.

'No,' he said, pulling a face, 'it's almost the same, but not quite.'

He stood up quickly, annoyed that his expertise had failed him, went round the tables and sat down at a small oblong machine whose function was hard to guess from its shape.

Sevran typed the first words of the message again, but not on a keyboard: this time a wheel turned until the right letter printed. He did not need to look at the metal disc, since he knew the order of letters by heart. He took the paper out and smiled.

'This is it. It must be from the Virotyp 1914. Show me the original again, inspector.'

The engineer compared the two pieces of paper.

'Yes, it's the Virotyp, no question. Do you see?'

'Yes,' said Guerrec. 'Can you type the whole thing, so we can check it in the lab?'

While Sevran was once more working the Virotyp disc, Guerrec was looking around the room. The table on which the Virotyp sat was near the door, but screened from the windows. Sevran brought him the second version.

'This time,' Guerrec said to him, 'can you put your fingerprints on it. Please don't take offence.'

'Well, I do take offence,' said Sevran, 'seeing that it's my house, and my machine, and I must be in the front line of suspects.'

He took off the gloves and held the paper in both hands, pressing his fingers down on it, before giving it back to the inspector.

'Kehlweiler, stay here, I'm calling my colleague to check the prints.'

Sevran stayed with Louis, his expression both anxious and intrigued.

'Is it easy for anyone to get in here?' Louis asked.

'In the daytime, yes, over the garden wall for instance. At night, or when we're not here, we put the alarm on. But this afternoon, after I'd buried Ringo, I took Lina to the cafe to distract her, and I forgot to switch it on, I had other things on my mind. In fact we often forget.'

'Aren't you worried about your machines?'

Sevran shrugged.

'You can't really sell them unless you know what you're doing. You have to find the right buyers, collectors, networks, addresses.'

'How much are they worth?'

'Depends on the model, how rare it is, its condition. This one, for instance, is worth five hundred francs, but that one over there might fetch twenty-five thousand. Who would know? Who would be able to choose the right one? There are some that look like nothing special and are very sought-after. The one in the back, with the lever inverted, see that? The very first Remington, 1874, and unique today, because the lever was badly engineered. Remington recalled them soon after bringing them out, and they reversed the lever, free of charge, for all their customers. But someone had brought that one over from America to France and Remington didn't chase after him to change the lever. So my machine must be unique. But who would ever know that? A collector, yes, but he'd have to be a real expert. And there aren't many of us, nobody would dare steal it from me, word would get out, and you'd lose your reputation, it would be professional suicide. So, you see, I don't run much of a risk. And I've fixed each machine to the base with metal feet. You'd need time and tools to unscrew them. Apart from the cellar, where the door was forced the other day, I've never had any trouble, and even then they didn't take anything.'

Guerrec came in with his colleague and pointed out to him the Virotyp, the door and the windows.

Then he thanked the engineer briefly, before leaving.

'I don't think we'll find any prints on the machine except Sevran's,' said Guerrec, as they went back towards the town hall. 'Yes, anyone could have typed the note, but Sevran's awkwardly placed all the same. Still, I don't see why he would be interested in secret couples. Nor do I see what motive he could possibly have to type the note on one of his own machines.'

'He can't have. Sevran can't have typed it, he didn't leave the cafe while I was playing Lefloch, he was still there when I went to the town hall with you.'

'Are you sure?'

'Sure.'

'Who else stayed there?'

'His wife, I think, though I couldn't see her when she was at the bar, Lefloch, Antoinette, Blanchet . . .'

'This business about the 7 ball bothers me. It seems pointless, gratuitous, meaningless, but it must mean something.'

'Whoever passed me the note didn't want to be identified. By mentioning the ball, he's making us think he was among the thirty or so people in the cafe when I was playing Sevran. Right? And what if he wasn't?'

'How else could he know about the 7?'

'By looking through the window. He waits, he listens, he finds the first significant detail which would place him as present inside the cafe. Nobody would be able to see him from inside, it was getting dark and pouring with rain, but he'd be able to see in.'

'Yes, I suppose he, or she, might either have been inside until you played the 7 ball, or outside. But it doesn't help us much. It's taking a lot of trouble not to be identified.'

'Either he's scared stiff of the murderer, or it's him.'

'Him? What do you mean?'

'He's the murderer. It wouldn't be the first time a murderer identified a scapegoat. We need to watch it, Guerrec, maybe we're being sent off on a false trail. Somewhere round here there's a truly evil person, that's the way I see it.'

Guerrec contorted his thin face.

'You twist things, Kehlweiler. Anyone can see you're not used to anonymous letters. They're common, terribly common. We had a case in Pont-L'Abbé six years ago, recent as that. It isn't murderers who write them, it's cowards, sneaks, beneath contempt.'

'So a murderer who premeditates his act and bashes an old woman over the head isn't beneath contempt?'

'Yes, but that's someone contemptible who acts. The writers of anonymous letters are passive, people who haven't been able to make any impression on others. There's a gulf between those worlds. It can't be the same person, it just doesn't fit.'

'Have it your own way. Keep me briefed about the prints, the alibis and Spain. If that's allowed, and if you're willing to accept my help.'

'I tend to work on my own, Kehlweiler.'

'In that case, our paths may cross.'

'It's quite true that you prompted this whole investigation, but you don't have the right to join in. I'm sorry to remind you, but you're just a man among others now, on the same footing as everyone else.'

'I hear you, I can live with that.'

Louis returned to the hotel at seven, but did not find Marc there. He lay down on his bed, phone in hand. He called the number of the police station in the 15th arrondissement, the one covering the rue de l'Abbé Groult. At this time, Nathan would still be at his desk.

'Nathan? This is Ludwig. Nice to talk to you.'

'It's the German, is it? How are you doing? Retired now?'

'I'm swanning around in Brittany.'

'Anything to do down there?'

'Lots of fish of course. But an old fish too. Marcel Thomas, rue de l'Abbé Groult, fell from a first-floor balcony, twelve years ago, can you give me any details?'

'Hold on, I'll have a look for the file.'

Nathan returned ten minutes later.

'Yeah,' he said. 'The guy fell, recorded as an accident.'

'Yes, I know, but the details?'

Louis could hear Nathan leafing through papers.

'Nothing special. It was the night of 12 October. The Thomas couple had had friends to supper, Lionel Sevran and Diego Lacasta Rivas, who left at 10 p.m. to go back to their hotel. The couple were in the flat with their two children, and Marie Berton, the nanny. Nobody came in after ten, the neighbours confirm that. The accident happened around midnight. Let's see, questions, colleagues, neighbours, I'll jump all that. The wife was questioned for several days. She was in bed, reading, nobody was able to find any evidence against her, or against Marie Berton who was also in bed. Neither one could have gone out without the other hearing. They were each in their bedroom until they heard the husband scream. Either the two women are backing each other up, or they were telling the truth. Lionel Sevran was also questioned, he was asleep in his hotel, and same goes for Diego Lacasta, he talked non-stop, there are pages of it. Wait, I'm skimming. Lacasta got very worked up, defended the two women with all his might. Then there was a reconstruction a week later. Wait. The inspector notes that everyone maintained their statements, the wife was in tears, so was the nanny, Sevran was very upset, and Lacasta said virtually nothing.'

'I thought you said he talked non-stop?'

'The week before, yes. He'd probably had enough. So, suicide was ruled out, murder was improbable and unprovable. The railing on the balcony was very low, he'd had a lot to drink. Conclusion, accidental death, permission given for burial, case closed.'

'Name of the inspector in charge?'

'Sellier. He's not there now, promoted captain.'

'Yes, to the 12th. I know him. Thanks a lot, Nathan.'

'Have you got some more on this story?'

'Two weddings, a disappearance and a death. What do you think of that?'

'Not exactly normal. Good fishing, Ludwig, but look out, you don't have any backup these days. Proceed with caution and follow to the letter the calm and moderate advice of your toad. That's my best advice.'

'I'll give him a kiss from you, and my love to your daughters.'

Louis smiled as he rang off. His friend Nathan had seven beautiful daughters, like in a fairy tale, which had always enchanted him.

Sellier had left the office. Louis found him at home.

'So, the bit of bone led to a murder,' said Sellier after listening carefully to Louis's summary. 'And all those involved in the Marcel Thomas affair are down there in Brittany.'

Sellier's voice was deliberate, a man who took care to recall things methodically.

'The investigation here is being handled by Guerrec. You know him?'

'A bit. He's rather annoying, doesn't say much, you wouldn't give him marks for GSOH, but he's pretty straight as far as I know. No miracle worker. But then neither am I.'

'From your interviews for the Marcel Thomas affair, is there anything that sticks out in your mind?'

'I'm trying to remember, but I can't think of anything. If it really was a murder, then I fucked up. But there wasn't anything to go on.'

'Could one of the women have crept out to the terrace?'

'You can bet I checked that out. They had an old parquet floor, Hungarian Point chevrons, that I remember very well, the blessed parquet. Every

249

section of it creaked. If one of the women killed him, it must have been with the connivance of the other, no doubt about that.'

'And no one came to see them after Sevran and Lacasta left?'

'No, that was clearly established.'

'How come you remember the case so well?'

'Because of, well, because of a few niggling doubts. Some of the cases I've handled, the killers have been caught, and I've wiped them from my memory, but the ones where there was a shadow of doubt linger in corners of your mind.'

'What kind of doubt?'

'About Diego Lacasta. He did a U-turn. He was a warm, expansive guy, all Spanish honour and emotion, determined to defend the two women, especially the nanny. Doesn't surprise me if he married her. He was obviously besotted with her. And when he came back with his boss a week later for the reconstruction, he'd retreated into being a proud haughty Spaniard, without speaking a word. He didn't defend anyone, he just let the situation take its course, in sulky silence. I thought it was his Iberian temperament – you have to remember I was young and prejudiced in those days. But still, because of him, I remember the reconstruction, the creaking floorboards, his closed face. He'd been the only one who had lit up the case for me, and the flame had gone out. That's all. It doesn't take much to plant a doubt, but that's just me.'

After hanging up, Louis lay on his bed for another five minutes, with arms folded. Time to get moving and have something to eat. As he left his room, he picked up a message slipped under the door, which he hadn't noticed when he came in.

If you want me, I've gone to the machine with some questions needing answers. Look out for your wretched toad, it's poncing about in the bathroom.
Marc

Louis asked at the hotel for some bread and two bananas, and set off on foot for the machine. He walked slowly. Guerrec didn't appeal to him, too much of a sobersides. René Blanchet certainly didn't appeal to him. The mayor, although more inoffensive, didn't appeal to him either. Nor did the anonymous letter. But Darnas *did* appeal to him, and he was precisely the man he'd have liked to demolish. He was out of luck. With Sevran, you could have a conversation if you kept off dogs, but the dog was dead. As for the women, Marie Lacasta's old face did appeal to him, he seemed to see it all the time, but she was dead too. Lina was also beginning to obsess him. She had killed the dog, in an act which was far from normal, despite what her husband said in his efforts to protect her. He seemed to want to protect her all the time, the hand on the shoulder to protect her, calm her down or hold her back.

As for Pauline, yes, she still appealed to him, and he was out of luck there as well. Because Pauline didn't seem to want to come near him, she was stiff, out of defiance or something. Well, he'd said he'd leave her in peace, better make an effort to keep his promise. Very noble to make promises, easily done, then you have to keep them, which is a pain in the backside. Just now, Mathias must be on the train, with the yellow folder. Thinking about that folder required an effort of him. It was a heavy and painful thought, and gave him a nagging headache.

He saw from a distance the weird black shape of the machine Marc had talked about. As he got nearer he could hear various rattles, clanks and squeaks. Kehlweiler shook his head. Marc was becoming obsessed with this pointless machine. What stupid question had he asked it now? And what machine could ever reconcile the incompatible contrasts of young Vandoosler, his nervous emotion and his capacity for concentrated study? Louis couldn't have said which had the upper hand, Marc's deep calm plunges into research, or his panic attacks like a swimmer about to drown. Would he have described him as a slender cetacean, a regular denizen of the deep, or a desperate pup, thrashing about on the surface of the waves?

Marc was standing there, reading the message the machine had just delivered to him by the flame of his cigarette lighter, and at the same time, singing a song. He didn't seem to be thrashing about. It wasn't the first time Kehlweiler had heard him sing. He stopped a few metres away to watch and listen. If it hadn't been for the murder of the old woman, which made him furious, and the difficult thoughts attached to the yellow folder travelling towards him, he would have appreciated the scene. The night was chilly, the rain had stopped, the stupefying machine had suspended its clanking, and alone in the dark, young Vandoosler was singing.

> *Farewell to life, farewell to love,*
> *Farewell to you ladies of France.*
> *The war goes on, the guns still boom,*
> *A soldier's the plaything of chance.*
> *In chalky Craonne, our bones will be laid,*
> *For death is leading the dance.*

'What did the machine answer?' Louis asked, interrupting him.

'The machine can go fuck itself,' said Marc, crumpling up the message. 'All it does is shit on everything, the Middle Ages, life, the solar system. You'll see, but ask it out loud, otherwise it doesn't work.'

'Out loud – is that the rule?'

'I just made that one up, so as to find out what you're thinking. Clever, eh?'

'What do you want to know?'

'Basically what you think of the murder, what

you think of Pauline Darnas, what you're expecting from the folder marked "M", for which you have made Mathias your slave. And as supplementaries, what you think about the future explosion of the sun, and about me.'

Kehlweiler went nearer the machine.

'We'll ask it. Is this the handle?'

'Yes, you do five turns, hard. Then I'll pick up the answer.'

The machine set in motion all its workings and Louis watched it with interest.

'Impressive, isn't it? Here's your message. Read it yourself, I don't poke my nose into other people's correspondence.'

'It's dark, I haven't got a lighter, or my toad, or anything. Read it to me.'

'"*Don't panic. Souvenir of Port-Nicolas.*" See what I mean? See how infuriating it is. Don't panic, but what else can you do?'

'You can wait. I don't have an answer to any of the questions you asked me. I don't understand the Marie Lacasta business, I fear I understand only too well the case of Pauline, and as for the file marked "M", we'll wait for your hunter-gatherer friend. Something new has turned up, a snide note that someone put in my pocket when we were in the cafe. *There was a couple in the Vauban cabin and nobody's letting on about it*, stuff like that. Not you, by any chance?'

'Why would I put something in your pocket? Take the risk of touching your filthy toad? Lose a chance to talk? You must be kidding. Tell me more.'

The two men walked slowly back towards the hotel. As Louis explained to Marc about the screw of paper, he kept looking at his watch.

CHAPTER 25

As soon as Mathias arrived at the hotel, Kehlweiler took the folder from him and shut himself up in his room.

'For the past half-hour I haven't been able to get a complete sentence out of him,' Marc told Mathias. 'Did you look inside the folder?'

'No.'

Marc had no need to add: 'Are you sure you didn't?' because when Mathias said yes or no, he really meant yes or no, no need to look further.

'You're a noble soul, St Matthew. I think I might have risked taking a peep.'

'I didn't have a chance to put my soul to the test, because the folder was stapled. I'm off to see the sea.'

Marc wheeled his bike to accompany Mathias down to the beach. Mathias didn't pass comment. He knew that Marc, even when he was on foot, liked to have a bicycle to push whenever he had a chance. It acted as his horse, the noble charger of a medieval knight, a peasant's old nag, or a Sioux brave's warhorse. Marc noticed that despite the cold, Mathias's feet remained stubbornly bare in his sandals, and he was dressed as ever with the utmost simplicity, cotton trousers held up with a rustic piece of string, and a sweater next to the skin. But he didn't comment either. No one would ever change the hunter-gatherer. At the slightest opportunity, Mathias took the whole lot off. If people asked him why, he just said he felt imprisoned in clothes.

Wheeling the bike, taking quick steps to keep up with Mathias, who had immensely long legs, Marc described the local situation while Mathias listened in silence. Marc could have given him a five-minute outline, but he liked detours, nuances, digressions, fleeting impressions, traceries of words, all the ornaments of speech which Mathias simply called chatter. Marc was now launched on what he called the dark squares on the chessboard: Lina Sevran's melancholy state, her two fatal shots at the dog, the inscrutability of the mayor, the hulking presence of René Blanchet, Marie's little hands poking about in the dustbins of the old brute, the disappearance of Spanish Diego, the poem denouncing some couple in the Vauban cabin, Kehlweiler's stricken face when he had asked for his yellow folder, the ruins of Louis's old love affair, Darnas's lively intelligence locked into the body of an ape with delicate fingers, when Mathias suddenly interrupted him.

'Hush!' he said, grabbing the crossbar of the bike to stop Marc in his tracks.

Mathias was standing stock-still in the dark.

Marc made no objection. He could hear nothing for the sound of the wind, nor could he see or feel anything, but he knew enough about Mathias to be aware that he was on the alert. Mathias had a way of using his five physical senses as captors, sensors, decoders and much else. Marc would willingly have marketed Mathias instead of those expensive inventions that pick up sound waves, detect pollen, read infrared signals and other complex things, the functions of which Mathias would have performed perfectly without costing a sou. He maintained that if the hunter-gatherer put his ear to the ground in the desert, he would be able to hear the Paris–Strasbourg express, although it was hard to see what use that would be to anyone.

Mathias let go the bike.

'Run!' he said to Marc, who saw Mathias rush off into the night, without understanding what they were chasing. Mathias's animal capacities – primitive, according to Lucien – always disconcerted him and cut short his constant talking. He dropped the bike to the ground and ran after the crazy prehistorian, who was moving silently and faster than him, taking no notice of the nearby cliff edge. He caught up with him two hundred metres further on.

'Down there,' said Mathias, pointing to the shingle beach. 'Go and see to him, I'm going to look around – someone else is here.'

Mathias disappeared at speed, and Marc looked

down at the seashore. A dark figure was lying there, someone who must have had a bad fall, of six or seven metres. Holding on to the rocks to make his way down, he wondered whether someone might have pushed this person from the path. Reaching solid ground, he ran over to the motionless form. He prodded it gently, his face tense, found a wrist, and felt for a pulse. It was beating slightly, but the man wasn't moving, not even moaning. Marc on the other hand felt the blood rushing to his temples. If someone had pushed this person over the edge, it must have happened only a minute ago, in a few rapid movements which Mathias had heard. When Mathias started to run, it must have prevented the murderer finishing off the job and now Mathias was after him. Marc didn't give the runaway much of a chance. Whether he lay low or plunged ahead, it was unlikely he would escape the primitive hunter, and illogically enough Marc felt no fear on Mathias's behalf, although Mathias was as vulnerable as the next man, after all, and didn't have thirty thousand years of accumulated strength, contrary to what one might think. Marc didn't dare move the head of the man on the ground, in case of damaged vertebrae. He knew just enough to know he shouldn't do anything. But he had managed to push aside the man's hair, and to fumble in his pocket for his cigarette lighter. He had to strike it several times before he recognised the youth whom Darnas had described as an inveterate dreamer, the young seventeen-year-old who'd been in the cafe a while back, sitting with the pale-faced buddy of the priest. He wasn't sure of this one's name – was it perhaps Gaël? When he touched the boy's hair, Marc had felt wet blood, and now, his stomach in cramps, he was squeamishly stretching his hand away from his body. He would have liked to go and wash it in the sea, but dared not leave the young man.

Mathias called softly to him from the top of the path. Marc climbed back up the seven metres of rocky slope, hauled himself over the edge and immediately wiped his hand on the wet grass.

'It must be Gaël,' he whispered. 'He seems to be alive so far. You stay here, I'll run for help.'

It was only then that he saw that Mathias was holding on to someone in the dark.

'Do you know who this woman is?' Mathias simply asked.

No need for the lighter. Mathias was holding Lina Sevran in an armlock.

'The engineer's wife,' said Marc in a sinking voice. 'Where was she?'

'Not far away, hiding in the trees. I heard her panting. Don't worry, I won't hurt her.'

Lina Sevran was neither moving, crying, nor speaking. She was trembling all over, as she had been at midday when she shot the dog.

'But hurry,' said Mathias.

Marc ran for his bike, jumped on and pedalled quickly towards the village.

He burst into Kehlweiler's bedroom, without knocking. Louis was not asleep, and looked up from a mass of papers spread out on his table, old documents from the yellow folder, covered with notes and drawings. Marc, as he drew breath, thought he looked the way he had earlier, like a Goth from the Danube basin, ready to do battle with the Huns. For a second, there flashed into his head a mosaic in Constantinople, of the fine head of a barbarian, dark locks falling over a pale forehead.

'Where've you been?' said Louis, getting up. 'In a fight?'

Marc looked down at himself. His clothes were muddied and wet from the rocks and there was still blood on his hand.

'Hurry!' he said. 'Phone for help. It's that young Gaël, he's at the bottom of the cliffs, he's bleeding. Just after the wooden cross. Mathias is there.'

Five minutes later, Marc was on his way back, dragging Louis along with him as fast as he could.

'Mathias heard something,' Marc said.

'Don't walk so fast and don't talk so fast. *You* didn't hear anything?'

'I'm not from primeval times,' said Marc, speaking more loudly. 'I'm a normal, civilised, educated person. I can't see in the dark, I can't hear anyone blink, I can't smell the micro-pheromones of sweat at twenty metres. But Mathias can still hear the aurochs thundering past the caves at Lascaux, so you can imagine. If he was in the

Sahara, he'd be able to hear the Paris–Strasbourg train, it's very practical.'

'Calm down, for Christ's sake! So Mathias has good hearing, but what happened?'

'What happened? Well, he dashed off and we found Gaël, at least I think it's him, he'd gone over the edge, further along, and while I went down to take a look at him, Mathias went charging after his prey.'

Louis stopped short on the path.

'Yes,' said Marc, 'I didn't have time to tell you everything. Mathias caught Lina Sevran, who was hiding nearby.'

'My God! What have you done with her?'

'Mathias is holding on to her, don't worry.'

'Could she get away from him?'

Marc shrugged.

'Back home, Mathias is the log-carrier. Without damaging them, mind, because he likes wood. I only carry little dustbin bags. Look, there are flashing lights, the emergency services have got here.'

Louis heard Marc draw a deep breath of relief.

Mathias was still standing on the clifftop, holding Lina in a stranglehold, with one hand. Down below, men were busy around Gaël's body.

'What's the news?' asked Marc.

'Don't know,' said Mathias. 'They took down a stretcher and first-aid stuff.'

'What about Guerrec?' said Marc. 'We'll have to call Guerrec.'

'I know,' said Louis, looking at Lina. 'But we don't have to do that this minute. We have time for a few words. Bring her over here, Mathias.'

Mathias gently propelled Lina away from the edge of the cliff.

'Guerrec will be along soon,' Louis said to her.

'I didn't push him,' murmured Lina.

'Why did you say "push"? He could just have fallen.'

Lina dropped her head, and Louis raised it again.

'He just fell,' said Lina.

'No, he didn't. But you know who pushed him and you almost said it. Gaël is from round here, he knows these cliffs like the back of his hand. Why were you hiding in a corner?'

'I was out walking. I heard a cry, and I was scared.'

'Mathias didn't hear any cry.'

'He was further away.'

'There was no cry,' said Mathias.

'Yes. Gaël cried out. I was scared, so I took shelter.'

'If you were scared, you wouldn't have been out walking alone at night. And when you hear a cry like someone falling, you run to help, don't you? No reason to hide, either way. Unless you pushed him.'

'I didn't push him,' Lina repeated.

'Then you saw someone else push him.'

'No.'

'Lina,' said Louis, more gently still. 'Guerrec will

263

be along very soon. He's a cop. A man falls off the cliff thirteen days after Marie's death. We find you here, hiding in the trees. If you can't find something better to say, Guerrec will simply do his job as a cop.'

Marc looked at the other three. Lina was still trembling, and Louis no longer looked like a Merovingian Goth.

'Well, what about you?' Lina spoke again. 'What job are you doing? I know who you are now, the mayor's wife told me. I don't see that you're any different from Guerrec.'

'Well, I am. You'd do better to talk to me.'

'No.'

Louis signalled to Mathias who took Lina to one side. She was trembling, but gave the impression of being quite removed from events, and that didn't fit.

An hour later, the scene was deserted. The Fouesnant gendarmes had been and gone, Guerrec had arrived and then left to take Lina Sevran home. Gaël had been transported, unconscious, to hospital in Quimper.

'I could do with a beer,' said Louis.

The three men had gathered in Kehlweiler's hotel room. Marc wouldn't go to fetch the beer, because Louis had put it in the bathroom with Bufo. Louis fetched three bottles. Marc contemplated the neck of his bottle.

'Lina Sevran,' he said softly, pressing the bottle

against his eye, 'was sleeping with Gaël. That was the couple in the cabin. Marie surprised them. So she kills her. Why?'

'Fear of a divorce,' said Mathias.

'Yes, she needs the engineer's money. Then afterwards she kills her fragile toy boy, to keep him quiet.'

'Come away from that bottle,' said Louis. 'If she was sleeping with Gaël, why not wait till the engineer was in Paris? Why go and freeze in an uncomfortable cabin at five o'clock, when you could have a nice warm bed at eight?'

'There could be reasons. She was there when Gaël fell. And she shot the dog.'

'I'm thinking of that,' said Louis.

'What did she say to you?'

'I didn't talk to her about the cliff or the dog. I talked to her about her first husband. He died falling off a balcony, remember?'

'An accident, surely?'

'A fall, like Gaël's. As a way of committing murder, it's simple and perfect.'

'And what did she say?'

Louis shrugged his shoulders.

'She said she didn't push him either, same as with Gaël. And she trembled more than ever. It seems she's still horrified by that business. I asked her about Diego Lacasta, who had changed from being as brave as a bullfighter in her defence one day, to becoming mute as if he had been struck dumb a week later. She confirmed that, and she added, even, that Diego always seemed to have suspected her. Before the accident, he was friendly and liked chatting with her, and he had ferociously defended her during the police inquiry. And then there was a sudden change in his attitude, he clammed up, he looked as if he didn't trust her any more. She says that without the constant support of Marie, Sevran and the children, she wouldn't have survived.'

'Does she know where Diego is?'

'No, but she must be pleased to be rid of him. He weighed on her like some old dumb ghost.'

Marc blew into his bottle.

'And the dumb ghost has disappeared too,' he said.

'Yes,' said Louis.

Louis paced round the small room and went to stand by the window. It was past two in the morning. Mathias was dozing on one of the twin beds.

'We need to know who the couple was,' Louis said at last.

'You think there really was one?'

'Yes. Once we know that, we'll be able to tell whether that's something solid or just a distraction. And whether the writer of the poem was simply a sneak, or a murderer providing a red herring for us. There must be someone who can tell us who Gaël's girlfriend was.'

'Darnas?'

'No. Darnas guesses, but he doesn't know. We

need someone who snoops on everyone for his own advantage.'

'The mayor?'

'Chevalier isn't the sharpest knife in the box, but he's not a sewer rat. If he had his own sources of information, he wouldn't have to resort to going through his rival's dustbins. No, I'm thinking of that arsehole Blanchet.'

'*He* won't want to help you.'

'Why not?'

Louis turned round. He stood still for a few seconds, then picked up his jacket.

'Are you coming?'

'Where are you going?' asked Marc sleepily.

'To Blanchet's, where do you think?'

Marc took his eye away from the bottle. He had a red mark now around his eye.

'At this time of night? Are you mad?'

'We're not here to preserve the man's beauty sleep. Two murders, that's enough. There's some kind of purge going on in this village.'

Louis looked into the bathroom, decided against taking Bufo, gathered up some papers from the table, and stuffed them into his inside pocket.

'Hurry up,' said Louis. 'You don't have any choice, because if I get punched on the jaw by Blanchet while you're snoring away in the hotel, you'll torture yourself with guilt until the end of time, and that will stop you working on your Middle Ages.'

'*Blanchet?* You suspect him? Just because you

don't like the way he looks, because he looks like he pisses vinegar?'

'You think it's normal to piss vinegar? You think you know something about the way he pisses?'

'Oh, give us a break!' shouted Marc, standing up.

Louis stood facing Marc and examined him calmly. He pulled Marc's collar up, pushed back his shoulders and lifted his chin.

'Right, that's better,' he said. 'Try to look dangerous. Come on, *dangerous*, we're not going to spend all night there.'

Marc felt sorry he'd come. He ought to have stayed in his nice cosy thirteenth century, in his house, in his bedroom, in Paris. This Merovingian Goth was completely crazy. Nevertheless, he tried to look dangerous. If he'd been a man, it would have been easy, oh, come on, he *was* a man, just as well.

Kehlweiler shook his head.

'Think of something nasty,' he insisted. 'Not food or the toad, something on a grand scale.'

'Simon de Montfort and the massacre of the Albigensians?'

'If you like,' sighed Louis. 'Yes, that's better, almost credible. The whole time we're there, think about that Simon chap. And bring *him* along,' he added, pointing to the sleeping Mathias. 'He could be useful.'

CHAPTER 26

Louis knocked several times at Blanchet's front door. Marc was on edge; little muscles were twitching all over his back. Every aspect of the massacre of the Albigensians went through his mind, he was gripping his beer bottle, one finger wedged in its mouth. Mathias had asked no questions, and was standing in the shadows, a giant in sandals, unmoving but ready for action. A sound came from behind the door. It opened slightly, on to the security chain. Blanchet was in his dressing gown.

'Let us in, Blanchet,' said Louis. 'Gaël has been pushed off the cliff, we need to talk.'

'What the fuck has that got to do with me?' said Blanchet.

'If you hope to be mayor one day, it could be in your interest to get involved.'

Blanchet undid the door, looking hostile, distrustful, but interested.

'If he's dead, what's so urgent?'

'That's just it. He isn't dead. He may be able to talk if he comes out of his coma. See how that might be awkward?'

'No, because it's nothing to do with me.'

'Take us inside, we can't stand on your porch all night. Not very welcoming, your porch.'

Blanchet shook his head. He adopted the persona he had paraded earlier: bluff, good-natured fellow, difficult at times, but rock solid. Marc thought that Mathias's size and Louis's Gothic expression might have had something to do with his yielding so quickly. Blanchet propelled them into a small office, pointed them to chairs, and sat himself down behind a large desk with gilded feet.

Louis sat facing him, arms folded, long legs stretched out.

'Well?' said Blanchet. 'So someone pushed Gaël off a cliff? If you hadn't come stirring up shit around here, that wouldn't have happened. You'll have him on your conscience, *Monsieur* Kehlweiler. And now you're looking for a scapegoat?'

'Apparently, there was some couple that used to meet in the Vauban Cove cabin. What I want to know is the name of Gaël's mistress. Come on, Blanchet, give us a name.'

'Oh, I'm supposed to know that, am I?'

'Yes. Because you collect all the gossip you can, in case it might come in handy at election time. I'd be most disappointed in you if you didn't know.'

'Well, you're quite wrong, Kehlweiler. Yes, I do want to be mayor, I've never made any secret of that, and I'll get there. But in a clean fight. I don't need to parade anyone's dirty linen.'

'Oh yes you do, Blanchet. You whisper in corners,

you say one thing to the right, another to the left, you discredit people, you set them against each other, you calculate, you manoeuvre and when the mix is right, you get yourself elected. Not just in Port-Nicolas, you're aiming for bigger things. You're too old for this game, give it up. So come on, what's her name, Gaël's mistress, girlfriend, whatever? Hurry up, we've got two murders on our hands, I want to make sure there's not a third, if you don't mind.'

'Especially if it's you, eh?'

'It could be me, yes.'

'So why would I help you?'

'If you don't, I'll use your own methods, I'll do some muck-spreading of my own tomorrow. I know a few good stories. A future mayor, who doesn't want to help in a murder investigation, that wouldn't look good.'

'You don't like me much, do you, Kehlweiler.'

Blanchet, insultingly, had started to call Louis 'tu'.

'No, not much.'

'So why don't you try to pin the murders on me?'

'Because, to my profound regret, you didn't do them.'

Kehlweiler was calling him 'tu' back now.

Blanchet smiled, and almost burst out laughing.

'You really have rubbish for brains, Kehlweiler. Gaël's mistress, that's what you want to know?'

Blanchet began to laugh quietly.

'If we have people like you in charge of justice round here, it won't flutter any dovecotes.'

Marc tensed. Louis was losing the advantage. And this man-to-man confrontation seemed both pathetic and tedious. A set of formal dance steps. In a moment, they had passed from polite but icy forms of address to an aggressive trading of insults. He didn't see the need for all this in the middle of the night, for one small piece of information. He glanced over at Mathias, but Mathias, who was standing against the wall, didn't look amused. He was waiting, arms dangling, watchful under his blond thatch, like a Neanderthal ready to pounce on the bear threatening his cave. Marc felt isolated, and thought about the Albigensians again.

Blanchet leaned forward.

'I suppose, Mr Too Clever By Half, you never noticed that Gaël was a nancy boy? You make me laugh . . . Try to find a murderer, and you can't tell a cock from a hen.'

'All right, the name of the *man* then.'

'You call that a man?' Blanchet laughed.

'Yes, I do.'

'Fantastic, Kehlweiler, fantastic. What a tolerant person, generous, politically correct and non-judgemental. Pleased with yourself, are you? Proud? With all that and your big heart and your victimised leg, you go charming your way around the ministries.'

'Get a move on, Blanchet, you're just being tiresome. What's the other man's name?'

'Even for that you need me?'

'Yes.'

'That's better. I'll give you your information, Kehlweiler. You can pass it on to Guerrec and much good may it do you. It's Jean, that pale-faced idiot who sucks up to the priest. And you hadn't spotted it.'

'OK. Jean and Gaël, that was the couple? In the cabin? On Thursdays?'

'And Mondays as well, if you want to know. The rest of the time, prayers, guilt, good resolutions on Sunday, but off again on Monday, dodging confession. That make you feel better? Now go and do your worst and lock him up. I've seen enough of you for one night, and I'm off to bed.'

Blanchet looked well pleased with himself. He'd had fun, and he'd worsted Kehlweiler. Standing up, he started round the desk with a confident tread.

'Just a minute,'said Kehlweiler, without moving. 'I haven't finished.'

'Well, I have. If I gave you Jean's name, it was because Gaël was pushed off a cliff, not because you impress me. I don't know anything about these murders, and if you persist in staying on my property, I'll call the police.'

'Just a minute,' Louis repeated. 'You're not going to call the cops over another little bit of information. All I want to know is where you're from. What's wrong with that? I'll tell you where I'm from, in exchange. I'm from the *département* of the

273

Cher. And what about you, Blanchet? Northern France, is it?'

'Yes, I'm from northern France!' Blanchet shouted. 'How much longer are you going to be buggering me about?'

'Not by any chance from the town of Vierzon? I'd have said you were from somewhere like that. Vierzon, yes.'

Oh, now we're getting to the point, thought Marc. What point, he couldn't say, but they were certainly getting there. Blanchet had stopped coming round the desk.

'Yes, Blanchet, make an effort. Vierzon, you know, in central France. Don't act stupid, I know it's a long way back, but make an effort. Vierzon, on the river Cher. No? Doesn't ring a bell? Don't remember? Need a bit of help?'

Kehlweiler was very pale, but he was smiling. Blanchet retreated quickly back behind the desk.

'No funny tricks, Blanchet! These two guys aren't here for decoration, don't underestimate them. The one on the right has fast reflexes and the hands of a gorilla. Wouldn't need any weapons to split your skull. The other one is quick on the draw, his ancestors were Sioux warriors. Got it?'

Louis stood up, pushed in behind the desk, and opened a drawer roughly, against Blanchet's stomach. He felt among the papers inside, extracted a handgun and emptied the magazine. Then he looked up at Mathias and Marc, who were now both standing against the wall, one each side of the door, blocking it. Mathias looked perfect, and Marc looked, well, almost dangerous.

He smiled, nodded and returned to Blanchet.

'You *are* from Vierzon, or do I have to piss on you to get you to admit it? Ah, yes, that rang a bell, didn't it, pissing? I can see a flicker of the eyelid there, it's coming back, isn't it. Nothing like early memories.'

Louis was standing behind Blanchet, holding the back of his chair with both hands. Blanchet didn't move, one eye was twitching and his jaw was set.

'In fact they used to call you the Piss-master, didn't they? And don't try bringing out some false ID, it won't fool me. Your real name is René Gillot, no distinguishing features, brown eyes, snub nose, stupid expression, but the artist's eye noticed the gap between your front teeth, the patch on your right cheek where the beard doesn't grow, your triangular earlobes, just little things, everyone has distinguishing features, you just have to remember them. René the Piss-master, despicable leader of the Vichyite Militia in Champon, near Vierzon, during the war. You had your headquarters in a corner of the forest, fifty-three years ago, yes, you were only seventeen at the beginning, you had rubbish for balls, and you started *very* young. On your little bike, you used to go to the *Kommandantur* to spew up denunciations of your fellow Frenchmen. And it was there in '42 that a German soldier on sentry duty, just a poor bloody soldier, in *Feldgrau* uniform, an anonymous Boche, saw you coming

275

and going. You should always watch out for soldiers on sentry duty, René, they get fed up standing around all day, so they look and they listen. Especially a soldier watching for a chance to desert – not so easy, believe me, with a German Army helmet on. I know, these are boring old stories from long ago, so long ago I wasn't even born, ancient history. But it's to please you. Because I know there are some bygone mysteries you still wonder about, you're still asking yourself how it was, and by what miracle, that some of the people you denounced got away in the nick of time. You suspected two of your own pals, and let me put this on your conscience right away, you wiped them out for nothing.'

Louis grabbed Blanchet's chin and turned his face towards him.

'And that German soldier, René? You never thought about him. Every week when people brought chickens into the marketplace, he was well placed to whisper, under cover of the cackling of hens, some information picked up at the *Kommandantur*. He didn't know much French, he just learned enough to be able to say things like: "It's tomorrow, dawn, get away." Ah, now you know the answer! Now you can see the face of that soldier you went past month after month. His features are a bit vague perhaps? So take a good look at me, René, that'll bring them back quite clearly, apparently I look very like him. Yes, you've got it, and with a bit of an effort, you'll even remember his name, Ulrich Kehlweiler. He'll be very glad to know I've found you, believe me.'

Louis let go of the back of the chair, and of Blanchet's chin which he had been squeezing. Marc couldn't take his eyes off him, he felt butterflies in his stomach, what if Louis were to strangle the old man? But Louis went across the room, and perched sideways on a large table.

'Remember the fuss there was when soldier Ulrich went missing? Every house was searched. And you know where he was? It'll make you laugh. Underneath the box bed of the schoolteacher's daughter. Ingenious, yes? And it creates friendships. One night in the box scared to death, the next in the bed, making love. That's how I came to exist and in fact Ulrich and the daughter fled together and joined a Resistance cell. But I'm not going to bore you with my family history, I'm getting to the bit that really interests you, the night of 23 March 1944, in your forest headquarters, where, with the help of the seventeen other *miliciens*, you had caught twelve members of a Resistance network, plus seven Jews who had taken refuge with them. Never mind how many there were of them, you were very pleased with yourself. You tied them up, you *pissed* on them, your pals did the same, you offered the women to them. My mother, who was among them, as you will have guessed, was raped by the big blond man, Pierrot. You tortured them for hours, you had so much fun, and you were all so drunk, that two women

277

managed to escape – yes, you pathetic arsehole, or I wouldn't be here to tell the tale – you realised that a bit late, but when you did, you decided to get serious. You put the others in the barn, roped them together and set the place on fire.'

Louis hit the table, Marc saw that he was livid, Gothic and dangerous. But Louis regained control of himself and took a breath. Blanchet could hardly breathe.

'The story had a happy ending for the girl, she got away, she found Ulrich again, and they were in love with each other all their lives. I hope you're glad for them. The other woman was older, the *milice* caught up with her in the woods and shot her down, just like that. Evidence? Is that what you want? You hope that history can be wiped out with your sleeve, by changing your ID card. Ask Vandoosler over there if history is ever forgotten, you piece of shit. I was twenty when my mother told me the story, with some sketches. Good pictures, very delicately drawn, she was gifted, as you might not have known. I would have picked you out of a thousand men, René. With her sketches and descriptions, I've managed to catch up with seven of your little friends so far, on my rounds, but none of them knew the new name of the Piss-master.

'And then, what do you know, I find you here, don't get excited, no such thing as chance. Twenty-five years I've been travelling the country, chasing those murderers, it wasn't chance but careful prospecting, I'd have found you one day or another. And now, you're going to give me the names and addresses of the nine others I'm after, if they're not already dead. Yes, you have, you've got all that somewhere, don't disappoint me, and above all don't make me angry. Then the affair will be closed. And you'd better get a move on, that's not the only thing I have to do in life. What? You're frightened? You think I'm going to *kill* them all, your old *milicien* friends? No, I wouldn't even piss on them. But if necessary I *will* neutralise them, dispose of the bombs. As I'm going to do with you. I'm waiting for the list. And then, René, while we're at it, I'm not just interested in the past, no, we'll think about today as well. You haven't been twiddling your thumbs since your pissing trips in days gone by. Now you want to be mayor, and you have higher aims. You aren't doing this all on your own. So I also want a list of your contemporary henchmen. The whole list, you hear. The sub-adults, the adults, the old fools, all ages, sexes and occupations. When I do bomb disposal I do it properly, I pull up the plant complete with its roots. Every bit. And you can leave me your slush fund too, that will be useful. You're hesitating? You realise, don't you, that old Ulrich Kehlweiler is still alive, and will recognise you at a tribunal? So you're going to dismantle the whole machine, you're going to give me the lists, papers, networks, you arsehole, or I can quite simply get you arraigned for crimes against humanity. Same thing if any of the little shits among your gang of today so much as lifts a finger. Or if you try anything against my father. Or if you try to escape, because there's not a chance.'

Louis stopped talking. Blanchet's head was still lowered, as he stared at his knees. Louis turned to Marc and Mathias.

'Right, we've finished here, we're off now,' he said. 'Blanchet, don't forget your instructions. Your pension, your army of bastards in hiding, your lists and your funds. You can chuck in your file on Chevalier too. I'll be along to pick it all up in forty-eight hours.'

Once in the street, the three men walked in silence, heading for the main square. Louis kept running his hand through his hair, now plastered on his forehead and damp with sweat. None of them considered going into the hotel; they went past it towards the harbour, where they sat down on some wooden crates. The howling of the west wind, the pounding of the waves and the metallic clang of the rigging replaced conversation. Perhaps they were waiting for Louis's hair to dry properly. Half past three struck, first from the church, then from the town hall a moment or two later. The double clang seemed to rouse Louis out of his sweat and from his immense fatigue.

'Marc,' he said suddenly, 'something's bothering you. Out with it.'

'No, it's not the time. There are moments in

one's life when one has to keep quiet about trivial matters.'

'As you like, but still, you've had that beer bottle stuck on your finger for an hour now, and you can't get it off. It's stupid, but something has to be done about it.'

Mathias and Louis, using a stone, managed with care to break the glass bottle, dangling from Marc's hand. Louis threw the shards into the sea, so that they wouldn't hurt anyone.

CHAPTER 27

Jean, so wan and unthreatening that the gendarmes had been in no hurry to take him into custody on the Wednesday morning, had escaped through the window with a start of two hundred metres on them. He fled, by reflex action, to his usual refuge and had barricaded himself inside the church.

Which meant that at nine in the morning, six gendarmes were stationed outside the building. Early customers at the Market Cafe had heard the news and turned up, passing comments and waiting to see what policy would be used to extract him. That policy was under discussion between Guerrec and the priest, who was refusing permission for anyone to break a sixteenth-century stained-glass window, or smash down a carved fourteenth-century wooden door, or in fact to touch anything at all in the house of God, full stop. No, he didn't have the keys, Jean had the only set in the village. The priest was lying with determination. Nobody was to count on *him*, he said, to help terrorise a desperate man who had chosen to seek the protection of the Lord. It was raining again, everyone was getting very wet. Guerrec remained calm, but his features were strained as he mentally examined every wall of the socio-religious dead end in which he now found himself trapped. From inside the church, Jean could be heard sobbing uncontrollably.

'Inspector,' said one of the gendarmes, 'I'll get some tools, we can bust the lock, and then turn the hoses on the faggot inside.'

'No, you don't,' said the priest, 'that's a seventeenth-century lock, and you're not going to harm the man inside either.'

'So you don't care if *we* get soaked because of that murdering queer? We'll replace your lock, padre. OK, inspector?'

Guerrec looked at the gendarme, felt like punching him on the jaw, but restrained himself. He was at the end of his tether. He'd spent the night at young Gaël's bedside with the parents, waiting for a word, a sign, but none had come.

'Why don't you try to go in?' Guerrec said to the priest. 'Talk to him. I'll send away the gendarmes, but I'll stay nearby myself.'

The priest went off through the rain, and Guerrec stationed himself on his own under a tree.

Louis, who hadn't slept a wink either, was watching the scene from the *calvaire*, sitting by the miraculous fountain, and trailing his hand in the water. Ever since he had recognised the Piss-master in the bar of the cafe – he'd known that cafe would bring him good luck – his thoughts

283

had been full of darkness and pain. He had only been following the affair of the dog through a mist of confusion and distress. Now the wound was still open, but the filth had been cleaned away. He had washed the hand that had touched the bastard, he'd called his father in Lörrach, he'd called Marthe in Paris. Now it was time to do some local bomb disposal. The boy was still hanging on between life and death in Quimper hospital, and despite his being under police guard, Louis knew that unless they moved fast, a skilful hand could well disconnect his life-support system, it had happened before, as Guerrec might say, and as recently as ten years ago in Quimper. His thoughts returned to the husband falling from the balcony, to Diego's sudden change of heart, his disappearance, Lina Sevran's face when she had been found as a runaway, her two shots fired at the dog, the engineer's protective stance.

Soaked to the skin as he was, it couldn't make any difference if he plunged his knee directly into the water.

Louis had placed Bufo on the fountain's edge.

'Eat up, Bufo, eat up, that's all I ask you.'

Louis was reordering his thoughts, chapter after chapter, one eye on the toad.

'Listen to me while you eat, Bufo, it might interest you. Chapter one, Lina pushes her husband off the balcony. Chapter two, Diego realises that Lina was the killer, but keeps his mouth shut, so as not to upset Marie, whom he loves. Are you following?

And how does Diego work that out? Between the police interviews in Paris and his return to Brittany, before he's brought back again for the reconstruction, he sees or notices something, but where and how? There's only one interesting thing between Paris and Quimper and it's the train, because they travelled here by train. So, chapter three, Diego sees something in the train, don't ask me what, and chapter four, Diego keeps his mouth shut for another seven years, same reason, same effect. Chapter five, Lina gets rid of Diego.'

Louis had put his leg to soak in the fountain which was freezing cold. You might perhaps have thought that miraculous waters would be warm, well, no, they weren't. Bufo had managed to travel a metre in clumsy and prudent little hops.

'Bufo, stop being so dumb, you're annoying me.

'Six, Marie is due to move in with the Sevrans. She is clearing out her little house, and Diego's possessions from his den, which she's not touched for five years. She finds some piece of paper, something, where Diego noted what he knew, because it's always hard to keep a secret like that. Seven, Lina Sevran, who is afraid, and is watching the preparations for the move like a hawk, immediately murders poor old Marie. Then the dog, the beach, the toe, the shit, we know the rest.'

Louis pulled his leg out of the cold water; four minutes of miraculous bathing ought to be enough.

'Eight, the cops turn up. Lina provides a red herring in the form of an anonymous note, a banal

285

but efficient ploy. She points the finger at the couple in the cabin, and pushes the boy Gaël over the cliff, then they are sure to accuse Jean, who will be incapable of defending himself. Nine, the husband suspects all this and protects her. Ten, she is crazy and dangerous, and is going to pull out Gaël's life support.'

Louis retrieved Bufo and stood up with an effort. The cold water had been like a hammer blow to his knee. He took a few steps, stretching his leg gently to get the muscles moving again. Another ten minutes in the miracle-working fountain and you'd be a goner.

But there was a catch. How had she managed to type the note on that Virotyp machine? Guerrec had made inquiries, which all corroborated each other: Lina had not left the bar before Louis himself went out with the cops, with that little screw of paper in his pocket. How had she done it? She couldn't have worked the machine by remote control.

Louis looked down towards the church. The priest had apparently managed to get inside. He went slowly downhill to where people had gathered and touched Sevran on the shoulder. He wanted to know what had happened with Diego, whether anything had happened on the train home, twelve years ago, on the Paris–Quimper line.

Sevran frowned. He didn't like the question. It was too far back, he couldn't remember.

'I don't see the connection. Don't you see this

is all about some local sex scandal,' he said, pointing to the church. 'Can't you hear him screaming his head off, that chap Jean, who's not all there?'

'Yes, I can hear him, but still. It was a special journey,' Louis insisted. 'Try and remember. Your good friend Marcel Thomas had just died, you'd stayed on in Paris a day or two for the police investigation. Think, it's important. Did Diego see anyone on the train? A friend? Perhaps a lover of Lina's?'

Sevran thought for a few minutes, looking down.

'Yes,' he said, 'we did see someone. I only saw him when we arrived. Diego and I were sitting separately in the carriage. But this was someone who travelled regularly, so it was perfectly normal. He didn't know Lina very well. They would have met occasionally when she and her husband came here on holiday, that's all, believe me.'

'And he knew about the death?'

'I suppose so, it was in the papers.'

'What if this man seemed happier than the circumstances warranted? And what if Diego could see that from where he was sitting? Where was his seat?'

'At the back of the carriage, the other man wasn't far from him, but I was further forward, in a space for four seats. I just caught up with them when we got out, I've no idea if they could have spoken.'

'Is it true that Diego had changed?'

'Yes, that's true,' Sevran recognised. 'I thought it

was delayed reaction to events. Then, because it went on, I thought it might be some trouble in Spain, he had a big and complicated family. But anyway, none of this makes sense.'

'Who was the man on the train?'

The engineer wiped raindrops from his face. He looked embarrassed and annoyed.

'It doesn't make any sense,' he said, 'just fantasy, Lina would never –'

'What was his *name*?'

'Darnas,' said Sevran.

Louis stood thunderstruck in the rain, while the engineer, clearly upset, moved away.

Over by the church porch, the priest was bringing Jean out, propelling him gently. Guerrec approached them. Jean still kept his face covered with his hands and cried out if anyone but the priest touched him.

Louis went back to the hotel to change out of his wet clothes. He kept seeing Darnas's face. Darnas twelve years ago, not so fat, very rich, and Lina's first husband, fond of her but older, short of money, a good exchange. But then something had gone wrong. It was Pauline who had married Darnas and Sevran had married Lina, so what was Pauline's role in all that? Louis squeezed Bufo in his pocket.

'Things are not looking good, old fellow,' he said, 'we'll have to think about it in the train.'

He picked up a note from Marc. Marc had a serious weakness for communicating by note.

Son of the Rhine, I'm taking the hunter-gatherer to visit the Machine for Pointless Messages. Don't let your toad run wild in the bathroom etc.
Marc

Louis walked up to the machine. Under Mathias's impassive gaze, Marc was turning the handle and passing on messages to him. Marc saw Louis approach and came to meet him. Mathias stayed where he was, near the plinth of the machine, looking down at the ground.

'I'm going to Rennes,' said Louis. 'I've got some books to consult. Back tonight. When you've finished with the oracle, can you keep an eye on both the Sevrans' house and Darnas's, all day if you can manage it?'

'Darnas?' asked Marc.

'I haven't time to explain now. It's a big tangle. Both Darnas and Pauline left the cafe after the 7 ball, but were back in before I left. Think about Gaël, and watch everyone. What's Mathias up to – looking for moles?'

Marc turned round to see Mathias who was now crouching down and examining the grass.

'Oh, he's always doing that,' he said. 'Don't worry, it's normal for him. Like I said, he's obsessive, archaeologists are like that. One dandelion out of place and it niggles him, he thinks there's some flint arrowhead underneath it.'

Louis's train got to Rennes at three. They had

to move fast, and he was anxious. He hoped Marc had stopped consulting the machine's Delphic utterances and that Mathias had been able to tear himself away from his archaeological suspicions. He needed them to keep watch.

CHAPTER 28

Louis spent the return trip making visits to the toilet to moisten Bufo's skin – his carriage was overheated, dry and uncomfortable for amphibians – and changing seats frequently. He was trying to observe what was reflected in the mirror running the length of the luggage rack along the carriage, while attempting to rearrange his thoughts, which his visit to the Rennes public library had sent off in a different direction. Without a shred of evidence, there was no way he could take direct action. It would have to be by ricochet, a three-ball French billiards game which was particularly delicate. What did that spectator in the cafe say? 'French billiards is more straightforward, you know straight away if you're useless'. You just don't have to miss your shot. He fell into a deep sleep, an hour before the train reached Quimper.

It was only at the last moment that he saw Marc, who was standing, dressed in black, on the dark station forecourt. This guy had the gift for appearing out of the blue and making you as jumpy as himself, if you didn't watch out.

'What the hell are you doing here?' Louis asked. 'Aren't you keeping watch?'

'Mathias is outside the Sevrans' house and Pauline and Darnas are having dinner with the mayor. I came to meet you. Nice of me, wasn't it?'

'OK, tell me what's happening, but please, Marc, make it snappy.'

'Lina Sevran is secretly planning a getaway.'

'Are you sure?'

'I climbed up on to the roof of the house opposite and looked in. She's packed a small case, a rucksack, just the bare minimum. When Sevran went out, she went to order a taxi for tomorrow morning at 6 a.m. Shall I give more details or the short version?'

'Find us a taxi now,' said Louis. 'We need to hurry. Where's Guerrec?'

'He's taken Jean into custody, and the priest is upset. This afternoon, Guerrec went and sat with Gaël, but nothing new. Mathias has been working very hard on his archaeological site.'

'Quick, a taxi!'

'But I was telling you about Mathias's site, dammit.'

'For the love of God,' said Louis, now getting agitated in turn, 'can't you give a bit of priority to what's urgent? What has Mathias's dig to do with anything? What's it to me if the pair of you are totally nuts?'

'You're very lucky that I'm a nice guy who lends

you my leg and my patience, but anyway, the fact is that Mathias's dig is a grave. And if you want me to be snappy and cut to the chase, it's Diego's grave, quite shallow, the body is covered with a layer of pebbles and the whole lot sealed by two of the feet of the colossal Machine of Pointlessness. There you are, that's it.'

Louis pulled Marc aside from the station entrance.

'Explain please, Marc. You've dug it up?'

'Mathias doesn't need to dig up the earth to know what's underneath. A patch of nettles that looks different from the others is enough for him. The rectangle made by the grave is right under the Machine, like I said. Machine for nothing, a likely story. It did surprise me that someone like Sevran would go to all that trouble for no reason, it's not like him. With the engineer, everything has to have a purpose. I can spot people who have a taste for the futile, because it takes one to know one. He has a very heightened sense of the useful, so his machine is certainly useful for something. To conceal Diego's grave, two big iron feet clamped on top, and no one's going to touch it. I found out a few things at lunchtime, from the mayor. It was on that spot that they were due to build the supermarket. See what would have happened when they started digging the founda-tions? But Sevran proposed putting up his machine, he convinced the mayor, he chose the exact spot in among the undergrowth. Out of love of art, they moved the ground plan of the supermarket 120 metres further back. And Sevran put his machine up on top of the grave.'

Looking satisfied, Marc shot across the forecourt to hail a taxi. Louis looked at him, biting his lip. Jesus, he hadn't been quick off the mark about the machine. Marc was quite right, Sevran wasn't a man who liked pointless things. A piston has to push, a lever has to lift, and a machine has to have a purpose.

CHAPTER 29

They stopped the taxi fifty metres from the Sevrans' house.

'I'll pick Mathias up,' said Marc. 'Where is he?'

'Over there, a black shape under a black shape, against a black shape.'

Screwing up his eyes, Louis made out the large form of the hunter-gatherer, pressed against a wall, under a fine rain, watching the door. With a sentry like that outside, it was hard to see that anyone could get away.

Louis approached the door and rang the bell.

'As I feared, they're not answering. Mark, break the French window.'

Marc stepped over the broken glass of the French window and helped Louis through. They heard Sevran running downstairs, and stopped him halfway. Wild-eyed, he was holding a pistol.

'It's all right, Sevran, it's only us. Where is she?'

'No, please, you don't understand –'

Louis pushed the engineer gently aside and went up to Lina's bedroom, followed closely by Marc and Mathias. Lina Sevran was sitting at a

295

small round table. She had stopped writing. Mouth too wide, eyes too big, hair too long, the hand gripping the pen, everything about her frozen and defeated posture alarmed Marc. Louis went over to her, picked up the paper and read in a murmur:

'I am guilty of the murders of Marie, Diego and my first husband. I am guilty and I'm going to disappear. I am writing this in the hope that my children . . .'

Louis put the paper down with a tired movement. The engineer was wringing his hands in a kind of tortured prayer.

'Please,' said Sevran, almost shouting, 'let her go. What would that change?. . . The children. Let her go away somewhere. Tell her, I beg you. I wanted her to run away, but she won't listen to me, she says it's all over for her, I found her writing this with the pistol beside her. Do something, Kehlweiler, tell her to go!'

'What about Jean?' asked Louis.

'What proof is there against him either! We could say it was Diego, couldn't we? Diego! We could say he's still alive, he came back to kill everyone, and Lina can get away!'

Louis pulled a face. He gestured to the engineer, who had collapsed on to a chair, and held a whispered conference with Marc and Mathias.

'Agreed?' said Louis.

'It's a big risk,' muttered Marc.

'We must try it for her sake, or she's had it. OK, Mathias, off you go.'

Mathias went downstairs and out through the broken window.

'All right,' Louis said to the engineer. 'We'll do it your way. But first we have to go round by the machine – there's a reason. Lina,' he said in a low voice, 'bring your suitcase.'

Since Lina hadn't moved, he raised her gently by both arms and pushed her towards the door.

'Marc, take her suitcase and rucksack, and bring her coat too, it's pouring with rain.'

'Where's the other one gone, the big man?' asked Sevran anxiously. 'Has he gone to tell someone?'

'He's gone to cover us.'

The three men and Lina walked through the rain. When they saw the giant silhouette of the pointless machine, Louis asked Marc to stay behind on guard. Marc stopped and watched them going on in silence. Louis was still holding Lina by the arm; she allowed herself to be pushed with no more reaction than a terrified madwoman.

'Here we are then,' said Louis, stopping at the foot of the installation. 'What do we do about this, Sevran?' he asked, pointing to the ground. 'That's where Diego is, right?'

'How did you know?'

'We have someone here who is able to distinguish between the really pointless and the fake pointless, and another who can read signs from underground. Between the pair of them, they realised that this monument to pointlessness actually served to seal Diego in. Am I right?'

'Yes,' whispered Sevran in the dark. 'When Lina realised that Diego had decided to accuse her of Thomas's murder, she lured him outside. Diego agreed to talk, but he took his rifle with him. The old man was fragile, she easily got it away from him, and she shot him. I had followed them, I saw Lina fire the shot, I was absolutely horrified. I learned it all that night, how Thomas had been murdered, and then this next crime. It only took me a few seconds to make up my mind, I decided I'd help her, always. I took her back into the house, I got a shovel, and I ran back. I dragged the body up to the woods, dug a grave, and put stones on top of it. I was scared stiff. I covered everything back up, stamped it down and spread pine needles over it. Then I went and left the gun by the quayside and untied a boat and sent it off. It wasn't a brilliant solution, but I had to improvise quickly. Then everything settled down, and Lina did too.'

Sevran stroked Lina's hair, while Lina, still supported by Louis's arm, did not turn her head.

'Later on, I found out they were going to clear the land to build right on the spot. They would start digging and find the body. So I needed a big idea to avoid disaster. That's when I thought up the machine. I needed something heavy enough that no one would think of moving it for a hundred years, but something that would be able to stand up, without digging big foundations.'

'Spare us the technical details, engineer.'

'Yes . . . yes, something that might seem attractive to the mayor, so that he would move the planning permission for the building. I sweated blood making this blessed machine, and nobody will be able to say it isn't unique in the world –'

'No, they certainly won't,' said Louis. 'It's worked very well up to now. But it would be better to dig Diego up, and take him somewhere else, it would be more –'

There was a sudden cry in the night, then another, weaker, more strangled. Louis looked up around him.

'It's Marc,' he said. 'Wait here, Sevran!'

Holding his knee, Louis ran back into the wood, and found Marc where he had left him, with the suitcase and rucksack.

'Some miraculous fountain,' said Louis, rubbing his knee. 'Quick, better go back, it should have worked.'

A hundred metres away, they heard a thud.

'That,' said Marc, 'is the sound of a prehistoric hunter falling on his prey. No need to hurry, he could fell a bison.'

At the foot of the machine, Mathias was pinning the engineer to the ground, his hands behind his back.

'In my view,' said Marc, 'you shouldn't leave Sevran too long like that, he'll be crushed.'

Louis put his arm round Lina's shoulders. He did so instinctively, since he thought she was about to fall over.

'It's all over,' he said. 'He wouldn't have had time, because Mathias was watching. Right, Mathias?'

'As you thought,' said Mathias, who was now sitting astride Sevran's back as comfortably as on a rolled carpet, 'as soon as you were out of sight, he pulled out a gun. He put it into his wife's hand and pressed it against her head. He didn't have much time to fake a suicide, so I had to move quickly.'

Louis undid the straps of the rucksack.

'OK,' he said, 'you can let the beast go. Pull him upright and tie him to the machine, and then, if you will, please go and fetch Guerrec.'

Louis stared at the engineer through the darkness. Marc didn't trouble to look at Louis's face, he was sure he had the expression of the Goth from the Danube, the one on the mosaic.

'So, Sevran, you want us to get some answers from your machine of death?' said Louis in a low voice, addressing the engineer as 'tu'. 'Why did you kill Thomas? To get Lina, and with her the unique collection of typewriters her husband owned? Go on, Marc, turn the handle.'

Without knowing why, Marc turned it, and the whole mass of metal began to vibrate. Marc went to fetch the little message; by now he had done it so often that he knew exactly where to put his hand, even though it was dark.

'How you did it, you'll have to tell us. Some trick to make him lean over the railing, I suppose, to see you down in the courtyard, calling up to him. How did Diego find out the truth? Go on, Marc, keep turning. He understood in the train, by looking at you in the mirror over the luggage rack. You can see everything in it, people's faces and even their hands if they're sitting in the space for four, if you're behind them. That's a detail one might forget. You think you're fine in the train, all by yourself, but the whole carriage can see you in the mirror. I know, I spend my time watching people. And what kind of expression did you have on the way home? Turn it, Marc, make the machine spit out the truth. Did you look like the devastated friend you had appeared to be in front of the police? Not at all. You were smiling, you'd won, and Diego saw it. But why did he keep quiet, the brave matador? Because he originally thought Lina had killed her husband, and that you were just her accomplice. To accuse Lina, whom Marie had cared for since her childhood, would be terrible for Marie. And Diego loved Marie, he didn't want her to find out. But with the pair of you after your marriage, he changed, and one night Diego found out that Lina hadn't been involved, that she knew nothing about it. How did he do that? Turn, Marc, keep turning. I don't know, you will have to tell us what he came across. A conversation with Lina, a letter perhaps, some sign that made him understand. Diego realised then that you had acted alone, and he had no reason to keep quiet any more. So he confronts you. You take him off somewhere to have a chat, you've been friends for so long. Still, Diego is worried and takes his rifle. But he can't hold his own against you, sentimental Spaniard versus steel machine: nothing must get in the way of your levers and pistons and gears, all well oiled with ambition, all clanking and tapping away to prove your power. You killed him and buried him here. But why did you kill Marie, poor old Marie who went on hoping her Spanish husband would return, as she went out to gather her shellfish? Because Marie was going to move house! Lina wanted her to move in with you. But that house move could be a problem. What if Diego had left some clues? Of course you'd already searched their house, but does anyone ever know what secret hiding place a couple may have? You get in your car to go to Paris, just like every other Thursday night, you park it somewhere, you stop off at Marie's place, and you take a look. She hasn't gone out after winkles, she is crying her eyes out in Diego's den, where she's packed everything up in boxes, she comes and goes in the empty room, she pushes furniture that holds memories and what does she find? Where? You may tell us, perhaps a few pages rolled up inside the old umbrella by the door. I say umbrella, because he wouldn't put it in a box, and there was an umbrella there, I checked. I see it like that, a simple hiding place, you'll know. She reads it, she knows. You get hold of Marie, you knock her unconscious, you carry her away, you finish her off in the cabin or in the wood somewhere, and you lug her down on to the beach. It doesn't take more than ten minutes. Finding her lost boot and putting it on makes you lose another ten. You leave for Paris, and that's when the drama starts. The animal drama that your mechanical mind couldn't have foreseen. Your dog leaves his shit on a grid round a tree. Nice, that, don't you think? Basic intestinal nature intrudes, to ruin the stainless-steel perfection of the turbines. In future, you'll know not to take nature for granted, and you won't take the dog. Then the cops turn up here, that wasn't in the script, but you set your machinery going, and you divert them, by using your mechanical know-how. You accuse Gaël and Jean, you slip a note in my pocket. Well played, engineer, you slowed me down, and my mind was on other things just then. But I've found out about your Virotyp 1914.

'A very unusual machine, the top can be taken off, and fixed to a little carriage, and that makes it a portable typewriter. So portable that it can be carried in a large pocket, and with some skill, which you have in spades, you can type a note with your hand inside your coat. How? How do you see the letters on the disc? You type blind? Precisely, that's what you do, because there's a Braille version of the Virotyp, made for men blinded in the Great War. That's the one you own, a very rare machine. I went and read up about it in Rennes, in the book by Ernst Martin, the collector's Bible, the one you have on the sideboard in your kitchen, I'd noticed it, you see, because it's a German book. Your Virotyp was an idea of genius. As everyone had seen, you stayed all afternoon in the cafe. You couldn't possibly have typed the note, you are free of all suspicion, perfectly protected by the secrets of the marvellous machine. I told Guerrec that myself. In fact, you typed your message on the spot, in your pocket after playing the 7 ball. You put your coat back on after the game. Then it was easy, just grab the paper with a handkerchief, crumple it, and drop it into my jacket. When you got home, you put the movable piece back on the base of the Virotyp. You'll permit me to go and take another look at it, I hope, it interests me, I admit, I'd never heard of it. Which is what you bargained for, because who on earth would know that? Who would imagine that an ancient typewriter could be put in a coat pocket? But because it was puzzling me, I went to consult some books, I sometimes do a bit of research, you shouldn't think the world is full of idiots, that's a big mistake. Then you pushed Gaël over the edge, although you had no connection with Gaël at all, he was just a cog in your revolting machinery.'

Louis stopped talking and stretched his arms. He looked at Marc and Mathias.

'Stuff this for a lark, as Marthe would say. Let's finish it off. Lina followed you, when you went out to find Gaël. If she followed you, it was because she suspected something. And if she suspected something, her fate was sealed. You let suspicions pile up against *her*. Jean's arrest didn't seem to be in the bag, Guerrec didn't seem too keen, this morning by the church, since the man was weeping desperately over his friend Gaël. So it was Lina who would have to pay, before she cracked. You must have done all you could to stop her talking. I presume you went for the simplest method: you threatened to harm her children. So Lina kept her mouth shut, she was paralysed with fear. She's been afraid ever since I arrived with my story about the dog. Good evening, Guerrec, I'm just finishing with this man, then I'll pass him on to you. What's the news on Gaël?'

'Coming round,' said Guerrec.

Guerrec seemed relieved, he had grown attached to the young lad.

'Just listen to the end,' said Louis. 'I'll tell you the beginning later. Lina got frightened because of the toe in the dog's mouth. Because on Thursday nights, the dog knows you are about to leave, and it follows you everywhere. Any dog would be the same, even your pit bull, but I've spent too long with my toad to have thought about that at first. But Lina knows. The idea festers. If the dog ate Marie's toe on Thursday night, it must mean you, Sevran, were nearby, the dog wouldn't have left your side the night you get the car out of the garage. The idea keeps on growing, it chokes her, she starts thinking about her first husband and Diego, the whole scenario comes out of the shadows, she panics, she thinks she's going mad, she can't act normally. She is so scared, and so silent, that she lays herself open to all kinds of suspicions. She watches you, she follows you. From that point, she's doomed, and we, like fools, follow the trail you laid, for a day too long. When I got back this evening, with the secret of the Virotyp, I knew I'd got you, but I didn't have any evidence. Just Lina's total ignorance of the type-writers, which didn't count. Or my evidence from the dog. He had excreted one bit of truth and he gave me something else post-mortem. The dog didn't like Lina, he wouldn't ever have followed her to the cove. With fragile bits of evidence like that, and with Lina refusing to talk because she was protecting her kids, she was cornered. So I had to create some evidence. Tonight, when I saw you forcing her to provide proof of her guilt, with the possibility that you would fake her suicide afterwards, you offered me a way. I came back from Quimper as fast as I could, when I heard she was planning to escape today. If Lina ran away, it would be too risky for you, so you would certainly want to eliminate her. And yet, I suppose, you loved her enough to take her from Marcel Thomas? – unless it was more that you wanted his machines, that's possible. I brought you out here for you to fake the suicide in the only moment when I left you alone, by running over to Marc, you couldn't choose the time or place, but there'd be no witnesses. And you know now that Mathias had been placed ready. I'd never have taken the risk without being sure he could jump you at the critical moment. You are one piece of shit, Sevran, I hope you've understood that, because I haven't the heart to go over this again.'

Louis returned to Lina and took her face in his hands to see if her terror had passed.

'Let's pick up your bag,' he said, 'and go.'

This time Lina said something. Or rather she said yes by nodding her head.

CHAPTER 30

Louis slept in until ten o'clock.
Then he picked up Marc and Mathias to go to Blanchet's house.

Since Louis had referred to him as a Sioux warrior, Marc was intent on looking the part, without going over the top. For once, when he fitted the appearance of his boots, it would have been a pity not to play the game. Mathias was also smiling, the annihilation of the former member of the *milice* had pleased him, though Louis's description of him as having the 'hands of a gorilla' had rather shocked him. No one had more sensitive fingers for uncovering fragile prehistoric remains and the tiny flint tools of the Magdalenians. Mathias hadn't combed his hair that morning, and he ran his hands through his blond thatch. He was prepared to admit to himself, however, that he wouldn't greatly have minded putting his sensitive fists together to knock Blanchet over the head.

But no one had to do anything of the kind.

'I've come to pick up my order,' said Louis.

Blanchet had everything ready. He passed over

without a word two old briefcases tied with string and a small cardboard box, then his door closed.

'Shall we go to the cafe before we leave?' asked Marc, who was holding the box.

'Give me till this evening to round everything off,' said Louis. 'And I need to see Pauline. I'll just say hello, then we'll go.'

'OK,' sighed Marc. 'Well *I'll* just take my medieval accounts to the cafe and you'll find me there.'

Louis went off to find Guerrec. Marc put his pile of papers on a table which Antoinette cleared for him, and began a game of table football with Mathias. Louis had said there was no need for secrecy any more, they could tell anyone anything in the cafe, and nothing could have helped Marc to relax better than that. Mathias raised no objection to Marc's elaborate explanations. Mathias acted the perfect gent. He waited as Marc talked, while continuing to play, watched by all the fishermen, the clerks from the town hall and old Antoinette, who kept an eye on the number of glasses of white wine being drunk. It meant Mathias won every game, but Marc's ego wasn't dependent on the tiny football.

Louis came to the cafe at about one o'clock. Sevran, after a fit of rage during the night so alarming that a doctor had been called, had agreed to be questioned in the morning by Guerrec and, trembling with hate and scorn, had thrown him scraps of information, like meat to a dog.

It didn't bother Guerrec to be constantly called

'you pathetic little man', as long as he got the information he wanted. To get Marcel Thomas to fall from the balcony, Sevran had used a simple method. He had come back to the house, once Diego was asleep in the hotel. Thomas was waiting on the terrace, they had made an arrangement between them. Lina had never taken any interest in typewriters, except for one unique model called the Hurter, simply for the childish reason that it was supposed to be impossible to track down. Nobody had ever possessed a Hurter. Sevran had got hold of one, and they thought he would give it to Lina for her birthday, a very special gift, a secret between the two enthusiasts. Sevran had brought along this heavy machine, wrapped it in a blanket and attached it to a long leather strap which he threw up to Thomas. 'Put it round your wrist to secure it.' Thomas buckled it round his wrist and began to haul the machine up, and when it was about two metres above the ground, Sevran leapt up, hung on to it, and pulled. Thomas fell over the edge and Sevran finished him off by banging his head on the ground. He cut off the strap round his wrist and was already out in the street before Lina rushed on to the balcony. The typewriter was damaged, a detail he vouchsafed, but it was actually a big old Olympia from the 1930s. The Hurter, no, you pathetic little man, he had never found one. And if he did, he certainly wouldn't tell anyone.

Louis took the mayor – it was aperitif time – into

the back room and stood warming himself at the fire. The mayor listened to Louis's account, and a few movements appeared below the surface of the pool. The carp were stirring.

'What exactly does it mean, "non-aligned"?' Louis asked.

Chevalier shifted from one foot to another, twisting his hands.

'Look here, Chevalier,' said Louis, who had ended up calling everyone in the village 'tu', 'if you want to do me a favour now and then, take a little time in bed in the morning, or over your cognac at night, whatever you like, I don't mind, and think about the Piss-master for instance, and try to draw your political conclusions, *not* too non-aligned, for a change, and that will make me feel better, but it's up to you. I'm going to do you a favour now, I'm giving you the entire file Blanchet had compiled about you.'

Chevalier looked worried.

'Yes, of course I've read it,' said Louis, 'I've read it and I'm leaving it with you. It's pretty well researched. Blanchet was good at digging the dirt, like I told you. Your scandals are rather negligible, non-aligned so to speak, nothing too serious, and they don't interest me, but yes, they could have cost you the town hall, that's quite possible. I'm giving it all to you, you can read it, burn it, and clean up your act. I'm giving you everything, nothing left out, you have my word. You don't believe me when I say that, Chevalier?'

Chevalier stopped writhing, and looked at Louis. 'Yes, I do,' he said.

Louis put a large file into the hand the mayor held out, and his arm dropped under its weight.

'Heavy, eh?' said Chevalier, with a nervous grin.

He leafed through it, and the carp started bumping into each other in the depths of the pond. They were seriously bothered, the carp, and it showed. A little more readability appeared on the surface.

'Thank you, Kehlweiler. I *will* think of you perhaps, but in the evenings. Don't count on me to start being an early riser.'

'That's OK,' said Louis. 'Not before midday, if we ever need to talk to each other.'

Louis came back to the bar, and asked Antoinette for the telephone. She gave him a disc – that was how the phone worked then in the Market Cafe – and brought him a beer without his having asked for it. Details like that let you know a cafe has entered your soul.

'Lanquetot? Hello, it's the German speaking . . . Murder, murder and blue murder, case closed, we'll try to put Paquelin on the spot. I need to contact a few people in the Ministry and I'll be over to see you the day after tomorrow with my sandwich . . . No, not before eleven.'

Louis looked round as he hung up. Jean, wan, red-eyed, and his body more shapeless than ever in his would-be clerical clothes, was hesitating in the doorway of the cafe. Struck by a sudden fear, Louis went to the door and caught his arm.

'What is it? Is it Gaël?' he asked, shaking him.

Jean looked at him without a word, and Louis dragged him over to the counter.

'Come on, say something, for fuck's sake!'

'Gaël is better, he's eaten something,' said Jean with a shaky smile. 'It was the Virgin Mary who spoke to me this morning, that's what made me cry, she says she forgives me.'

Louis gave a sigh of relief. He hadn't realised how much he had wanted Sevran's last victim to survive the massacre. That they let the kid live was all he would ask of Port-Nicolas now.

'The Virgin Mary –' Jean began.

'Yes,' said Louis, 'the Virgin Mary is quite happy, she says you've a perfect right to see Gaël again, that's OK with her, she's a kind woman at heart. Have a drink.'

'No,' said Jean anxiously, 'she didn't say that, she –'

'No, no, no, Jean, you heard wrong. What she told you is what I just said. You trust me, don't you? You're not under arrest, you're not going to spend the rest of your life in the church, are you? You're going to live a bit outside as well. Trust me?'

Jean smiled a bit more.

'Are you sure?' he said.

'Of course. Cut off my leg if I'm not. Right, have a drink.'

Jean nodded. It was at that moment that Louis realised by the silence reigning in the cafe, apart from the noise of the table football, that if he

313

hadn't gone to fetch Jean from the doorway it wasn't evident that the wall of glances would have let him come in.

'Antoinette,' he said, 'Jean could do with a drink.'

Antoinette poured out a glass of Muscadet and put it in Jean's hand.

Louis went over to see Lina; her children had arrived home that morning, things would settle down. Then he found himself once more on the empty road to the health spa. He had to go and say hello. He hadn't dared ask Marc to push him there on the bike, but the icy bath in the miraculous spring had done his knee no good whatsoever. He'd just go and say hello. And perhaps ask if it was because of the leg that she'd left. Perhaps ask for more, and too bad for Darnas. Too bad for Darnas if she said yes. If she said no, of course, that would be different. Or perhaps just say goodbye and leave. Louis stopped halfway down the wet road. Or perhaps just leave a note, something mean like 'my toad is misbehaving in the bathroom, got to go'. Like plenty of other people would do, and just move on. Because if Pauline really had left him because of the knee, or, worse, if she didn't love him, and she really preferred Darnas, best not to know. Or perhaps it was. Or not. Or just say hello. Louis looked at the large spa building in its vast grounds, turned back and went as far as Sevran's machine. It was surrounded by police – they were going to excavate Diego's grave. He pushed aside a cop standing in front of the handle, without taking any notice of the dirty looks he received. He worked the mechanism, and picked up his strip of paper. '*Why hesitate? Souvenir from Port-Nicolas.*' 'Bloody fool,' said Louis between gritted teeth.

He went slowly back to the cafe, sat at the counter and asked Antoinette for some paper. He wrote half a page, folded it and taped it down.

'Antoinette,' he said, 'could you give this to Pauline Darnas when you see her?'

Antoinette put the paper inside the cash register. Marc came over from the football.

'So you're not going to say hello and off we go?'

'I don't want to hear hello, well, well, now, and bon voyage. I'm packing my doubts in my case and we're leaving.'

'That's funny,' said Marc, 'that's my system too. Do you want me to explain it again?'

'No. Look out, your medieval lord is getting soaked.'

Marc turned round and ran to the table where he had left his papers: a glass had been knocked over, and liquid was running gently over them.

'It does it on purpose,' cried Marc, as he wiped the damp papers with the edge of his jacket. 'History gets wet, and crumpled, and wiped out, so it panics, it starts crying like a child, and you go rushing to help it, and you don't even know why. That's the way I always fall for it.'

Mathias nodded. Louis watched as Marc desperately tried to rescue the wrinkled papers. He was

315

unsticking and unfolding the accounts of Hugues de Puisaye. Antoinette and Jean helped him, bringing cloths and blowing on the pages. Mathias put the saved sheets over the backs of cafe chairs. Louis would tell his old man about that, over in Lörrach. He'd like that. And then the old man would tell the Rhine, you could bet on that.

'I could do with a beer,' he said.